He continued to regard the ring steadily until Elizabeth startled him by saying: "I have not taken it off, not since the night you put it there."

He drew her roughly into his arms, bringing his lips down on hers in a kiss that was hot and hungry and demanding. His fingers were gripping her so tightly that she knew she would be bruised by them, but she didn't care, and she clung to him, allowing the wonderful closeness of their bodies to wash over her. For so many months she had felt desolate and alone. She'd yearned to have him hold her, dreamed of having him want her, and now, in his arms, she knew she had come home. . . .

A
RECKLESS
WAGER

Lois Menzel

FAWCETT CREST • NEW YORK

A Fawcett Crest Book
Published by Ballantine Books
Copyright © 1987 by Lois J. Menzel

All rights reserved under International and Pan-American Copyright Conventions. Published in the United States by Ballantine Books, a division of Random House, Inc., New York, and simultaneously in Canada by Random House of Canada Limited, Toronto.

Library of Congress Catalog Card Number: 86-91816

ISBN 0-449-21283-1

Printed in Canada

First Edition: May 1987

1

Julian Ferris, Viscount Stanton, tooled his high-perch phaeton expertly through the narrow space between an old-fashioned landaulet and a hackney carriage and swept into Grosvenor Square without appearing to even slightly check his pair. His perfectly matched bays were well-known in London, and today he was counting on them to rescue him from what he knew would be a long and tedious conversation with his godmother.

This formidable lady, the Dowager Duchess of Kern, would be incensed to find that he had driven himself in answer to her summons, but even she would not expect him to keep his horses standing long in the high wind of a chill September day.

Lord Stanton leaped gracefully down from the carriage as his groom ran to the horses' heads.

"I do not plan to be long, Jenkins, but if I am above fifteen minutes, walk 'em." He spoke over his shoulder as he sounded the knocker and a moment later was admitted to the house by a portly and disheveled butler. Stanton gave his caped driving coat into this worthy's hands, along with his high-crowned beaver and gloves, and found himself wondering if his godmother kept any servants under the age of sixty. If there were some younger ones, he mused, they would appear sadly out of place, for the whole musty heap spoke of a bygone era.

Twenty-five years ago the London town house of the Duke and Duchess of Kern had been a showplace for the aristocracy, and invitations to any function there were jealously coveted by the haut ton. Everyone who was anyone could be seen strolling the gracious rooms, conversing with only the cream of London society. But it had been many years since any strain of music rumbled through the formal reception rooms, and longer still since the ballroom had been closed for the last time. Even in those rooms the duchess now used there were unmistakable signs that time marches relentlessly on, leaving nothing untouched. Once-bright carpets and window hangings were dulled by exposure and age. Vaulting molded ceilings showed peeling gilded paint, and on many of the high walls priceless portraits hung in dusty frames, too high and too numerous for the hands of elderly servants to tend.

The viscount knew his way well and did not stand upon ceremony with his godmother, but he permitted the butler to lead him upstairs to the drawing room and announce him properly.

"Lord Stanton, your grace."

The dowager raised her head as the viscount entered the room, and a smile lit her heavily wrinkled face. "Well, Julian, you have been prompt! I sent my note only yesterday."

Stanton eyed the frail, white-haired lady with patient indulgence. She vexed him with her efforts to direct his life, yet he held her in considerable affection. "I fancied that your need to see me was urgent, ma'am, and I had no desire to keep you waiting."

He crossed the room to her as he spoke, and she noted with approval his claret-colored cutaway coat and dove-gray skintight pantaloons. As he seated himself in a chair she indicated near the fire, a reflection of the flames danced in the polish of his Hessian boots. He was a strikingly handsome young man, but the duchess realized he would not consider himself so, for vanity was not one of Julian's vices.

"It is fitting that you should call today, Julian. You have given me an opportunity to offer my felicitations." As his brows drew together in inquiry, she knew she had guessed correctly, and he had forgotten. "You are eight-and-twenty today, Julian! Never tell me that you have forgotten your own birthday!"

"I am afraid that I have," he admitted ruefully. "But it is not at all surprising. Such milestones mean little to me."

"Well, you may believe me when I say they are not so meaningless to others of your family."

"Yes, I know, Godmother. Eight-and-twenty and still unmarried! At my age my father and grandfather both had children in leading strings. How remiss of me."

"Sarcasm ill becomes you, Julian, and I cannot believe that you are as indifferent to this subject as you pretend. You must have some thought for what is due your family and your noble ancestors? For over two hundred years, the title you bear has passed from father to eldest son in an unbroken chain. Is it your intention to destroy such a proud heritage?"

"I have never understood why so much attention is paid to that accident of history," Stanton replied. "Sooner or later, one of the Viscounts Stanton will die in a war, or sire only girls, and then the chain will of necessity be broken."

"Nonsense, Julian! The Ferrises always produce sons— strong sons. And so also will you, if you will convince yourself that it is time to take a wife."

This was not the first time the viscount and his godmother had had this conversation. Since his return to England in the spring, she had taken every opportunity to introduce the subject. The theme was always the same;

only the characters changed. She was relentless in urging him to marry and never met an eligible debutante without considering the girl as a possible candidate for the future Viscountess Stanton.

"I know your feelings in this matter, Godmother. You have made them plain enough. But I cannot think that marriage is the answer for me. Henry would make a much better husband than I, or even Giles, when he is older."

"That may well be, Julian, but your brothers are not the head of this family. You are. And the responsibility is yours."

"I would not wish to see any wife of mine trapped in the existence my mother had to bear," he responded.

"Your mother had too much sensibility for her own good, which was undoubtedly the result of her being a Frenchwoman. But I agree that she received very shabby treatment from your father, very shabby indeed. He did not comprehend the meaning of the word *discretion,* a fault that you, my dear Julian, have not inherited. He married on a whim and for love—or call it passion if you will—and he found that passion soon dies. If you wish for a sensible marriage that you can be comfortable with, then you must carefully choose the proper woman. You insist that you are not a romantic. Very well. Choose a woman who is not desirous of having your heart at her feet. You must find a girl who is willing to fill the position of wife and mother and accept the fact that you would not be constantly dancing attendance upon her."

The duchess paused for a moment, and when he did not speak, she continued cautiously. "My niece by marriage, Louise Sherwood, has two charming daughters. The eldest, Charlotte, is an exceptional girl. She is just twenty-one and has had several seasons. An excellent family, good connections, and the girl is handsomely dowered."

"I believe I have met Miss Sherwood, Godmother, but

I assure you, the thought of making her an offer has never crossed my mind."

"Then let it cross your mind!" she snapped. "You cannot remain a bachelor forever! Marry you must, sooner or later. Now that the war is over and you are finished with soldiering, the time is ripe. Charlotte Sherwood is a sensible girl, with no silly romantic notions in her head. She is also remarkably lovely. It would be no penance to take such a girl to wife."

Stanton turned away impatiently, walked to the brandy decanter, and poured himself a liberal portion. He had every right to be annoyed with his godmother for this meddling in his private affairs, but he found that he couldn't blame her. Her feelings were, after all, in harmony with those of most of his family and friends, and indeed with those of society in general. A man of his age and social standing was expected to marry and produce an heir to secure the direct line. But even though he accepted these things, he still found the idea repellent.

Stanton had been to his share of weddings, and he knew the vows as well as any man, but regardless of his godmother's wishes, he had no intention of taking them. Perhaps he was a romantic after all, for he could see no sense in promising faithfulness and then breaking faith at the first convenient moment. His strong innate sense of fairness rebelled at the unwritten social ethic that expected wives to remain faithful while husbands could philander at will, provided, of course, that they were discreet. He had watched his mother suffer endless humiliation as his father had flaunted one mistress after another before the ton. Better not to marry at all than to involve oneself in a situation where pledges were made to be broken and honor sacrificed to desire.

His godmother had implied that Miss Sherwood, if he married her, would be sensible. In other words, she would

5

be willing to accept his behavior even if she was disapproving or resentful.

Is that what he wanted for his life? Marriage to a woman who would not be particularly concerned if he shared another woman's bed? Such a marriage was a sham—meaningless promises, empty vows, hollow honor. He wanted no part of it. He had known his share of women, and he would be content to continue as before. When an interlude ended, when interest flagged and attraction faltered, he would just walk away—no commitment, no ties, no disillusionment, and, most importantly, no guilt.

The dowager duchess was beginning to lose hope that her godson would ever marry, and she was distressed for more than one reason. She wanted the family name protected, it was true, but she also wished to leave her not inconsiderable personal fortune to Julian and had convinced herself that she would not change her will in his favor until he should be safely wed. She had not previously mentioned this subject to him, but she had decided that today she would put her last card on the table and hope that it would be enough to force his hand.

"I am an old woman, my boy, and not in the best of health," she continued. "It would please me to see you comfortably settled."

The viscount smiled tenderly at the old lady and took her frail hand in his. "I have always thought that you would outlive us all, my dear."

"Don't speak nonsense, Julian! Only a fool would wish to live forever. But you change the subject. I wish not to speak of me, but of you, and of those who will come after you."

"But I am a ramshackle fellow, Godmother. We both know I would make the deuce of a bad husband."

"I am not convinced of that, Julian," she argued. "A wife and family could have a steadying effect on you, bring some sense of purpose to your life. I am a very wealthy

6

woman, Julian, as you know. I am willing to settle my entire estate on you if you will please me in this matter."

The smile instantly disappeared from Stanton's lips, and he dropped her hand as his brows drew together sharply. "A bribe, ma'am? This is not in your style, surely?"

She could not miss the clipped resentment in his words. "Not a bribe, Julian, rather an inducement. I know you have no need of my money, but few prudent people would refuse a large inheritance out of hand. I ask only that you choose a suitable girl and marry; I place no other condition on the bequest."

Stanton turned away and crossed to the windows overlooking the square below. The dowager maintained a prudent silence. She knew he was not pleased, but she had said all she intended and was now willing to allow the matter to rest. She could see that he was eager to be off, but she had not dismissed him, and his manners were too pretty to allow him to offer her any slight. She knew that he cared for her in his way, and for herself, she had loved him all his life.

The duchess had never borne her husband any sons, but Julian was a perfect example of the son she would have liked to have had. He was of moderate height with a quick, athletic figure. He had fine shoulders and a good leg, and the tight-fitting styles of the day suited him well. His handsome features were topped by a head of thick, medium brown hair that curled slightly. His slate-gray eyes were fathomless to most, but the dowager had discovered over the years that they were always her best means to discover what he was thinking. He had a fine, passionate mouth, which, unfortunately, rarely smiled.

As he turned now to face her, she focused her eyes on the grim lines of that mouth as she forced her own into a smile. "Will you be attending Lady Selfridge's ball tomorrow night, Julian?"

"Yes, ma'am, I had planned to go."

"Then, no doubt I shall see you there."

Recognizing his dismissal, Stanton made the proper farewells and took himself off. He saw no sign of his carriage in the street and knew that he had taken longer than the prescribed fifteen minutes. His groom, walking the horses as instructed, soon reappeared, and as the viscount mounted onto the driver's seat, Jenkins handed over the reins.

The dowager stood at the window overlooking the square and watched her godson drive away. Lord Stanton was a nonpareil with the ribbons, and seldom a week went by when he was not challenged by one man or another to race one of his teams or pairs. His name was often to be seen in the betting books, for he could never resist the opportunity to race his bloodstock. This partiality for racing did not concern his godmother, for his wagers were never outrageous, and he seldom lost.

The dowager sighed and turned from the window as Stanton disappeared in the direction of St. James. He had grudgingly given her less than half an hour of his time but now would go on to White's and amuse himself for hours on end. If Stanton was to be at Caro Selfridge's tomorrow, the dowager had every intention of making a push at least to see that he and Miss Charlotte Sherwood should become better acquainted.

2

Lord Stanton and Sir Hugh Broughton sat silently as the last course of their dinner was cleared and the port decanter placed upon the table. Stanton dismissed his footman with a nod and then reached to pour wine for his friend. Sir Hugh was a taller man than the viscount, slimmer, and fair. Both were attired in strict evening dress, for they were to proceed shortly to Lady Selfridge's grand ball.

Earlier in the evening, the viscount had made his friend privy to the previous day's conversation with his godmother, and now he eyed Sir Hugh speculatively.

"What do you know of the Sherwood family, Hugh?"

"No more than the next man, I suppose. Lord Sherwood is in his early fifties; came into the title about two years ago. There are the two girls, a younger son in the army, and of course, Richard."

"Richard?"

"Yes. Richard Sherwood."

"Good Lord! Are you telling me this is the same family?"

"Yes. Of course. I thought you knew."

"No. I hadn't made the connection. If I recall Miss Sherwood, she is dark and slight."

"Yes. And Richard is a blond giant. I agree there is

9

little resemblance, but they are brother and sister nevertheless.''

Stanton smiled reminiscently. ''Remember how much we missed him when he sold out?''

''I lost count of the times he rescued you from one of your harebrained schemes, Julian. When I look back now, I can see that some of your plans for our entertainment were really quite mad.''

''One must have something to occupy one's time between battles,'' Stanton said defensively. ''Even forced marches were preferable to sitting bivouacked in one spot for days on end. London is starting to bore me, too. There is a sameness about each day that makes one long for a change.''

''You felt that way about Oxford.''

''So did you, and we never knew a happier time than those days when we shook the dust of those august halls from our boots, bought our colors, and shipped off to Portugal. Now that the war is over, how do we occupy ourselves, Hugh? Have you given it any thought?''

''I plan to look about me for a wife. I'm the last of the line, after all, and I am not as opposed to the idea of marriage as you are, Julian. You might be wise to at least consider your godmother's advice.''

''What! Are you taking her side in this?''

''No. Of course not. But as long as I've known you, Julian, you've had the habit of selling yourself short. I think you would make a fine husband.''

''Your confidence is gratifying, Hugh, but I will stand by my decision. I must admit, however, to some little curiosity about Miss Sherwood. My godmother seems convinced that this girl would be the perfect wife for me.''

Lady Selfridge's ball was an intolerable squeeze and no doubt would therefore be put down as one of the highlights of the Little Season. As Lord Stanton and Sir Hugh

Broughton made their way through the press of people, they estimated that there were nearly four hundred persons present.

"I should have talked you out of coming here, Julian," Sir Hugh protested. "We will most likely be suffocated in this crowd."

"I promised my godmother that I would be here, Hugh, and I will bet you a monkey, and even offer you odds, that she will have Miss Sherwood at her side."

"I won't take that bet," his friend replied. "You have been too damnably lucky all week. But I don't see how you can be so certain that she will have the girl in tow. She did no more than mention Miss Sherwood to you yesterday. Surely she won't *thrust* the girl into your arms."

"Oh, I would place no assurance on that, my dear Hugh. My godmother has no scruples when it comes to the matter of my marriage. If she could arrange to have me compromise a young lady—a lady of unquestionable suitability, of course—she would do it without a moment's hesitation. She is mad to have me married."

"And you are equally determined not to be leg-shackled. Although how you can turn your back on nearly eighty thousand, just to preserve your solitude, is something I cannot fathom!"

"I don't need my godmother's money, Hugh."

"Then marry the girl and give her grace's money to me," Sir Hugh suggested, "for I could certainly find a use for it."

"You know that I would do almost anything to oblige you, Hugh—but marry to improve your fortune?—no, my friend, I am afraid that there I must draw the line."

The two gentlemen made uneven progress through the reception rooms, full to bursting with elegant ladies in gowns of every color and description and equally elegant gentlemen in more sober darker hues. They were greeted by dozens of friends and acquaintances but managed slowly to gain the ballroom. Stanton methodically scanned the walls, certain that he would find his godmother there.

Stanton laid a hand on Sir Hugh's arm to claim his companion's attention. "You were wise to refuse my wager earlier, Hugh, for if you will look ahead, against the far wall, and to the left of that green urn, you will see my godmother, and, unless I miss my guess, the matron to her left is Lady Sherwood."

Sir Hugh followed the direction of his friend's gaze but only mumbled, "Very handsome woman. And the two young ladies?"

"The Misses Sherwood, of course. Charlotte, the elder, we have met. She is in the rose gown. And her younger sister, very properly, in debutante white."

Stanton had paid little attention to Charlotte Sherwood on first meeting her, and if she had not been with his godmother tonight, he doubted that he could have recognized her again. But now, with his godmother's praise of her person ringing in his memory, he took a moment to observe her. She was a brunette, her dark hair cropped short in the latest fashion and curling about her face attractively. Her rose gown was simple but elegant and set off her excellent figure to advantage. She stood speaking quietly with her sister, a gentle smile hovering on her lips. Her complexion was flawless, her features feminine and harmonious. For one fantastic moment he tried to imagine her as his wife. If her personality matched her physical attractions, she would certainly be a woman of whom a man could be proud.

In the next moment, Lord Stanton and Sir Hugh stood before the duchess and she beamed happily upon her godson and his tall, fair friend. "Julian, and Sir Hugh, how good of you to seek me out. Allow me to introduce my niece, Lady Sherwood . . . This is my godson, Louise—Viscount Stanton, and his friend, Sir Hugh Broughton."

Both gentlemen took Lady Sherwood's hand briefly in

theirs, and then she made them known to her daughters. Stanton had time only to note that Charlotte's voice was low and pleasant and her eyes a rich brown, and then he turned from her placid and serene face to make the acquaintance of her younger sister. He had to drop his gaze an inch or two, for Miss Elizabeth was shorter and slighter than Charlotte. The first thing he noticed about Elizabeth Sherwood was her smile, for it was warm and welcoming, and an indication of her extreme youth and innocence, he thought. Women better versed in the social graces did not bestow smiles so generously upon strangers. Elizabeth's hair, a shade darker than her sister's, was piled high on her head with only a few long curls permitted to escape onto her shoulder. As he took her hand, she sank into a curtsy deep enough for royalty, and as he raised her again, he found her staring boldly into his eyes. He was accustomed to having chits of this age stammer and blush and cast their eyes down upon meeting him. But Miss Elizabeth met his gaze directly, her brown eyes twinkling and mischievous, and despite himself, his rare smile appeared.

A moment later he turned to Charlotte again and solicited her hand for the next dance. Sir Hugh invited Miss Elizabeth to stand up with him for the same set, and the couples moved off to join the other dancers. The dowager smiled approvingly, even though she realized that her godson had asked Miss Sherwood more from a desire to satisfy an old woman's whim than from any desire to please himself.

Both the Misses Sherwood had been popular since their arrival upon the social scene. Their father had come into the title quite unexpectedly when his father and elder brother had drowned together in a yachting accident. Jarvis Sherwood had been, all his adult life, a seagoing man, rising on his own merits to the rank of captain under Lord Nelson. He was proud of his career and proud of the years he had spent serving his country. But overnight, at the age

13

of fifty, he had become a peer of the realm, and the transformation had been overpowering. He had inherited not only the title, but a large fortune as well, and considerable property in Surrey. His eldest son, Richard, was now heir to a barony, and his daughters were expected to be presented at the Queen's Drawing Room and make their debut in society.

The Sherwood family had moved from their modest home in Sussex to the handsome manor house at Sherwood Park. Lord Sherwood had, of course, lived there as a youth and was not unaccustomed to it. His children, however, found it very grand and were delighted that their fortunes had taken such a turn. The girls were both eager to enter Society, and their father generously settled twenty-thousand pounds on each of them. They could marry, or if they preferred, they could remain single, assured of independence through their own income.

Lady Sherwood watched her daughters move gracefully about the room. Elizabeth was smiling at something Sir Hugh had said to her but never faltered in the intricate steps of the dance.

"If you were brought out last year, Miss Elizabeth, how is it that we have never met?" Sir Hugh asked.

"I was not presented at court until this year, sir, so I did not attend such grand parties last year. Also, I don't think that you, or Lord Stanton, for that matter, often attend functions of this sort."

He smiled broadly. "It is true that we enjoy rather less crowded gatherings as a rule. But I am glad we came tonight."

On the opposite side of the room, Lord Stanton and Charlotte were having an equally pleasant conversation. "It seems you have a very military family, Miss Sherwood. Your father was in the navy, was he not?"

"Indeed, my lord. His last command was captain of the frigate ____."

"Then, he was with Nelson at Trafalgar?"

"Yes, he was. He says it was the most glorious action of his career."

"I can well believe it. I served with your brother Richard in the Peninsula, and I think you have yet another brother in the army."

"My brother Jonathan is with the 1st Guards"—she nodded, smiling—"though he complains that it is dreadfully dull since the peace was signed."

"So you are Richard Sherwood's little sister," the viscount said thoughtfully. "I would never have guessed it. You are not very like him."

Charlotte smiled again but could not answer, for the dance was ending. Stanton returned her to her mother's side, thanked her politely, and begged her to convey his regards to her brother.

Lord Stanton and Sir Hugh stood for a few moments in conversation and then parted company as Sir Hugh asked another young lady to dance and the viscount strolled toward the library, which he expected would be a male stronghold tonight, where he could sit and enjoy a glass of brandy and some masculine conversation.

Even though he managed to find congenial company, Stanton's thoughts strayed more than once to Miss Charlotte Sherwood. His godmother was right. Miss Sherwood was a beauty. She was also intelligent, modest, and unassuming—altogether a very comfortable female. He found himself thinking that a man might search long and hard before finding another such paragon. And yet, if he were to allow such a woman into his life, he would be in many ways answerable to her. Simple civility demanded that, at least. For most of his life he had been answerable only to himself. A wife would drastically alter his life-style, placing upon him responsibilities that he did not desire.

Nearly an hour later, Stanton quit the library, determined to search out Sir Hugh and, if necessary, drag him bodily from the ball. The library was some distance removed from the public reception rooms, and Stanton stepped out into the quiet, empty hallway, closing the door behind him. He turned toward the ballroom and had just reached a spot where two corridors converged, when he suddenly collided with a young woman hurrying heedlessly from the other direction. She was nearly running down the hallway, yet her face was turned back, watching behind, as if she feared pursuit.

The sudden collision brought a startled exclamation from the young lady as she stumbled and lost her balance. Stanton reached quickly to steady her and for the briefest moment held her close against him, but in an instant his hands were at her waist as he set her away, holding her only long enough to be certain that she had regained her balance. It was then that he realized the young lady was not unknown to him, for he was staring into the startled dark brown eyes of Elizabeth Sherwood. Earlier in the evening he had written her off as an attractive child, but as she tumbled against him he was brought to realize his mistake. Young, she might be—but a child, definitely not!

"My Lord Stanton! Excuse me!" As she realized her hands had come to rest against his chest, she drew them quickly away and busied them in smoothing the front of her gown. "How foolish of me not to watch where I was going. Pray forgive me."

She glanced over her shoulder again as she spoke, and the viscount murmured: "Think nothing of it, Miss Sherwood." Her heightened color and obvious agitation were hard to ignore, yet the viscount was hesitant to intrude into what was clearly none of his concern. "Surely you are not alone in this part of the house, ma'am? What brings you here?"

"Lord Granbrooke offered to show me the picture gallery. It is said to be very fine, and I was eager to see it." She paused, glancing down at her hands in confusion.

16

"But . . . ?" he coaxed.

"But I did not enjoy it . . . Lord Granbrooke . . . he . . ."

"You need say no more, Miss Sherwood. I am acquainted with Granbrooke. Sometimes he enjoys his wine too much."

Her face brightened perceptively at this possible explanation for the excess civility Lord Granbrooke had treated her to. "Yes, of course. It must have been the wine. Gentlemen sometimes do tend to overdo, don't they?"

"Some certainly do. May I escort you to the ballroom? I am sure that the duchess and Lady Sherwood will be wondering what has become of you."

"Yes, thank you, my lord. You are very kind."

She took the arm he offered, and they returned slowly to the ballroom. They did not encounter Lord Granbrooke, but Stanton sensed the young lady's anxiety and guessed that she was making a supreme effort to keep from turning to look behind them. There was no doubt in his mind that Granbrooke had taken her to the gallery to make some sort of improper advance. Granbrooke was a fool. If he really wanted to win this girl, he would never do so using such tactics. A young and inexperienced miss could only be frightened by that kind of behavior. He considered dropping a word in his godmother's ear about warning Lady Sherwood but then decided that a word to Miss Sherwood herself would not come amiss and would possibly be better taken from him.

"If you wish to avoid such confrontations in the future, ma'am, you need only direct your admirers to a place where others are present. A crowd of people will generally dampen the ardor of the most passionate cavalier."

As he offered this advice in the most conversational tone, and accompanied by a gentle smile, Elizabeth could not take it amiss. She smiled in return, and he thought again how warm and lovely a smile it was, turning up the corners

17

of a generous mouth to show a row of perfect teeth, denting both cheeks with tempting dimples, and lighting her eyes with a rich, warm glow.

"I thank you for the advice, my lord, and I promise that I will heed it." She wondered if he included himself in that advice and then chided herself for thinking that she could inspire any passion in the lofty Viscount Stanton. Even though she had never met him before tonight, she had heard a great deal about him. People said he was a confirmed bachelor, and his tastes ran to older, experienced ladies.

Elizabeth found herself thinking that the man at her side was not what she had expected. He seemed more friendly than aloof, and genuinely concerned for her welfare. He need not have inquired into her distress, nor was he obliged to escort her back to her mother or offer her friendly advice. Charlotte had said after her dance with Stanton that he had admitted knowing Richard. Perhaps he had been kind to her for her brother's sake, or perhaps because of the distant relationship they shared through his godmother. Whatever his reasons, she was pleased with him, and disposed to like him.

Shortly after Viscount Stanton had returned Miss Sherwood to her mother, he encountered Sir Hugh again, and together they quit Lady Selfridge's ball. When Sir Hugh suggested they go on to Watier's, the viscount demurred, insisting he felt more reckless than Watier's. They went instead to Victor's, off St. James, a house that had lately been enjoying a spate of popularity. Victor's was most certainly a gaming hell, but it was a cut above some of the more disreputable places. Its owner kept an excellent cellar, admission was by private invitation only, and although the play was deep, it was fair. The gentlemen settled down to a friendly game of macao and a bottle of excellent cognac.

Lord Stanton and Sir Hugh had arrived at the club sometime after midnight. By three o'clock they were well into their second bottle of brandy, and both feeling a trifle above par. They were tiring of their game when Robert, Lord Granbrooke, approached their table. His flushed complexion indicated that he, too, had been imbibing freely, and he addressed the viscount jovially.

"Well met, Stanton. I have wanted to speak with you anytime these past several days. I have bought myself a new pair, and I think I may have found some cattle at last that will take the shine out of your grays."

Sir Hugh laughed rather loudly, but it was a sound totally devoid of humor. "Will you never learn, Granbrooke? How many times is it now that Julian has beaten your unbeatable horses? Is it three or four?"

"It has been four times," the viscount replied solemnly, "but I am not opposed to taking your money for the fifth time, Granbrooke. Name the day and the distance, and my horses and I shall be at your disposal."

"Don't you care to see my animals first?" Granbrooke asked.

"Not at all. I am sure they are everything you say they are, and we will have a fine race. What should you care to chance on your pair this time?"

They mutually agreed upon a wager of one thousand pounds, although Stanton was certain that Granbrooke could ill afford it. It was generally known about town that his lordship was under the hatches, and the fact that he had been dangling after several heiresses indicated to most observers that he intended to mend his fortunes by making an advantageous match. The knowledge that he was a gazetted fortune hunter would not deter certain ambitious mamas from attempting to secure a title for their daughters.

Lord Granbrooke moved away and soon afterward left the club. Mr. Duffney, one of a group of gentlemen who had been standing nearby, offered his opinion on the proposed race. "I don't see why you bother to race him, Stanton. The fellow is a damned loose-screw."

"I bother to race him because he is an excellent whip, and he provides me with good sport. It is no concern of mine how he chooses to conduct himself in his private life."

"Lately," Duffney continued, "he has been most marked in his attentions to the younger of the Sherwood girls—Elizabeth, I believe her name is. I feel sorry for the young lady who accepts him, for in a very short time he will gamble away whatever money she has brought him, and she will then find herself sharing his poverty."

Sir Hugh's interest was immediately caught. "I do not think you need concern yourself over Miss Sherwood's falling into his trap, Duffney," he replied. "I only met her for the first time tonight, but I assure you, she is quite above his touch."

Stanton added in support of his friend's statement, "Miss Elizabeth Sherwood also has a father and two brothers who will waste little time in taking Granbrooke's measure. My godmother assures me that it is a most unexceptionable family. Miss Elizabeth can look much higher than Granbrooke."

As Stanton turned from Duffney back to Sir Hugh, his attention was caught by a man across the room. In his present inebriated state the viscount found the strange gentleman's puce coat to be of a most offensive hue. "Who the devil is that purple popinjay?" he demanded. "That coat of his fairly pains my eyes!"

Sir Hugh turned to see to who Stanton was referring, and his face lit with sudden pleasure. "That, my dear Julian, is Reginald Fielding!" he exclaimed. "The fellow I have been telling you about!"

"The marksman?"

"The same. I swear I have never seen anything like it!

I watched him for more than an hour at Manton's and never once saw him miss his mark!''

"Invite the fellow over here, Hugh. I will try to suffer his coat, for I would very much like to meet the man who can shoot so well.''

Sir Hugh soon brought Mr. Fielding to the table, and introductions were made. "I have heard a great deal about your talent with a pistol, Fielding,'' the viscount said. "I will look forward to seeing you in action sometime soon.''

"Your lordship's own skill with pistols is not unheralded,'' Fielding returned.

"I am accounted, I believe, to be tolerably accurate. Would you care to make a match between us, Fielding?''

"Certainly, my lord. Anytime you like.''

"Why not now?'' the viscount asked.

"Now, my lord? You cannot be serious!''

"I assure you that I am,'' Stanton continued. "It won't be the first time pistols have been fired in this place. "Sir Hugh tells me that you can shoot the spots from a playing card across the room. Shall we try such a contest?''

"I will be more than happy to oblige you, my lord, but not tonight. You have, as you know, been drinking. I, on the other hand, have not. Such a contest would be unfair.''

Sir Hugh saw that Stanton was about to expostulate strongly, and he hastened to intervene. "He's right, you know, Julian. You wouldn't care to race your horses against a man who wasn't cold sober. Same thing holds true for shooting. You'll have your fairest match if you wait until you can meet on an equal footing.''

This logic was inescapable, and the viscount lapsed into a brooding silence, but even after Fielding had departed, he still could think only of how much he would like to shoot the spots from a playing card. "I am certain I could do it, Hugh.''

His friend smiled at him. "Perhaps, if you were sober,

you could. But in your cups, I doubt if you could hit the card, let alone the spots.''

Lord Stanton rose unsteadily to his feet. ''Drunk or sober, my dear Hugh,'' he said defiantly, ''I will wager you that I can shoot the spots from a five of spades across this very room.''

''You are hopeless, Julian.'' His friend laughed. ''Is there nothing you will not bet upon?''

''Find me a pistol, name your stakes, and we will see just how steady this brandy-soaked hand of mine really is. What shall it be, Hugh? I am weary of the same hundred-pound wager. Let this be one with some teeth in it. We shall each pledge something we would truly be loath to part with.''

''Very well,'' Sir Hugh replied, considering. ''I am so sure that you cannot do it, that I will wager my brown hack, the one I bought from Sorington.''

''I thought it likely that sooner or later I could get you to put him up,'' Stanton said. ''But what have I of equal value?''

There was silence for a moment while they both pondered this question, and finally Sir Hugh spoke. ''There is only one thing that you have, Julian, that you truly value.''

''And what would that be, my friend?''

''Your freedom.''

''My freedom? What do you mean?''

''If you are so certain that you can accomplish this amazing feat of marksmanship, then wager your freedom against my horse. If you succeed in hitting all five spots, then the horse is yours; but if you miss any of them, you will follow your godmother's advice before the week is out and try your luck with the young lady.''

The viscount's eyes opened in astonishment at the stakes his friend suggested. There were several men gathering about their table now that news of a possible contest had spread through the various rooms of the club. Stanton knew

22

that Sir Hugh was referring to his offering for Miss Sherwood, but he would not, of course, mention her name in public and in connection with a wager.

"Those are very high stakes indeed, Hugh," he said, meeting the challenge in his friend's eyes. "But I accept them."

This conversation was lost on the men listening, but they did glean from it that the viscount had decided to try his luck at the target and several of them set about preparations. It was found that the proprietor had an accurate pistol that he was willing to lend to the contest. Several tables were dragged against the far wall and multibranched candelabra placed on each to provide the best possible lighting. Duffney shuffled through a deck of cards to extract the five of spades. One of the waiters had been sent to procure a target board that was kept on hand for just such occasions as this, when young gentlemen who frequented the establishment insisted on such sport.

Stanton was permitted several practice shots to familiarize himself with the pistol, and then the playing card was placed upon the board. Total silence reigned as he raised his arm to fire the first round; the report was deafening in such a confined space. While the viscount carefully reloaded the pistol, the target was examined and found to have one of its spots removed, quite neatly, through the center. Many of the onlookers were amazed, for even those who knew the viscount to be a dead shot could hardly credit his accuracy after the amount of brandy they had seen him consume.

The second spot, and the third, were removed just as neatly, and Stanton was reloading for the fourth try. Sir Hugh was surprised to see that small beads of perspiration had appeared on Stanton's forehead, for Julian's was the coolest head under pressure he had ever known. Watching the steadiness of his friend's arm as he raised it for the fourth time, Sir Hugh was nearly ready to admit that he had lost his favorite hack. The trigger was pulled, the report sounded, and once again the target was checked. The ball had gone wide! It had touched no portion of the card's spot!

Some conversation broke out then, and several of the men wandered away, the entertainment being over. But the viscount continued methodically to reload the pistol. "I shall try for the fifth spot, Hugh," he said, "and if I hit it, I shall have four of five. Then the next time I try, I shall endeavor to improve my score."

Sir Hugh watched his friend in silence, suddenly feeling very sober indeed. He had won his wager and kept his horse, but he was beginning to believe that the stakes he had insisted upon were too dear.

The fifth round was fired, and although the hit was not dead center, it had definitely struck the spot. "Damned fine shooting, Stanton!" Duffney exclaimed. "You must let me know when you plan to meet Fielding. That is one match I must see!"

Soon afterward, as the dawn was breaking, Lord Stanton and Sir Hugh walked slowly toward Sir Hugh's rooms in Ryder Street. The morning air was cold, and the more sober Sir Hugh became, the more he regretted the night's events.

"You know, Julian," he said finally, "Tonight's wager was private between us, and no one would be any the wiser if we simply forgot the whole thing."

Stanton stopped abruptly and turned to his friend in surprise. "You know me better than that, Hugh! A wager is a wager, whether two people or two hundred are involved. You have won fairly, and when I play, I pay. Miss Charlotte Sherwood will receive my offer before the week is out."

Sir Hugh shook his head sadly. "If you end up in a miserable marriage, you will blame me for pitching you into it. I would not lose our friendship over this, Julian, even to satisfy your honor."

The viscount laughed aloud at his friend's concern. "There is no danger of that, Hugh. You and I have been through too much together to allow a mere exchange of marriage vows to come between us. And besides, you are forgetting one thing. My godmother has merely suggested that I make an offer for Miss Sherwood. Who knows? My luck may yet be in! The lady may refuse me!"

3

In the book room of his London residence in Mount Street, Lord Jarvis Sherwood sat at a large desk liberally spread with papers of every description and found himself wishing for perhaps the tenth time that his son Richard had not been detained in Surrey. Lord Sherwood had no head for business and was the first to admit it. His naval career had satisfied him, and he had never wished to step into his father's shoes. Born the third son of a baron, he had been sent to Eton, and eventually to Cambridge, but he had never settled there. From his earliest recollections, he had wanted only to be a sailor, for the open sea to him was a magical, mystical place. He had badgered his father relentlessly, until finally, when he had come down from his second year, his father had capitulated. For the next thirty years the sea had been his life, and he had never regretted it. He had married well, settled his wife in a comfortable home on the outskirts of Portsmouth, and fathered four hopeful children. All in all, life had dealt him, he thought, a very fair hand.

As a young man with two older brothers, it had never occurred to the present Lord Sherwood that he would ever succeed to the title. His eldest brother, John, had never married, and when he had succumbed to a heart condition ten years previously, any thought of inheriting still had not crossed Jarvis's mind, for his brother Rupert already had two daughters and would no doubt have sons as well. But Rupert never did produce sons, and when he and his father were lost together in the yachting accident, Captain Sherwood became the new Lord Sherwood. Lord Sherwood found himself master of a large estate, a situation for which he had little training and even less inclination.

In addition to his two daughters, Lord Sherwood had two sons: Richard, the eldest, now twenty-seven, and Jonathan, aged twenty-two. Lord Sherwood had always hoped that his sons would embrace a military career. Richard had finished at Oxford and gone on to the Peninsula to join the army there, and although he had served well for more than four years, he was not enamored of the military, and when informed of the fatal accident to his grandfather and uncle, he had resigned his commission and returned home. Jonathan, on the other hand, was eager to join the army, and no sooner had he finished school than he was off to the war. He was understandably disappointed when the hostilities ended within a year of his joining, for as he complained to his sister Charlotte, there was little opportunity for a man to advance himself during peacetime. Jonathan's regiment was part of the Army of Occupation in the Low Countries, but Jonathan himself had just arrived in London for a month's furlough.

Lord Sherwood had turned to Richard for help at the time of his succession and had found his elder son to be an excellent manager. He had dealt admirably with the lawyers, made sense of the mountains of documents, and taken over the reins of the estate as if he had been born to it. Lord Sherwood once apologized to Richard for thrusting so much work onto his shoulders, and was more than a little surprised at his son's reply.

"Don't mention it, sir. I like the work. It gives me something constructive to do with my time, and I enjoy it that much more because I know you find it irksome."

27

Irksome was a much milder word than Lord Sherwood would have chosen to use. Farmers and tenants, cows and sheep, fodder and wool, were all matters that he preferred never to think of at all. So from that time forward, Richard handled all the affairs of the estate, and his father enjoyed the first true leisure he had known in his adult life.

England had been at war for more than twenty years, and Lord Sherwood had spent the large majority of that time away from his country, family, and home. He was proud of his sons and daughters, and very much in love with his wife, and he was determined to enjoy the good fortune that had come his way. He retired from active military duty, a decision made easier for him by the peace with France, but he still held a post in the government as adviser to the Admiralty. This position required that he spend a great deal of time in London, which he was able to do so long as Richard was willing to take responsibility for the Surrey property.

Lord Sherwood looked once again at the mass of work that had accumulated on his desk during the weeks of Richard's absence. "Thank God the boy will be back in town soon," he said to himself.

He was interrupted at that moment by the entrance of his butler. "Excuse me, my lord, but Lord Granbrooke has called and wishes an audience with you."

"Give me a few moments, Williams, and then show the gentleman in."

"Very good, my lord."

As the butler disappeared, Lord Sherwood opened a large drawer at the side of his desk and slid all the offending papers into it. They filled it nearly to the top, and he shoved in the last pages and closed the drawer as Lord Granbrooke was announced.

Usually when a gentleman with whom Lord Sherwood was barely acquainted made a request to speak with him in private, he expected to receive an application for permission to address one or the other of his daughters. And, indeed, he had correctly guessed the reason for Lord Granbrooke's visit. Today the lady in question was Elizabeth, and Lord Granbrooke had called to make a very proper offer for her hand in marriage.

On the first floor at the back of the Sherwoods' town house was a small sitting room where the Sherwood ladies habitually gathered when they wished to be private. Miss Sherwood entered this room now, and both her mother and sister looked up as she announced with a voice of doom, "Lord Granbrooke is with Papa in the book-room."

Elizabeth looked imploringly at her mother. "Oh, Mama, what shall I do?"

"Come now, Lizzie, there is no need for such distress. This visit is, after all, no more than you expected."

"But, Mama, I did everything I could to discourage him. I even hinted that I had developed a *tendre* for someone else."

"Well, it clearly didn't serve," Charlotte said dampingly. "But I don't see why you should be in such a taking. You have only to politely refuse him. Or, better yet, have Papa do it for you."

This idea had not previously occurred to Elizabeth, and she grasped at it now. "Do you think he would do so, Mama?"

"I am sure your father would willingly do so should you ask it of him, Lizzie. But do you not think that Lord Granbrooke deserves, at the very least, the courtesy of a direct answer from you? It is not every day, after all, that a man asks a woman to be his wife."

"I'm sure you are right," Elizabeth said, "but I must admit that I am rather afraid of him."

"Afraid of whom?" This question from the doorway caused all three women to turn their heads as Jonathan Sherwood entered the room, resplendent in his Guardsmen's uniform of scarlet and gold. He was a well-made young man of above-average height, with an open, smiling countenance. His hair, like that of his sisters, was dark brown, but his eyes, unlike theirs, were gray.

"Lord Granbrooke is with Papa and has come to make an offer for Lizzie," Charlotte explained.

Ensign Sherwood flung himself down on the sofa beside his youngest sister and offered gallantly, "Shall I go down and send him to the rightabout?"

"I wish you would," Elizabeth returned with feeling, "but Mama feels that his lordship deserves to have my answer personally, however much I may dread giving it."

"Do you think so, Mama?" Jonathan asked. "I would agree with you if I thought for one moment that Granbrooke's affections were involved. But we are all agreed, are we not, that it is Lizzie's fortune and not her admirable person that has taken Lord Granbrooke's fancy? I see no reason for her to meet him if she has an aversion to the task."

Elizabeth's hopes rose at her brother's words but fell quickly as her mother spoke again. "We may think that we understand his lordship's motives, Jon, but it would be folly to pretend that we are certain of them. If Elizabeth has engendered those feelings in a man that would lead him to offer for her, for whatever reasons, then it is her responsibility to explain to the gentleman why she cannot, or will not, accept him."

Hearing the finality in her mother's voice, and realizing that she was undoubtedly right, Elizabeth rose from the sofa resolutely. "Well, I must go then. Wish me courage."

Jonathan laughed outright. "That you have never lacked, little sister! When you have finished making Granbrooke the unhappiest of men, hurry back, and bring my father with you, for I have some news of my own to impart."

Elizabeth went quickly down the stairs to the ground floor and there encountered Williams, preparing to come in search of her. "Lord Sherwood would like you to wait on him in the book-room, Miss Elizabeth."

"I suspected as much, Williams. Thank you." She glanced at her image in the hall mirror, pushed one stray curl back from her forehead, and made sure that her blue sash was neat. Then she followed the butler to the book-room door.

Lord Sherwood, who had perforce spent months and sometimes years away from his family, had missed a great deal of his children's adolescent years. But during the past two years, he had taken advantage of the opportunity to know them better, and he could see now that his Lizzie was not looking forward to this interview. He walked forward to meet her and took her hand firmly in his. Elizabeth was not shy in company, but this was the first offer she had received, so the situation was unusual and therefore uncomfortable for her.

"Lord Granbrooke would like a few moments of private conversation with you, Elizabeth," her father said simply. "You may use this room. I will see that you are not disturbed."

He left on the words, and Elizabeth found herself nervously confronting Lord Granbrooke. If she was dispassionate about his lordship, she had to admit that he was an attractive man. He was not above medium height, but he had a strong-looking, muscular figure. She had heard that he was a noted Corinthian, and she could readily believe it. She had also heard that he was addicted to the gaming tables, and although this predilection did not exhibit itself upon his person, she was nevertheless convinced of its veracity. His interest in her hand, she felt, had always been feigned, and she had not the slightest doubt that were her dowry to vanish overnight, her suitor would vanish just as quickly.

She had not met him since their misadventure in Lady Selfridge's picture gallery, and she wished now that she had confided that incident to her mother. She had hesitated to do so, knowing that she had been foolish to accompany him there and that her mother would be displeased.

It had seemed harmless enough at the time. She had wished to view the paintings and had enjoyed the early part of their stroll down the long, narrow gallery. A full-length portrait of the present countess was exquisite, and Elizabeth had stopped to admire it, even though the cut of the crimson gown the countess wore revealed enough of her ample bosom to make Elizabeth blush.

"The countess is a lovely woman, is she not?" her companion had asked, noting her heightened color.

"Her gown is stunning," Elizabeth had answered.

". . . if a bit revealing."

Elizabeth had returned no answer, and Granbrooke had continued smoothly. "Married woman have a great deal of license in the matter of dress. You would look enchanting yourself in such a gown, Elizabeth, and I would willingly buy you a dozen."

Elizabeth had turned startled eyes to him, shocked as much by his use of her name as by the meaning of his words. In the next instant he had taken her shoulders in his hands and bent his mouth to hers, but as she had instinctively pulled from his touch, his lips had never reached their goal.

"Please, my lord . . . you . . . I . . . please, excuse me." And with only that, she had fled, unable to voice the anger she felt, unable to command a glib rejoinder to gloss over the moment, unable to remain one instant longer in his presence, wanting only the busy ballroom and the security it provided. Moments later she had collided with Viscount Stanton outside the library.

Now as Lord Granbrooke stood before her she felt the unease of that evening returning as she slowly crossed the room and held out her hand to him, more from unconscious habit than from any desire to touch him. He took it and held it longer than she would have liked.

"My dear Miss Elizabeth, it is good of you to see me," he said very formally. "I am sure you must have guessed the reason for my visit. I think that you cannot be unaware of my sentiments upon this occasion." He paused briefly, and Elizabeth felt that she should say something, but not a single word would come to her lips. His lordship seemed undaunted by her silence, no doubt attributing it to maidenly modesty, and he continued smoothly. "I have spoken with your father, and he has given me permission to address you. It is my most earnest wish that you would consent to become my wife."

He is persistent, she thought, but still said nothing, and after a moment, he continued. "Please allow me to apologize for my precipitate behavior the other evening. I frightened you, and you must believe me, I had no intention of doing so. I was swept away by your loveliness—"

Disliking the direction his thoughts were taking, Elizabeth finally found her voice. "My Lord Granbrooke," she interrupted, "I am honored by your proposal, but I am afraid that it is impossible for me to accept it." She had planned to say that she could not return his regard, but the words would not come. Instead, she heard herself saying, "I had tried to hint to you that such a declaration would not be welcomed by me." To her credit, Elizabeth was steadily regarding him as she uttered her totally fabricated refusal. She watched as the hope slowly died form his eyes, and then she dealt it the final, fatal blow. "The fact is, my lord, that my affections are otherwise engaged."

"I see," he said rather tightly. "I had no idea. Well, of course, if such is the case, then I perfectly understand. I am sorry if I have caused you any embarrassment, Miss Elizabeth."

"No. None at all, my lord."

It only remained for Lord Granbrooke to take his leave,

which he promptly did, begging Elizabeth to convey his compliments to her parents. He then made her a stiff, formal bow and left the house. Elizabeth decided that his lordship had not expected to meet with a rejection and was having some difficulty in believing that he had. She did not regret the impulse that had made her mislead him, for she was certain that had she given him any other answer, he would have continued his pursuit of her.

The interview was disquieting for Elizabeth, but once relieved of her suitor, her spirits rebounded, and remembering that Jonathan had bade her hurry back, she returned at once to the sitting room.

"Back so soon, Lizzie?" Jonathan teased.

"It does not take a great deal of time to say no, after all," Charlotte said practically.

"Did you refuse him, then, Lizzie?" her father asked.

"Yes, Papa. I did. I have not the slightest wish to marry Lord Granbrooke."

"Lizzie is determined to marry only for love," Charlotte added scornfully.

"There is no fault to be found with that," Lady Sherwood said. "Your father and I made a love match, and it has served us well. But, come. Jonathan has some news that he wishes to share with us, and I am sure we are all most anxious to hear it."

"Yes, well, I do have an announcement to make," Jon said, "and although I daresay I should wait until Richard returns, I am bursting to tell someone. I have asked Harriet Putnam to marry me, and she has accepted!"

This communication had the effect of causing the Sherwood family to all suddenly begin speaking at once, and then just as suddenly to stop in midsentence, as they heard their voices mingling in confusion.

Jonathan laughed. "I can see that I have not surprised you!"

"Certainly not," Elizabeth said. "We have been expecting you to offer for Harriet forever."

Lord Sherwood crossed the room to his son and reached to take his hand. "Allow us to wish you happy, Jonathan. You know, of course, that we all hold Harriet in affection and esteem."

Jonathan did know this to be true, and indeed, it would have been difficult to find someone who did not like Harriet. She was a quiet, handsome girl, possessed of both pleasing manners and excellent sense. The Sherwoods had known her all her life, for she was the only child of their nearest neighbor in Sussex. As boys, both Jonathan and Richard had admired Harriet, and had even gone so far as to vie for her attention when they were home from school over the long vacations; but their interest had been neighborly amicability, with nothing of the romantic in it.

Squire Putnam, always ambitious for his daughter, had sent her at nineteen to spend a season with his sister in London. With the signing of the peace that spring, Jonathan's regiment had been billeted outside London, and he had been granted the opportunity to see his young neighbor in all her London finery. Harriet was much admired but seemed to smile more often upon her childhood playmate than upon any of her London beaux. It was not many weeks before Jonathan had become most marked in his attentions, but before anything could be decided between them, he had received orders to sail for Belgium with the occupational army and had not been back to England since. Now on furlough, he was determined to make good use of his time. He had been home only two days and was already engaged to be married.

"Have you spoken to Squire Putman, Jonathan?" his father asked.

"Yes. I stopped at Portsmouth on my way home."

"And what did he say?"

"I think he had hoped Harriet would make a great match

and not settle for a younger son," he said ruefully. "But he was a brick about it. He said that if I was Harriet's choice, he would do nothing to throw a rub in the way."

"Have you chosen a date for the wedding, Jonathan?" Lady Sherwood asked.

"Yes, Mama, we have. Three weeks from today—if you think we can manage it."

4

Sherwood Manor stood in a deep wooded valley, under the shadow of the Surrey Downs. The barony of Sherwood had existed from Saxon times, but the present manor house was of a much later date. During the reign of Charles II, a previous Baron Sherwood, considering his medieval home to be anything but comfortable, had had the entire building razed, with the exception of the chapel, and had had the present house constructed in its place. It was a two-and-a-half-story red-brick structure, handsome and symmetrical, weathered by the passage of time. The house faced east, and the large leaded, mullioned windows of the breakfast parlor sparkled in the early-morning sunshine.

Richard Sherwood sat in solitary state at the breakfast table, finishing a hearty meal. He was a tall man with very broad, square shoulders and a strong, athletic figure. He was the only one of the Sherwood offspring to have inherited his mother's coloring, for in striking contrast to his dark-haired brother and sisters, Richard's hair was bronzed gold and his eyes were blue.

From where he sat, Richard could see a groom leading his mare, Sultry, to the front of the house. He rose, and pausing only to take an apple from a bowl on the sideboard, he passed through the entry hall and down the shallow steps to the drive. He was promised in London tomorrow, but now, as he mounted his horse and set off, he considered how he would spend his last day in the country.

There were several tenants to see this morning, but with any luck he would finish by midday and beg a luncheon somewhere along the way, perhaps at the vicarage, where he planned to call and say good-bye. Then he would make one final stop at the receiving office, in the event there was any last-minute correspondence awaiting him. He should be home again in good time to spend a few hours with his father's agent before dinner. The following morning he would be off at first light, and with little more than thirty miles to travel, he could be in town by midday.

The majority of the park at Sherwood Manor lay before the house, to the east, wedged between two upstanding hills that ran parallel for a distance of half a mile. A pair of wrought-iron gates marked the entrance to the drive, and beyond them a winding country lane crossed at right angles. A left-handed turning led northward over several tree-covered ridges and gradually diminished into a cart track and finally a sheep walk as it rose over the grassy chalk country of the Downs. A right-handed turning, which Richard now took, led down to the fertile valley of the Tillingbourne, with neat fields at the foot of the hills and lush pastures stretching to the banks of the gentle river.

By the time Richard had finished with his tenants, the sky was clouding over, and what had begun as a bright late-summer day now held the promise of rain. Turning his horse still farther south, he crossed the Tillingbourne at the ford below the village and made his way toward the church steeple at the far end of the street. Dismounting, he tied his mare to the picket fence surrounding the vicarage. As he had suspected, he was invited for luncheon. The vicar and his wife begged him to carry their good wishes to his family in London, and he promised to do so, but it was almost two o'clock before he managed to get away. One look at the darkening sky told him that he must hurry if he wished to avoid a soaking. He made a quick stop at the receiving office, and then turned Saltry toward home.

Richard had nearly reached the gates of Sherwood Manor when, coming round a corner at a canter, he saw a small boy and dog in the road and had to pull Sultry up sharply to avoid running them down. Richard thought the lad could be no more than eight or nine, and he was struggling to lift a large sheep dog that was clearly too heavy for him. The boy looked up apologetically as Sultry tossed her head in response to the unexpected pull on her tender mouth.

"I'm so sorry, sir," he said. "I could hear you coming, but I couldn't move her out of the way in time."

Richard dismounted, noting as he did so that this was no village boy, as he had at first suspected. His speech alone declared him to be gently born, and Richard saw that his short coat and breeches were well-made, even though covered with large quantities of both dust and dog hair. "What ails your dog, lad?" he asked.

"Sheba has injured her paw, and can't walk on it, and she is too heavy for me to carry. Aren't you Captain Sherwood, sir? From the Manor?"

"I am. And who might you be, young man?"

"Jimmy Ellis, sir. From Ellis End."

"I have met Sir Winston Ellis," Richard replied. "A relative of yours?"

Jimmy nodded. "He is my grandfather."

"Well, Jimmy Ellis, you happen to be in luck, for Sultry here has no objection to dogs, and I am sure she would be more than willing to help you carry your dog home. We will put Sheba up first, and then I shall mount and pull you up behind me."

Jimmy hesitated. "I must not trouble you, sir. I can manage myself."

"How will you get her home without my help?" Richard challenged. When the boy didn't answer, he continued.

39

"You should not hesitate to accept help when you truly need it, Master Ellis. When a helping hand is offered honestly and willingly, it can be accepted honorably and without obligation. Come now, for if we don't hurry, we are both likely to get a soaking." Even as he spoke several drops of rain fell, while to the north over the Downs, heavy black clouds were bearing down upon them.

Sultry turned an inquisitive muzzle round to her master as he hoisted the injured dog over the saddlebow but made no objection. Young Master Ellis held the dog steadily in place while Richard mounted, and then, reaching down, Richard took Jimmy's hand and pulled him easily up behind the saddle.

"Your home is to the north, Jimmy, is it not?"

"Yes, sir. Follow this road to the end of the wood, and then eastward along the Downs."

They had covered only a short distance before the rain began to fall in earnest. "You would have been safely home by now, sir," Jimmy said, "if you had not stopped for us."

"Indeed I would, but don't let it trouble you. This will not be the first time I have been caught in a storm."

A little farther on, the trees ended abruptly as the lonely ridge of the Downs rose before them. The rain was being driven now in sheets before the wind, and Richard was thankful to be able to turn his horse eastward, putting the wind at their backs. They came at length to Ellis End, and although the house itself was not prepossessing, Richard thought the situation charming, with the stark, forbidding commons rising on the one hand, and the gentle protection of a tree-covered ridge on the other.

As the house came into sight, Jimmy spoke suddenly. "If you would leave me here, Captain Sherwood, I'm sure I could manage myself."

Richard could not see the boy's face, but he could hear

the uneasiness in his voice. "Something is troubling you, Jimmy. What is it?"

"Well, sir, the thing is that my mother isn't likely to be pleased to see me bringing Sheba home."

"No? Why not?"

"She told me I was not to go looking for the dog. Actually, what she said was that I should leave it to the servants. But she didn't make me promise that I wouldn't go, so I haven't really disobeyed her, have I?"

"Yes, young man, I am afraid you have. But I think I understand. When you have lost something that you care for, you are convinced that no other efforts at searching can be nearly as effective as your own."

"Yes, sir, that's exactly right! But the thing is, I'm sure my mother won't see it that way. And if she finds that I've troubled you, and gotten you wet into the bargain, she will be more angry still."

Richard considered the boy's request but finally shook his head as he replied, "I see your problem, truly I do, but I don't think I would be doing you or your parents any service by leaving you here in such weather." Jimmy made no reply, and in a moment Richard continued. "Where shall we take Sheba? To the stables?"

"Yes, sir, for Victor, our groom, will tend the paw, and we can shut Sheba into one of the loose boxes, to keep her from wandering off again."

They rode past the house and on to the stables beyond. Richard gave Jimmy a hand down, and then Jimmy led the big hunter while Richard carried the wet dog inside. There they discovered Victor and were just beginning to examine the wounded paw, when Mrs. Ellis swept through the stable door.

She had seen their approach from the front windows of the house, where she had been anxiously waiting since the moment she learned that her son was out in the storm.

41

When they did not stop at the house, she had donned a hooded cloak and hurried to the stables in their wake.

Throwing the hood back, she directed a stern look at her son, but as she spoke, Richard thought there was more concern than anger in her voice. "James William! I might have known that you would disobey me and go searching for that wretched animal. You will answer to me later. For now, give that dog to Victor, and go to the house immediately and remove those wet things."

Richard had intended to give the boy an encouraging smile, but as Jimmy turned to leave, Richard had no thought to spare for him, for his complete attention was captured by Mrs. Ellis. He saw a tall, elegant woman of striking beauty, with an abundance of auburn hair, braided intricately and piled high upon her head. Her features were fine-drawn and delicate, her complexion extremely fair, with just a touch of color in her high cheekbones. In contrast to her pale skin, her brows were dark, and her lashes long and thick. Her cloak lay open to reveal a simple country gown of dark green wool, finely molded to a figure with full, rounded bosom and neat, trim waist. As she turned her direct gaze upon Richard, he realized he should have guessed that her eyes would be green and magnificent.

Victor walked away with the injured bitch, and Mrs. Ellis held out her hand to Richard. "I must thank you, sir. You have clearly aided my son, and at no small cost to yourself."

He took her hand briefly as he said, "Allow me to introduce myself, ma'am. I am Richard Sherwood, from the Manor."

She smiled. "I am pleased to make your acquaintance, Captain Sherwood. I have heard my father-in-law speak of you. It is unfortunate that we must meet under such circumstances."

"You make too much of it, Mrs. Ellis. I assure you, a little rain doesn't concern me."

"A little rain, sir! You are quite soaked to the skin, and I dare you to deny it."

His ready smile appeared as he said ruefully, "Very well, I admit it, but believe me, I was more than willing to help Jimmy. He was in quite a fix, for the dog was too heavy for him, and he was determined not to leave her when he knew she needed help." He considered that this view of the escapade may not have occurred to her, and he was determined to soften her displeasure if he could. "It hasn't been so many years since my younger brother, Jonathan, was getting into scrapes of this sort, but he always seemed to land on his feet."

"I can see that you think I am being overly protective, Captain Sherwood, but Jimmy has been gone for hours and has just recently recovered from pneumonia. When it started raining so heavily, I was frantic, and I am most obliged to you for bringing him safely home."

"I am happy to have been of service, ma'am. And now, if you will excuse me, I must be going. I leave for London in the morning and have still some business to attend to today." He moved to where Sultry stood waiting but then turned once more to speak. "Mrs. Ellis, there was one more thing. I know Jimmy expects to be punished for his disobedience today, and that, of course, is between the two of you. But he expressed a concern that you would be angry with him for involving me in his adventure. You must know that he tried to refuse my help, but that I . . . insisted. I would not like to think that any insistence on my part resulted in a harsher punishment for him."

"Very well, Captain, if that is what you wish, I will not tax him with it."

He thanked her briefly and then led his horse out into the stable yard and mounted. Raising a hand in farewell, he turned the mare and set off once again into the storm.

Mrs. Ellis stood at the stable door and watched until he had disappeared into the grayness of the falling rain. She said a silent prayer of thanks that he had come upon Jimmy when he had, and that he had been disposed to help. Then suddenly she realized that she should have offered him shelter until the storm had passed or, at the very least, a coach to carry him back to his home. She chided herself for her bad manners, but recalling how the captain had shrugged off the storm, she thought it more than likely that he would have refused any offer she might have made, for he had said he was in a hurry and did not seem the type of man to pamper himself.

5

Richard dined early, as was the country custom, but it was a simple meal and soon finished. When the family was not in residence, he insisted upon austerity in the household. Of all things, he disliked being fussed over, something the servants were apt to do when the family was in London and the captain in solitary residence.

Upon his return to the Manor earlier, he had endured a full twenty minutes of his valet's sullen silence after he had removed each piece of the captain's ravaged clothing. Henchly knew better than to voice his disapproval, but the unspoken reproach was thick enough to cut with a knife. Richard always took particular care in his dress and appearance, but tonight he was preoccupied and refused to concern himself over a wet coat and a few dog hairs.

The meeting with his father's agent had been brief and fruitful, and now as he sat overlong at his port, he had leisure to reflect upon his meeting earlier in the day with Mrs. Ellis. What was her given name? he wondered. Why had they never met before? What manner of man was her husband? He had a partial answer for the second question. The Sherwood family had spent very little time in the country during the past two years. As long as the war with France had continued, it was necessary for Lord Sherwood to remain in London. When Richard came to Surrey alone, he came to work, and, residing as a bachelor, he was not expected to entertain. He wondered briefly why he had never been invited to dine with Sir Winston and his family at Ellis End, for they were the closest neighbors of his own class. Perhaps the Ellises, like his own family, were not often to be found in the country.

His reverie was interrupted by the entrance of Jepson, his butler. "Sir Winston Ellis has called, Captain. I told him you were still at dinner."

"Show him in here, Jepson, and bring another glass."

Moments later, Sir Winston was shown into the room. He was a burly man in his late fifties, with a ruddy complexion, overly long curling gray hair, and a heavy, unkempt beard. Richard rose to greet his guest, and Sir Winston replied with bluff informality, "Evening, Sherwood. Sorry to interrupt your dinner. Good of you to see me."

"You do not interrupt, Sir Winston. As you can see, I am merely lingering over my port. Please, share a glass with me."

"Don't mind if I do," Sir Winston replied, seating himself at the table. "Sarah tells me that you came to Jimmy's rescue this afternoon."

Sarah, Richard thought. It fits her. But he said, "If you have come to thank me for that small service, Sir Winston, let me assure you that both young James and your daughter-in-law have already done so."

"I did wish to add my thanks to theirs, but that was not the primary reason for my visit, Captain. Sarah mentioned in passing that you were traveling to London tomorrow, and you could do me a favor, if you would be so inclined."

"If I can, I will be more than happy to do so," Richard replied amiably.

"The thing is," Sir Winston continued, "Mrs. Ellis is traveling up to London herself, taking my daughter, Virginia, to spend some time doing the social whirl during the

Little Season. Sarah insists upon traveling with only the servants. She says she don't need any other escort when she has her maid with her and a coachman and footman to do for her. And perhaps she's in the right of it. But I don't mind telling you, sir, that I can't be comfortable with the arrangement, especially when she will have Virginia with her, and young Jimmy as well. Sarah's forever coming the staid matron with me, but she's fair and far off if she thinks her widowhood lends her any protection, for she's a damned handsome woman withal, make no mistake about that!''

Richard found himself extremely interested in Sir Winston's disclosures, but his tone was carefully bland as he spoke. "I will be more than happy to lend my support to the ladies' journey, Sir Winston. When did they plan to travel?''

"Sarah said you were leaving tomorrow, Captain Sherwood, and we have no intention of detaining you. I am sure they could be ready to leave by noon, if that would be convenient?''

It would make him half a day later than planned, but Richard made no objection to this proposal. Within several minutes, the gentlemen had settled all the details of the journey between them, and then Richard refilled his guest's glass and spent the next thirty minutes learning what he could about Sir Winston's intriguing family. Sir Winston was easily led to volunteer the information that his only son, James, had been dead for almost five years, and young Jimmy was now his heir. His only other child, Virginia, now aged twenty, had enjoyed her London debut the previous spring. His wife he did not mention, but Richard had gathered from the vicar that Lady Ellis had been dead for many years.

Sir Winston returned home that evening shortly before eight o'clock and threw his household into turmoil by announcing that the departure date for London had been

47

moved forward two full days. "Captain Sherwood has agreed to escort you to town, and you must leave by noon tomorrow so as not to inconvenience him."

Mrs. Ellis, who under normal circumstances would not consider contradicting her father-in-law, was moved to expostulate. "But, Sir Winston, how can we possibly be ready in such a short time? We have only just begun packing."

"Nonsense. The servants do most of the work. Pack tonight what you will need for the first few days of your stay, and take it with you in the post chaise. The rest of your gear can follow in a few days time."

Sarah had to admit that this plan was workable, although she was mortified that Sir Winston had foisted them upon Captain Sherwood. She already owed him a debt of gratitude, and now she was forced into being under further obligation to him. She blamed herself for mentioning the captain's plans at dinner. She should have known that Sir Winston would seize the opportunity to have his own way. She was well accustomed to her father-in-law's autocratic nature, and more than aware that she was no match for him, but as a rule he tended to display his high-handed tactics within the privacy of his own home. To consult Sarah concerning any plans he wished to make would never occur to Sir Winston. Any time she made the slightest bid for independence, as she had in suggesting that she travel to London on her own, he took umbrage, overset her wishes regardless of their suitability, and, more often than not, succeeded in having his own way in the end. This time his weapon had been Captain Sherwood.

Sarah wondered if the captain knew that their plans were being changed to accommodate him. It would not have surprised her in the least! Men were so pompous! Why should they care if she should be up half the night hurrying to be ready on time? What concern of theirs if she arrived two days early in London? What was it to them if her hostess, Sir Winston's sister, should be inconvenienced?

The questions could go on endlessly, but to what purpose? It was a man's world, plain and simple, and no man of her acquaintance had ever missed an opportunity to drive the point home.

London, at least, would offer some peace from Sir Winston's tyranny, for their host, Lord Kemp, did not hold women in contempt. Rather, he chose to ignore them entirely, which suited Sarah well enough. Better to be ignored than oppressed.

Mrs. Ellis managed to find her bed shortly before midnight but slept fitfully and awoke with the headache. When she descended the steps to the drive some twenty minutes before twelve, it was to find the captain already arrived and her son gazing in awe at the four matched chestnuts harnessed to his curricle. The day was fine, the storm of yesterday having passed off as quickly as it had come. Thin white clouds riding high in a blue-gray sky promised a pleasant day for travel.

The captain turned to Mrs. Ellis immediately and smiled as he greeted her. "Good morning, ma'am. We are to have good weather for our journey it seems."

Sarah, embarrassed that her father-in-law had maneuvered the captain into his present role of escort, was prepared to offer him an apology. They were, after all, relative strangers, and she had no right to make demands upon his time or good-will. But his ready smile and good-natured civility made an apology seem inappropriate, so she merely smiled and said, "It it good of you to accompany us, Captain Sherwood."

"Not at all, ma'am . . . My pleasure. Your coachman has been telling me that Jimmy is an indifferent traveler. Do you think he would feel less queasy if he were to ride in the open carriage with me?"

Sarah glanced toward the captain's curricle, where Jimmy was in earnest conversation with Captain Sherwood's groom. "I appreciate the offer, Captain, but we should not inconvenience you."

"It would be no inconvenience, Mrs. Ellis. I would enjoy his company." When he thought he saw a trace of anxiety in her eyes, he added, "He will come to no harm with me, I promise. And we will be close behind your coach at all times."

It was clear to Sarah that he would press her until she gave her permission, and indeed, this did not surprise her. The captain was clearly, like her father-in-law, a man accustomed to having his own way—and she was a woman accustomed to relenting. So more from habit than inclination she said, "I do not fear for his safety, Captain Sherwood." She wanted to add: "But I would rather not be under any further obligation to you." Impossible to say that, of course.

Richard was quick to pick up the note of restraint in her voice, and his next words surprised her considerably. "I have said nothing to Jimmy about taking him up, so there can be no question of disappointment for him if you refuse your permission. If you feel so strongly about his not traveling with me, then you need only say so and there will be an end to it. I will not press you to agree to anything you would not like."

She was convinced that that was precisely what he had intended to do. With his last words he had dropped his guard, but it was she who was completely disarmed. Left in full possession of the field, with the choice totally hers, she chose in her son's interest. "I have no objection to his going with you, Captain, if he wishes it."

Jimmy was therefore applied to, and finding him eager to take a seat in the curricle, Richard dismissed his groom, instructing him to travel with the valet in the baggage chaise. Jimmy climbed into the curricle, and Richard stepped back to take his leave of Sir Winston, who had just come out of the house with his daughter, Virginia. She was a diminutive brunette, quite dwarfed by both her father and sister-in-law. Richard was introduced to Miss Ellis and then the ladies were handed into the coach. Within a few moments the traveling-chaise rumbled off down the uneven drive.

Mounting into the curricle, Richard set his restive horses in motion. Thanks to yesterday's rain, there would be no dust, and they would be able to follow as closely as they liked. Their progress for the first several miles was of necessity slow, for the country lanes and roads were not well maintained for coach travel. As Richard had suspected, the motion of the open carriage had less negative effect on Jimmy than the sway of a closed one, and although Richard watched the boy surreptitiously, he saw no sign of nausea. Even when they reached a better surface, Sir Winston's coachman did not push his horses unduly, and Richard was pleased to note it, for although the chaise horses would be changed as soon as they reached the London Road, Richard intended his curricle team to cover two stages. He didn't plan to make a change before Croydon, if he could avoid it.

6

Elizabeth Sherwood sat in the window seat of the front salon, a worn copy of *The Taming of the Shrew* open on her lap. Lady Sherwood sat at her embroidery. There had been no conversation for some time, as both ladies were content in their separate occupations.

Elizabeth glanced up as her sister, Charlotte, entered the room. "Is Richard not yet arrived? I thought he wrote that he would be leaving early, Mama?"

"Indeed, he did, my dear, but it is only twelve-thirty, after all, and he may have started later than he planned. And then, you know, one can never foresee the condition of the roads or the traffic one may encounter."

"Mama is right, Lizzie. Don't you remember the last time we journeyed from Brighton? We were stuck behind that plodding farm cart for miles and could not pass for the vehicles coming in the opposite direction."

"Yes. It was most vexing." A movement in the street below caught Elizabeth's eye, and she gazed down curiously. "We have a visitor, Mama, a gentleman, driving a curricle."

"Not Richard?"

"No, Mama. There is only a pair, and the driver is certainly not Richard, although I cannot tell who it might be from this angle, for his hat is hiding his face."

The visitor was admitted to the house, but some time passed and he was not shown up to the salon. "Perhaps the gentleman called to see your father," Lady Sherwood suggested. She meant the words innocently enough, but Elizabeth and Charlotte looked at each other and smiled. They were both remembering Lord Granbrooke's offer for Lizzie only yesterday and wondering if perhaps someone else had called on a similar errand.

Laying down her book, Elizabeth slipped quietly from the room. She tripped lightly down the stairs and found the butler lingering outside the door to the book-room. "Is there a gentleman with my father, Williams?"

"Yes, Miss Elizabeth. Viscount Stanton."

"Viscount Stanton?"

"Yes, miss. Arrived just a short time ago and asked to speak with his lordship."

Elizabeth spun around without another word and walked back up the stairs at a decorous pace. The moment she knew herself to be out of sight of the hall below, she broke into a run and dashed the remaining distance to the salon, throwing herself through the door.

"Lord Stanton is with Papa," she said without preamble, "and I will be willing to bet you a monkey that he has come to offer for Charlotte."

"Elizabeth!" her ladyship admonished. "As much as you admire your brothers, I must beg you not to speak like them. Such language is hardly becoming."

"I beg your pardon, Mama. But don't you think it's possible—about Lord Stanton, I mean? What other reason could he have for calling here? He has never done so before."

"But, Lizzie," Charlotte complained, "I am barely acquainted with Lord Stanton."

"What has that to say to anything? You are forever saying that marriage should be a civilized, well-planned *arrangement*, with nothing so vulgar as love to taint it. Well, just such a marriage would appeal to Lord Stanton, I daresay. You are well suited, and the duchess, *his godmother,* did say just the other night that she had reason to think he was considering marriage."

"That is true, Charlotte," her mother agreed. "And there is no denying it would be a magnificent match for you."

Charlotte looked thoughtful, but Elizabeth jumped up, clapping her hands. "A viscountess, by all that's wonderful! And he's so handsome, *and* wealthy, and his *horses* . . ." She paused, enraptured. ". . . his horses are spectacular, and they say he has no equal in handling the ribbons."

"I think he is also quite a ladies' man," Charlotte said dampingly.

"Well, I daresay he may be," Elizabeth returned, "but it can't signify! His wife would be quite another matter, and I am sure he is much too aware of his own consequence to offer her any slight."

"Honestly, Lizzie," Lady Sherwood complained. "How you talk. Such topics should not be discussed by young unmarried girls."

"You always tell us to be realists, Mama," Elizabeth countered. "We know you and Papa have a love match, and personally I think it's wonderful and will not marry myself unless it is for love. But Charlotte is not romantic, and if she enters into marriage with a man of Lord Stanton's stamp, she must be willing to look the other way when he appears to have *another interest.*"

Lady Sherwood shook her head resignedly. It was unfortunate that Elizabeth was so outspoken, and yet, she thought, her very outspokenness was one of her most endearing qualities. When other members of the family were all aflutter, Lizzie would utter some totally inappropriate banality that would bring them quickly to earth. And if someone happened to be in the sulks, just let Lizzie tell them they were dull as ditch water, and they would be well on the road to recovery. Lord Sherwood had been heard to say on more than one occasion that his little Lizzie had enough ballast to keep the whole family on an even keel.

Elizabeth felt that the truth, plain-spoken, was the only truth worth listening to, and this was a maxim she lived by. She had no patience with pretense or artifice and was appalled to find herself using such tactics herself, when all her life she had abhorred them. Take for instance Lord Granbrooke's offer of the previous day. She had employed every pretense she could think of to put him off, and when that didn't answer, she was actually forced to *lie* to him, first saying that she was honored by his proposal and then telling him that her affections were otherwise engaged. How odious the man was to force her into compromising her principles just because he was too proud (or too thick-headed) to see that she wasn't interested in his presumptuous proposal!

The door opened at that moment to admit Williams. All three women looked up expectantly as Lady Sherwood asked, "Yes, Williams?"

"His lordship desires Miss Charlotte to wait upon him in the book-room, my lady."

"Aha!" exclaimed Elizabeth. "You see, I was right! Hurry downstairs, Charlotte. You are about to receive the offer of every girl's dream."

Elizabeth's tone was mocking, but Charlotte knew that she was being teased to give her courage, a commodity that she often lacked, which Lizzie possessed in abundance.

Charlotte rose calmly and faced her mother. "What do you think, Mama?"

"The choice, as always, is yours, Charlotte, but your father and I would be pleased to see you so well established. You are old enough to make your own decision, and you alone can decide whether Lord Stanton will suit

55

you, and whether or not you think you can build a life with him."

"Thank you, Mama." Charlotte kissed her briefly on the cheek, and then with a fleeting smile at Elizabeth, turned and followed Williams downstairs.

Charlotte entered the book-room to find her father on the point of leaving. "Ah, here you are, my dear. Lord Stanton would speak with you privately, Charlotte."

"Yes, Papa, thank you." He winked broadly as he passed her, and she smiled in return. The viscount, standing near the middle of the room, was struck by the sweetness of that smile and by the gentle beauty of Miss Sherwood as she advanced and extended her hand to him. He had meant only to take it briefly in his but suddenly changed his mind, carrying it to his lips instead. She blushed slightly but spoke calmly. "How do you do, Lord Stanton?"

He inclined his head. "Your servant, ma'am." Charlotte was certain she should ask him to be seated, but he continued almost immediately. "I think you know the reason for my visit, Miss Sherwood."

"Yes, my lord."

"I have spoken with your father, and he has given me his permission to address you. He has also told me that in the matter of your marriage, you shall make your own decision, and whatever course you choose shall have his blessing."

"That is quite true, my lord."

He took her hand again and held it gently. "I think you are aware of my circumstances, Miss Sherwood, so we need not discuss them. Suffice it to say that I am twenty-eight years old and have decided that I should marry. I feel that we would suit admirably and would feel both honored and privileged if you would consent to become my wife."

Charlotte had been unable to look at him as he spoke,

but now she forced herself to raise her head until her eyes met his. "I am equally honored and privileged to accept your gracious offer, my lord."

He found himself smiling down at her. Only yesterday he would have found it impossible to believe that making an offer of marriage and having it accepted could be so pleasant an experience. "Thank you, ma'am. You have made me most happy." He bent his head and kissed her briefly on the lips and then, straightening, said, "I will leave you now. With your permission I will see that the proper notices are made, and I will call on your father again tomorrow. Good day, Miss Sherwood."

"Good day, my lord."

Then, with a formal bow, he was gone, and Charlotte stood rooted to the book-room floor, totally incapable of motion of any kind.

7

Sir Winston Ellis's strong coach team reached the London Road without mishap, and the first change was made. Jimmy confided shyly to Captain Sherwood that he had never been driven in a curricle before, and this served as a basis for much of their conversation. He was full of questions about a four-in-hand, and Richard was more than happy to be his tutor.

"You are not too young to learn to drive, Jimmy, but you should begin with a single horse, and a less sporting carriage, perhaps a tilbury. I have one in London. If I took you up in it sometime, would you care to try your hand with one horse?"

Jimmy responded enthusiastically, and Richard realized belatedly that he should have spoken first with Mrs. Ellis. Remembering her reticence at the beginning of the journey, he thought it likely that she would be vexed with him, so he added, to cover his blunder, "We must, of course, check first with your mother. She may consider you too young."

"Did you learn at my age?" Jimmy asked.

"No. But I should have liked to. When I was your age, my father was at sea, and I was at Eton. My uncle let me drive his pony cart when I was eleven. I did very well," he said reminiscently.

"I was to start Harrow this year," Jimmy replied, "but

then I became ill, and Grandfather decided to hire a tutor instead. I was disappointed, for I had looked forward to starting school.''

Interspersed with their talk of horses and schooling were Jimmy's questions and Richard's answers concerning the countryside and the villages through which they passed. All in all, Richard considered it the most pleasant journey he had ever made along this road. His groom could never be credited with conversation as ingenuous or as diverting as Jimmy's.

Richard immediately perceived that traveling with Jimmy would give him a rare opportunity to learn more about the entrancing Mrs. Ellis. But almost as quickly as he entertained the thought, he rejected it. It would be unchivalrous to extract from a young boy information concerning his mother. If he was to discover more about Mrs. Ellis, then he must set about it for himself—a not altogether unpleasant prospect.

Within the traveling-carriage, Mrs. Ellis was occupied from time to time with her own thoughts about Captain Sherwood. Miss Virginia Ellis said she thought the captain handsome, and Mrs. Ellis agreed that he was indeed a well-looking man. It was his manner, however, and not his appearance that most interested Mrs. Ellis. For some reason she felt a need to get the man's measure, and just as she thought she was making some progress in that direction, he had deferred to her in that unsettling way. He had been compelled, politely, of course, to accompany them. But there was no clear reason why he should put himself out for Jimmy. She voiced this last thought to her sister-in-law, for even though there was little sympathy between them, they were wont to confide in each other, for in their situation neither of them had any freedom in choosing a confidante. They had each other or no one.

"Perhaps the captain has a naturally agreeable personality," Virginia mused.

Sarah grimaced. "Has any man?" They laughed together at the thought and decided that the majority of the men of their acquaintance were most disagreeable.

"Perhaps he shows an interest in Jimmy to advance his own interest with Jimmy's mother," Virginia suggested.

Sarah frowned. It was entirely possible, for it had happened before. During the past five years since her husband's death, Sarah had not gone unnoticed—women of her beauty rarely did. She did not encourage men to dangle after her; rather, she discouraged them, but several of her more determined suitors had attempted to reach her through her son. Needless to say, such tactics did nothing to advance their cause. Sarah had been inclined to like the captain at their first meeting, but his present behavior seemed to be falling into a pattern that she knew only too well, a pattern not at all to her liking.

Both carriages changed horses at Croydon, and at this point Richard thought it best that Jimmy leave the curricle and finish the journey with his mother. The handling of a strange team would demand his attention, especially once the town was reached and the traffic grew heavier. Even though Richard had no lack of confidence in his own ability, he felt that Mrs. Ellis might and would be more comfortable having the boy with her.

Having arrived in London, Richard escorted the ladies to their destination in Upper Berkeley Street, took civil leave of them, and turned his curricle toward his own home in Mount Street. Traveling without a groom, he drove around to the mews himself and moments later entered his father's house through a service door at the rear. He encountered Charlotte on the first-floor landing, and she hurried him to the sitting room, where he was surprised to find the entire family gathered.

There was a general outcry at his lateness. They had expected him hours earlier. He delivered kisses and handshakes about the room, explaining the while that he had been detained and unable to leave until midday. Everyone seemed in excellent spirits, and the reasons were soon revealed.

"Jonathan and Charlotte both engaged!" Richard exclaimed. "How can so much happen so quickly? I have been gone only four weeks."

"You need only have been gone two days, Richard," Elizabeth chimed in, "for Charlotte became engaged today, and Jon only yesterday!"

"Well, who are the lucky spouses to be?" he asked, and then, looking at his younger brother, answered half of his own question. "No need to ask you, Jon . . . Harriet, of course, and a lucky devil you are! You don't deserve a woman half as good." Looking his brother over critically, he added, "You've gained weight since last I saw you, and it looks well on you. Army life must agree with you."

Richard moved to take Charlotte's hand in his own. "Don't tell me, Charlotte, that you have finally met a man who can measure up to the high standards you demand in a husband."

"Charlotte has received and accepted an offer from Viscount Stanton," Lady Sherwood said proudly.

A slight frown crossed Richard's brow. "Really? You surprise me."

"You are acquainted with Lord Stanton, are you not?" Charlotte asked.

"Yes. I know him well. We served together in the Peninsula." Richard refrained from saying more, simply wishing his sister joy, and leading the conversation to other topics. He soon went away to wash after his journey and change for dinner.

Elizabeth waited half an hour and then slipped out of the sitting room, up a second flight of stairs, and down the hall to Richard's bedchamber. Her gentle knock on the door was answered by Pull, Lord Sherwood's valet, summoned to wait upon Richard until his own Henchly should arrive.

61

Pull ushered Elizabeth into the room and then busied himself tidying the remnants of Richard's bath. Richard sat before his dressing table, wholly absorbed in the delicate operation of tying his cravat. He was completely dressed for dinner, with the exception of his coat, which lay over a nearby chair.

Elizabeth knew better than to speak while he was concentrating on his neckcloth, so she kept a prudent silence, idly toying with one of his silver-handled brushes while she waited. Elizabeth stood directly behind her brother, and as he finished he glanced up at her image in the mirror. She was staring down at the top of his head with what amounted to a look of resentment on her pretty face. "You know, Richard, it's a terrible waste for a man to be blessed with hair of this color." She ran her fingers through it as she spoke, noting that it was still slightly damp from washing. "Such beautiful, golden richness," she continued. "I would I had Mama's coloring as you do."

He reached up to take her hand and turned to meet her eyes directly. "Your own coloring does you no disservice, Lizzie, and well you know it. But you have not come to pay me compliments on my hair. You have something on your mind. Is it that you have no beau of your own, with all this talk of love and marriage?"

She shook her head. "No. Nothing like that. It's about Charlotte and Lord Stanton. I could see that you didn't like it above half."

He grimaced. "Little Miss Perspicacity. Let us hope that my feelings were not so transparent to everyone else. I should have guarded my reaction better, but I was taken by surprise."

"You think Charlotte and Lord Stanton will not suit, don't you?"

"I think Charlotte is a fool to seek a marriage of convenience, and I cannot think that any woman could be happy for long married to Stanton."

62

"You are very harsh, Richard. Do you dislike him so much?"

"No. You misunderstand me, Lizzie. I do not dislike him at all. In fact, I like him. He was a good officer, and is a fine man, and I will always be proud to call him my friend, but I can't think marriage will suit him."

"Perhaps not. But if he wants an heir, surely he must marry."

"That's true enough. But in that case I would prefer that he didn't marry *my* sister. Charlotte pretends to be tough and independent, but underneath she has the same fears we all have and the same need to be loved and cherished. She doesn't like to admit it, but I know it to be true, as do you."

"What will you do?"

"I will do nothing until I have taken time to consider the matter more carefully. And in the end, there may be nothing I can do, Lizzie. After all, if Father and Mother have both given this match their blessing, and Charlotte wishes it as well, it would be inappropriate for *me* to raise any objection."

"Even if you thought Charlotte would be made unhappy?"

He rose and reached for his coat. "Yes," he said resignedly, "even if I thought she would be made unhappy."

The entire family was home to dinner that evening, with the exception of Jonathan, who was dining with his betrothed. Many topics presented themselves for discussion, including the Sherwoods' ball, an event that was to be held in four days' time. Lady Sherwood had initially planned the evening as a grand entertainment for their friends and acquaintance, to coincide with Jonathan's furlough. But now it had begun to take on the form of a lavish engagement party.

"The girls and I have worked very hard planning it,"

63

Lady Sherwood said. "It should be quite a lovely evening."

Lord Sherwood smiled lovingly at his wife. "My dear, your parties are always exceptional, and with two engagements to announce, this one will no doubt be the grandest yet."

"If it's not to late, Mother," Richard put in, "there is someone I should like you to invite." She raised her brows inquiringly as he continued. "The reason I made a late start this morning was because I waited to escort some of our neighbors to town."

"Which neighbors?" Charlotte asked.

"The Ellises. Sir Winston's daughter-in-law, Mrs. Ellis and her young son, and Sir Winston's daughter, Miss Virginia Ellis."

"I would be more than happy to invite them, Richard," his mother said. "I had been hoping to make their acquaintance and was planning to invite them to the Manor during our next stay in the country. If you will give me their direction, I will call upon them in the morning and invite them personally."

"I will accompany you, if you like," Richard returned. "They are staying with Lord and Lady Kemp, and you should issue the invitation to Mrs. Sarah Ellis and Miss Virginia Ellis only, for Mrs. Ellis is a widow, and Sir Winston has not come to town."

The following morning the proposed call was duly made. Richard, Charlotte, and their mother presented themselves in Upper Berkeley Street and found the Ellis ladies and their hostess at home. Lady Sherwood and Lady Kemp were not acquainted, so it was necessary for both Richard and Sarah to take part in the introductions. Lady Sherwood then issued her invitation, which was graciously accepted. With the two older ladies conversing amicably, and Charlotte and Virginia becoming acquainted, Richard took the opportunity to speak with Mrs. Ellis.

"I hope you were not fatigued by yesterday's journey, ma'am?"

"Not at all. I am a good traveler, Captain Sherwood."

"And Jimmy? Did he manage the last stage well enough?"

"Yes, quite well, but then the roads are so much better closer to town. I'm sure it was the pleasantest journey he has ever made. You must know that he talked of little else all evening. He so enjoyed your taking him up. I must thank you again."

"You will not perhaps be so quick to thank me, ma'am, after I have made a small confession. Did Jimmy tell you that I offered to take him driving with me while he was in town?"

"No, he didn't mention it."

"Well, I did tell him that you might not approve, so perhaps he thought it best to say nothing. I was carried away by his enthusiasm and made the offer without thinking. I know I should have said nothing without consulting you first. I have a tilbury in town, and a very well-behaved older horse, and I thought Jimmy might like to try his hand at driving him. Perhaps early in the morning, in the park, when there is little traffic."

Why did this man insist upon insinuating himself into her life? she thought, but she said, "I am afraid I don't think that would be a very good idea, Captain Sherwood."

"No? You think he is too young? I think he has an aptitude."

"No. I do not think him too young, Captain," she answered hesitantly.

Richard regarded her critically. "Then you must question my skill. I assure you—"

She interrupted him irritably. "I do not question your skill, sir. I question your motive." How could she have said that? Surely she meant only to think it!

"My motive?" He was dismayed. "My motive is to

65

teach the boy something of handling the ribbons. What other motive could I have? I thought that since he seemed so keen to learn, and has no father, I could be in some part a substitute. . . ."

"And you do not consider this substitution to be an intrusion into my affairs, Captain?"

He stood silent for a few moments as she stared frostily at him, and finally he spoke. "I must beg you to forgive me, ma'am. You're right. I am intruding, and I apologize. I will not mention the subject again." He took a step back and bowed. "If you will excuse me?" He turned and crossed the room to join his mother and sister, and within a few moments they took their leave, but neither he nor Mrs. Ellis was to forget their conversation for some time to come.

8

On the evening of the Sherwoods' ball, they sat down ten to dinner. In addition to the six members of the Sherwood family, Jonathan's betrothed, Harriet Putnam, and her aunt, Mrs. Satterly, were present, as well as Lord Stanton. To keep her numbers even, Lady Sherwood had invited a friend of Richard's, the Honorable Charles Warmington. Richard and Charles had been at Oxford together, and, finishing there, had joined the same regiment and continued their friendship abroad. Little more than a year into his military career, Charles had suffered a severe shoulder injury that had left him disabled and unfit for active service. He was a handsome young man with black hair and dark blue eyes, and although Lady Sherwood thought him too staid and serious, he could always be counted on as a perfect dinner companion whether he was seated beside a lively debutante or a half-deaf dowager. He was also a younger son of the Earl of Haigh, and a first cousin to Lord Stanton, and would soon be related to the Sherwoods through Charlotte's marriage.

They dined formally but at a table small enough to make some general conversation possible. Elizabeth had ample opportunity to observe her sister and Lord Stanton and saw nothing in their behavior to cause alarm. She thought Richard was studying them as well, although she had noticed that he seemed preoccupied for the last several days. The meal passed pleasantly, and presently they adjourned to the reception rooms to await the arrival of the first guests for the ball.

Charles Warmington stood near Jonathan at the side of the room. His eyes rested on Charlotte and Elizabeth with undisguised admiration. "Your sisters are looking lovely this evening, Jon."

"You must tell *them* so, Charles, not me," Jonathan answered, but knew his brother's friend to be right.

Handsome girls to begin with, they sparkled in their ball dresses. Charlotte was in pale yellow crape worn over a slip of white sarcenet. A sash of darker yellow marked the high waistline, and a matching yellow ribbon was wound skillfully through her dark curls. Elizabeth wore white, a color her mother preferred for her at her age, but her gown was finely embroidered in a silver floral pattern. Silver dancing slippers peeped from beneath the hem, and a sparkling silver sash set off her trim figure to perfection.

Elizabeth glanced up at that moment to see Jon and Charles regarding her. She crossed the room to join them, and the conversation turned to a subject she was to hear mentioned many times throughout the coming evening.

"Have you heard of my cousin's exploit this morning, Miss Elizabeth?"

"No, Mr. Warmington. What exploit?"

"He and a fellow by the name of Reginald Fielding had a match at Manton's Shooting Gallery. Fielding is some kind of a marvel, it seems. They say he never misses."

Jonathan confirmed this last statement. "I have watched him at practice myself and have never seen a more accurate aim. Is it true, Charles, that Stanton matched him shot for shot?"

"I had it from Sir Hugh Broughton, who was present," Charles confirmed. "They continued the contest for over an hour, with neither of them ever missing the mark. Finally they agreed to call a halt and declared the match a stalemate. There was a huge amount of money wagered on the outcome, but it was all for naught, for no winner was declared.''

Elizabeth left the gentlemen when her mother beckoned her, for within a very short time the rooms had become quite full. The orchestra had finished tuning, and the dancing was about to begin. Elizabeth turned to find Lord Stanton at her elbow. ''Miss Elizabeth, my brother wishes to be made known to you. Miss Elizabeth Sherwood . . . Mr. Henry Ferris.''

''How do you do, Mr. Ferris? I am pleased to make your acquaintance.''

''I was hoping you would honor me with this dance, Miss Elizabeth.''

''Thank you, sir. I would be delighted!'' She went off with him and soon discovered that he was an excellent dancer. Mr. Henry Ferris could not be many years younger than the viscount, Elizabeth decided. He was a man of medium build, like his brother, and although she would describe him as being rather more striking than handsome, she decided almost immediately that she liked him very well.

''How well you dance, Mr. Ferris!'' she exclaimed.

''Certainly I should be saying that, Miss Elizabeth,'' he expostulated.

''Only if you think to say it first, sir. I didn't know Lord Stanton had a brother. Have you a large family?''

''We have another brother, Giles. He is just twenty, and at Oxford at present.''

''No sisters, then?''

''No. No sisters, ma'am. My father didn't believe in 'em.''

She smiled, and he thought her smile enchanting, and when the dance ended, he led her to where Charlotte stood with his brother. Mr. Ferris thanked Elizabeth for the dance, expressed his hope that she would honor him again later, and moved off through the throng.

Elizabeth had been instructed to stay with Charlotte or Harriet or one of her brothers until Lady Sherwood had finished greeting her guests, so when Charlotte's hand was solicited for the next set, Elizabeth looked about for Jon or Richard and found her eldest brother only a short distance away. As she moved to his side she saw him staring fixedly toward the top of the stairway where their parents stood. She followed his gaze and immediately understood why he was staring. A tall, red-haired woman had just entered the room. She was wearing a gown of emerald-green, cut low over her full bosom, and even from this distance, it was plain to see that she was exquisitely handsome.

"Do you know her, Richard?"

Startled from his reverie, Richard looked down at her. "Yes. She is our neighbor from Surrey."

"Mrs. Ellis?"

"Yes, Lizzie, Mrs. Ellis."

"When you were describing her to us the day you arrived home, you failed to mention that she was beautiful."

"Did I?"

Elizabeth stared at her brother in disbelief. Could it be that Richard had been smitten at last? And by a widow who must be his own age or older? Elizabeth certainly saw admiration in his eyes, and there was something else as well, but exactly what, she couldn't tell.

"Will you introduce me?" she asked.

Richard seemed to be pulling his thoughts back from a great distance as he answered her. "Yes, certainly, if you wish it."

Together they made their way across the room, and Richard made the proper introductions, although to Elizabeth's ear his manner seemed more formal than usual.

"I am happy to meet you, Mrs. Ellis. Richard tells us you have a son and have brought him along to town."

Elizabeth was only making polite conversation, but Richard stiffened perceptibly at her side as he said, "If you will excuse me, I must speak with Lord Stanton." They nodded their dismissal, and as he turned away, he heard Mrs. Ellis respond to Elizabeth's last comment.

Richard could not deny that he was strongly attracted to Mrs. Ellis, but it was clear that the lady had not the slightest interest in him, so there was an end to it. He soon joined Lord Stanton, and they stood together watching the dancers.

"I have heard of your meeting with Fielding this morning, Julian," Richard remarked. "The whole town is talking of it."

"Yes. I am aware," the viscount answered. "I am beginning to regret that I met the man at all. Such an uproar over a mere shooting contest."

"I always knew you to be a fine shot, Julian, but I had no idea you were a nonpareil."

"I have improved."

"You are to be congratulated."

"On my marksmanship?"

"Yes, certainly on that, and also on your engagement to my sister."

"I was wondering when you would find time to offer your felicitations."

"There has been little opportunity for us to speak privately."

"True enough, yet I have the unmistakable impression that you don't approve of this engagement."

"Nor do I precisely disapprove. I would say rather that I am *concerned.*"

"I thought we were friends, Richard."

"And so we are. But I love my sister. Is it so surprising that I should wish to see her happy?"

"You have some considerable influence with Charlotte,

71

I think. You could use it to protect her interest, if you feel she needs protection."

"I could. But I will not. Charlotte has made her decision, and it is not my place to interfere. The advisability of such an engagement must be a matter for her conscience—and, of course, for yours."

Mrs. Sarah Ellis was favorably impressed with Elizabeth Sherwood. She thought her a very prettily behaved young lady, with forthright and friendly manners. Sarah glanced at Elizabeth now, where she stood speaking with Lord Granbrooke at the side of the ballroom. As Sarah watched, she was surprised to see Lord Granbrooke take Elizabeth's hand and Elizabeth quickly pull it away, a flush mounting to her cheeks. Elizabeth then turned abruptly and walked away, and Sarah watched in dismay as Lord Granbrooke followed in her wake.

Instinctively Sarah crossed the room in their direction, but the crowd impeded her progress. She finally reached the doorway through which they had passed but saw no sign of them in the next room. She moved quickly into the hall and approached one of the Sherwood footmen on duty there.

"Have you seen Miss Elizabeth?" she asked.

"Yes, madam," he said. "She went on down the hall just a few moments ago."

Sarah thanked him and moved in the direction he indicated. The rooms in this part of the house had not been opened for the ball, and she had proceeded some little way along the corridor, wondering where Miss Elizabeth had gone, when she heard raised voices in the room directly to her right. She was sure Elizabeth was being confronted by Lord Granbrooke, and she felt just as sure that Elizabeth would welcome her intervention.

Without a moment's hesitation, she knocked, called Elizabeth's name, and then opened the door and entered.

72

As she had suspected, Lord Granbrooke was with Elizabeth. They stood very close, and although he was not touching her, it was obvious that he had just put her from him as they were interrupted. Elizabeth was shaking, and there were tears in her eyes. She either could not or would not speak.

"I think your presence is not wanted here, my lord," Sarah said steadily. "You will please leave us." She made no effort to be civil, contempt sounding clearly in her voice.

More than aware that there was nothing he could say to defend himself, Granbrooke glared angrily at her and, without a word, turned and left the room. Sarah closed the door behind him and went to Elizabeth but after a few moments realized that she would not be much help. The girl was considerably shaken, and Sarah knew that a relative stranger was not the person needed in the present situation.

"Please wait here, Miss Elizabeth," she said. "I will be right back. Do you promise you will wait?"

Elizabeth didn't answer, but she nodded her head, and Sarah quickly returned to the ballroom. Her eyes swept the room for some member of the Sherwood family, and she was relieved to see Captain Sherwood standing nearby. Momentarily forgetting the recent awkwardness between them, she hurried to his side, and when she placed her hand on his sleeve and spoke his name, he started and looked down at her in some surprise. Light as her touch was, she communicated her anxiety with it, and he instinctively laid his own hand over hers.

"Ma'am?"

"Please, sir, come with me." The words were spoken lowly and urgently, and Richard did not question the appeal but accompanied her without comment. Once free of the crowded rooms, she said, "Your sister, Elizabeth, needs your assistance, Captain. I am afraid she has had a rather unpleasant scene with Lord Granbrooke."

He followed her into what was known in the family as the yellow salon and found Elizabeth there, struggling to regain her composure. He moved immediately to the sofa where she was seated and sat beside her, taking her hands in his. "Lizzie, what has been happening here?"

"Oh, Richard . . . He is such a horrible man!"

"Who? Granbrooke? What were you thinking to come here with him?"

"I didn't come here with him," she objected. "I came alone. Partly to get away from him, and partly to be on my own for a while. But he followed me, and he . . ."

"Lizzie, tell me what happened," Richard demanded. "How long were you here with him?"

"It was only a few minutes, Captain Sherwood," Sarah offered. "I saw them leave the ballroom and followed immediately. It didn't take me long to find them."

She had remained standing nearby, and he looked up at her as she spoke. "I am obliged to you, ma'am." There was no doubting the sincerity in his voice as he turned his attention to his sister once again. "You must tell me what took place here, Lizzie. Did Granbrooke force his attentions upon you?"

"I'm not sure what you mean by that, Richard," she said in a small voice.

"Did he kiss you? Or touch you?" he asked impatiently.

"No, he didn't try to kiss me, but he backed me against that table and pressed his body against mine in the most disgusting way."

"Damn!" Richard muttered wrathfully.

"But it was what he said that frightened me," Elizabeth continued.

"What did he say?"

"I couldn't begin to repeat the words he used, Richard, but I know no gentleman would speak so. And his tone . . . his tone terrified me."

Richard rose suddenly to his feet. "Damn him! He shall

74

answer to me for this!'' He turned to Sarah. ''I would appreciate it, Mrs. Ellis, if you could stay with my sister until she has composed herself and then see her back to the ballroom and into my mother's care. It will cause comment if she is too long absent.''

As he turned to leave, Elizabeth asked quietly, ''What do you plan to do?''

''I plan to see that Lord Granbrooke offers no further insults to ladies!''

His tone was grim, and as Elizabeth was assailed by a new thought, she sprang to her feet and, hurrying to her brother, took hold of his arm. ''You will not call him out, Richard? You must not do so!''

''You need not concern yourself, Lizzie. I will deal with his lordship.''

''Yes, I see that you must deal with him, of course, but not in such a way as that!''

He tried to disengage her hand, but she only held on more tightly. ''Lizzie, it is not your concern, believe me.''

''You're wrong! It is my concern. *I* am the one he insulted. Throw him out in the street, or knock him down, or anything else you like, but not a duel, Richard, *please,* I beg of you. *Swear* to me that you will not consider it!''

He took her chin in his hand. ''Always the sensible, levelheaded Lizzie. Don't you think your honor worth protecting, little one?''

''Nothing I have is worth protecting at the risk of any harm coming to you. If you love me, Richard, you will not endanger yourself just because Lord Granbrooke is a sore loser and a complete fool.''

Richard gazed down at his sister with a great deal of tenderness, and Sarah realized that she was witnessing an excellent example of how a woman could bring a man round her finger if there was a strong bond of love between them.

"Very well, Lizzie, you win," he said finally. "I will not demand that he meet me."

"You swear it?"

"I swear." Bending, he kissed her gently on the cheek, and then, turning to Sarah, he said, "I am in your debt, Mrs. Ellis, and I will not forget it." Then before she could answer, he passed through the door and was gone.

Sarah turned to Elizabeth and smiled. "Well, Miss Sherwood . . . may I call you Elizabeth?"

"Yes, please do. And I would like to thank you, too, Mrs. Ellis, for noticing that I was in trouble and for coming to help me."

"You're very welcome, Elizabeth. But if we are to be friends, then you must call me Sarah. Shall we go up to your bedchamber and ring for your maid so that she can repair the damage Lord Granbrooke has done to your hair? Then we shall return to the ball and find you a suitable partner for the next set, for I have noticed, Elizabeth, that you love to dance."

When they finally returned to the ballroom, Charlotte wondered aloud where Elizabeth had been, but Sarah fobbed her off with a tale of how one of Elizabeth's partners had trod upon the hem of her gown and they had retired upstairs to pin it. Henry Ferris claimed Elizabeth for the next dance, and she was soon restored to spirits, for he was unquestionably one of the best dancers in the room.

As the dance ended, Mr. Ferris led Elizabeth to where Lord Stanton stood in conversation with his future father-in-law. "Julian, dear fellow," Henry said to his brother, "the next dance is a waltz, and you really must stand up with Miss Elizabeth. She is as light on her feet as a rose petal!"

Elizabeth blushed at the compliment, but her father supported Mr. Ferris. "That's true enough, Stanton. My youngest girl is the best dancer in the family."

Stanton inclined his head and held out his arm to Elizabeth. "Will you honor me, ma'am?"

"Certainly, my lord, but it cannot be pleasant to have a partner foisted upon you." With a withering look at both her father and Mr. Ferris, she went with the viscount to join the other dancers.

"How can it be that we have never stood up together, Miss Elizabeth?"

"I only made your acquaintance early last week, my lord, and I think you don't grace the dance floor as often as you could."

"I don't dislike dancing, Miss Elizabeth."

"Then the explanation must be that you find your partners insipid."

He raised a brow at her insight and started to enjoy the conversation. "Perhaps I do, ma'am. Present company excluded. And Henry was right. You dance delightfully."

"Thank you, my lord. So do you. I have not yet congratulated you on your engagement. I suppose I should do so."

He looked at her quizzically. "You *suppose* you should? Are you opposed to the engagement, Miss Elizabeth?"

"No, sir. I am not opposed to the engagement. I am opposed to marriages of convenience."

"And you think that is what your sister and I are planning—a marriage of convenience?"

"Well, of course, my lord. It could scarcely be anything else, when you have only recently met and were barely acquainted when you proposed."

"I take it that you don't believe in love at first sight, then, Miss Elizabeth?"

"No, certainly not! I am sure there can be *attraction* at first sight, but love is not something that *is,* it is something that *grows,* and it cannot grow in an instant. Anyone can see that."

"I am sure you must be right," he agreed. "Your logic

is irrefutable. But haven't you considered that four, or shall we say five, days would be adequate time for love to grow, given the proper circumstances?''

Elizabeth had not considered this option. Could it be that Stanton had offered for Charlotte as a matter of convenience, and then proceeded to fall in love with her? It was not impossible, and the very idea struck her as so romantic that she blurted out without thinking, "Have you fallen in love with Charlotte, my lord?''

He smiled down at her indulgently but did not answer and then was truly amused as the enormity of her statement struck her. She blushed scarlet and stammered incoherently, "Oh, my lord . . . I'm so sorry . . . I beg your pardon . . . How rude of me . . . How could I be so impertinent?''

"I don't know," he answered. "How *could* you be so impertinent?'' He still seemed amused, and she felt enormously relieved that he didn't snub her.

"It is my besetting sin," she confided.

"What is?''

"My outspokenness. Mama is always warning me, and I try, I do really, but my tongue seems so often to have a mind of its own and will say just what it pleases. Please say that you will forgive me, my lord. I truly did not mean to be insinuating.''

"No forgiveness is necessary, Miss Elizabeth, I assure you. I was not offended, and I would never consider you insinuating. I would much rather describe you as 'a breath of fresh air.' ''

9

Perhaps thirty minutes later, Mrs. Ellis noticed Captain Sherwood speaking with his brother, Jonathan, on the far side of the room. She had seen nothing more of Lord Granbrooke and knew not whether he had departed after his encounter with her or whether Captain Sherwood had shown him the door. If the latter were true, the captain's immaculate person showed no signs of a struggle. His dark silk coat was still set straight across his broad shoulders; his smallclothes and elaborately tied cravat seemed not to have been disturbed. She allowed her gaze to travel down his entire person, and then slowly up again, and when she brought her eyes to his face, she found to her dismay that he was fixedly regarding her. She felt a hot flush rise to her cheeks but would not now look away and continued to hold his gaze as he moved across the room to her side and said softly, "Such steadfast regard, ma'am. I was beginning to think that I had forgotten to finish dressing."

"I was only searching for some evidence of—"

"Of a mill, ma'am? And, as you see, there is none. So sorry to disappoint you."

"I am not disappointed, Captain. I only wish you to understand that I had no ulterior motive in staring."

"No need to convince me of that," he replied, his eyes roving out over the dancers. "I have it from Sir Winston himself that you consider yourself a 'staid matron,' and I am sure I need not worry that you may have designs upon my person.''

She smiled. "How ridiculous you are, Captain Sherwood! But certainly my father-in-law never said such of me."

He turned his intense blue gaze upon her. "On my honor, ma'am. Those were his exact words."

"Then, I shudder to think what else he may have said."

"Nothing to your discredit," Richard replied, smiling, "I assure you. Shall we dance, Mrs. Ellis?" He held out his hand, and she put her own into it, and then, drawing her arm through his, he led her onto the floor.

The dance was a waltz, and Sarah could not repress a feeling of exhilaration as the captain's arm encircled her waist and he turned her onto the dance floor. She kept her eyes downcast, studying the pattern of his watered-silk waistcoat. A few moments later she happened to glance at her right hand, held firmly in his left one, and after a moment's scrutiny said, "Your knuckles are bleeding, Captain Sherwood."

His gaze idly followed hers, and he agreed dryly, "So they are, Mrs. Ellis. It cannot signify."

"Perhaps not to you, Captain. But if you should brush against some lady's ball gown, which has cost her two hundred guineas, believe me, she would not consider it insignificant. As you can see, your glove is quite soaked through."

"What would you have me do, Mrs. Ellis?"

"I would have you direct me to the edge of the floor, sir, and thence to some place where we could procure water and a cloth."

"You would treat my wounds, ma'am?" he asked, a smile lurking at the corners of his mouth.

"Certainly, Captain, if you will permit me."

She soon found herself at the side of the room. Disassociating themselves from the dancers, they made their way through several adjoining rooms, and as the crowd thinned, Richard spoke again. "Where shall we go?" he asked provocatively, "my bedchamber?"

She gave him a quelling look. "Your levity is not amusing, Captain. Show me the way to the kitchen."

"The kitchen! Surely you must be joking!"

"I assure you I'm not. I assume you *know* your way to the kitchen?"

"Of course I know my way to the—why the kitchen?"

"Because I am sure we will be able to find what we need there."

They soon made their way to the kitchen, which was in a great bustle with preparations for supper. One of the maids fetched them a cloth and a basin of cold water with ice, and they retired into the servants' dining hall, which was deserted and relatively quiet. Sarah noticed that Richard left the door standing wide, despite the fact that closing it would have offered them considerable relief from the din of the kitchen beyond.

"Concerned for my reputation, Captain Sherwood?" she teased.

"No, ma'am, for my own," he answered glibly.

As they seated themselves at the table, she stripped off her gloves and held out her hand imperatively. He put his own in it, saying, "This really isn't necessary, you know."

She silenced him with a look and surveyed the damaged hand critically. Three of the knuckles were actually split and bleeding, and the fourth was scraped. The fingers were rapidly turning black and blue, and, to her eye, looked very painful. She started carefully to soak the blood away and apply ice to the swelling.

Richard winced, and she looked up apologetically. "I'm sorry," she said. "I'm sure it must hurt dreadfully."

There was so much sympathy in her voice that he laughed aloud. "If you think that, ma'am, you can know nothing of wounds. Compared to a saber cut or a bullet-hole, this is child's play, believe me!''

He was smiling, and she knew he intended the comment to lighten her mood, but in fact it had the opposite effect. She stared at the hand she held. It was nearly twice the size of her own, strong and shapely. She paused in her work to look across at him. ''You were wounded, then, during the war, Captain?''

''A few times,'' he admitted, and then grinned. ''More than I care to remember.''

''I had hoped that Lord Granbrooke would be gone by the time you returned to the ballroom.''

''No. He was still there, and mighty cool, too. Tell me, Mrs. Ellis, is Miss Virginia Ellis an heiress?''

Sarah looked puzzled at the question but answered it readily. ''Jimmy is Sir Winston's heir, but as his only surviving child, Virginia will have a very handsome portion, yes. Why do you ask?''

''I found Granbrooke ingratiating himself to her. You have been in town only a few days and he is already aware of her circumstances. The man is a damned loose-fish.''

''You have not told me how you came by this hand, Captain.''

''I had intended only to show him the door, although an exposé on his personality in general, and his manners in particular, would have been much more to my liking. I politely informed him that I would see him to his coach. We were just descending the steps outside when he tried to excuse his behavior by informing me that my flirt of a sister had been encouraging him, and she had received no more from him than she deserved. If he had more to say, I will never know, for it was at that moment that my hand came to grief. He fell like a stone. Didn't even give me the pleasure of hitting him a second time. I would I had my promise back from Lizzie. I would willingly rid the world of scum such as he.''

"You don't mean that, Captain. Surely such a man should be beneath our contempt? If you had insisted on making more of it, then Elizabeth would have done so as well. As it is, she has almost forgotten the incident and is upstairs dancing and enjoying herself, as she should be."

She finished with his hand and used a towel to dry it. "There," she said, "it should feel somewhat better. If you are careful, I think it will not start bleeding again."

He looked at her consideringly. "Thank you. You never did mention why you involved yourself in this affair, Mrs. Ellis?"

"I happened to be watching your sister and Lord Granbrooke just before they left the ballroom. I could see that Elizabeth was angry, and I suppose I sensed that his lordship might cause trouble."

"But that does not explain *why* you followed them."

"I don't understand you, Captain."

"I am trying to discover your *motive*, ma'am." He had no sooner uttered the word than he regretted it, for she flushed and rose suddenly from the table. "I'm sorry," he said quickly. "I didn't mean to distress you."

"No. You meant to expose my bad manners," she replied, "And you are perfectly within your rights to do so. I followed your sister to offer her my help if need be. And you offered the same to Jimmy, and through him to me. *Your* intentions were both innocent and honorable, Captain, and *my* behavior was disgraceful. I beg your pardon."

He had risen to his feet as she did, and, taking her arm once again, they left the kitchen and made their way upstairs. As they came along the ground floor past the door to the book-room, Richard paused and turned to face her. The corridor in which they stood and the hall beyond were both deserted.

He spoke quietly. "I was startled more than angered by your behavior the other day, and once I had time to consider the conversation, it didn't take me long to understand

83

what you must have been thinking. I am not an advocate of oblique tactics, Mrs. Ellis. When I want something, more often than not I prefer the direct approach. If I had any intention of trying to fix my interest with you, I would not employ your son as a stepping-stone. I hope you can believe that, because it's the truth.''

"I do believe you, Captain."

"Good," he said, taking her arm again and strolling on. "Then, if you have no objection, I will call for Jimmy tomorrow morning. Shall we say—nine o'clock?"

"Nine o'clock will be fine, Captain Sherwood."

Despite the fact that Richard had not retired until three-thirty on the morning of the ball, he was up at eight o'clock, ate a quick breakfast, ordered his tilbury brought round, and presented himself in Upper Berkeley Street promptly at nine. He found Jimmy eagerly awaiting him, and they set off together for the park.

Richard soon saw that he was not mistaken in thinking Jimmy would have an aptitude for driving. He listened carefully to Richard's instructions, and when Richard finally handed him the reins, he was pleased to see that the boy had light, even hands.

They stayed out only an hour and made plans to meet another day. Dropping Jimmy in the street outside Lord Kemp's house, Richard bade him carry his compliments to his mother and, turning his horse, set off again for home.

As he entered the house, Williams stepped forward to relieve him of his hat and driving coat. "His lordship is in the book-room, Captain, and said he would like a word with you when you returned."

Richard crossed the hall to the book-room, stripping off his gloves as he went, and entered to find his father puzzling over some papers on the desk before him. Lord Sherwood looked up as his son entered and spoke to the footman who was moving to close the door behind him. "Wait outside, Matthews, and please see that we are not disturbed."

There was no mistaking the seriousness of his lordship's tone. Richard glanced at the footman as he left the room, assured himself that the door was properly closed, and then advanced to stand near his father's desk. "Something is worrying you, sir. What is it?"

Lord Sherwood motioned his son to a chair. "Please, Richard, sit down. I have been doing some work this morning, and I have found something that troubles me greatly. As you know, I have little patience with accounts and estate matters. But you also know that when it comes to the matter of my position within the present government, I cannot bear disorder."

"Yes, sir, I do know it."

"Then you will understand my concern when I tell you that this file I hold before me is not as I left it yesterday. The pages are out of order, several have been turned upside down, and I suspect . . . no . . . I know, that it has been tampered with!"

Richard frowned. "Does it contain vital information, sir?"

"The contents would not be considered highly confidential, otherwise I would not leave them unguarded as they are. But they must be considered delicate, as they deal with such things as sailing orders, fleet movements, and various troop strength. We may be at peace with France, but we have no cause to relax our vigilance."

"I assume you think that one of our guests last night was responsible for this . . . encroachment."

"Yes, I think it highly likely," his lordship replied, "but every person present last night pretends to be a loyal British subject. What we seem to be discussing here, Richard, is not encroachment or trespass—but treason."

The word hung for a few tense moments between them,

and finally Richard spoke. "Do you have any suspicions, sir, as to who this traitor might be?"

"No. I have asked your mother for a list of those who accepted her invitation, without arousing her suspicions, of course, and will have it compared to a list of those who have been suspected in the past. And then, of course, one always thinks first of those who have French blood."

"That will get us nowhere, sir, for surely dozens of our guests last night can claim a French progenitor or two. Your own grandmother was a full-blooded Frenchwoman. And think of Stanton—his mother is French, yet I have fought side by side with both Julian and Henry Ferris and would not doubt their loyalty any more than I would my own."

"Nevertheless, those persons with French blood must stand high on the list. On the other hand, we could find that the perpetrator is no more than a poor misguided Englishman who sees the offer of gold in return for services rendered as a thing of greater value than his, or her, own honor."

"Have you mentioned this incident to anyone else in the family, Father?"

"No. I have not. Nor do I intend to."

"Well, of one thing at least we can be certain. If this person hopes to collect additional information from you, it will be necessary for him to attach himself through some member of the family. Not a very pleasant thought."

"No. Not pleasant at all," his father agreed. "But if he is to be encouraged to find this house an easy mark, then we must make no mention of anything being amiss with my papers. We will not change any of the household routine. We will continue to leave this room unlocked and accessible as always. But you and I, Richard, shall keep our eyes open, and if in the natural course of things an opportunity should present itself, perhaps we will make an effort to capture this . . . person."

10

If there had been an uproar in the Sherwood house in the days preceding the ball, it was as nothing compared to the activity that now reigned. In little more than two weeks Lady Sherwood would see her younger son married, and even though he had given her very little notice, she was determined to make the day memorable.

There would be a small, private ceremony at St. George's, Hanover Square, followed by a lavish wedding breakfast at Sherwood House. Jonathan and Harriet planned to leave early and travel the same day to Sherwood Manor, where they would spend the remaining days of Jonathan's furlough together. Afterward, Harriet intended to return to her aunt's house in London until her husband could make arrangements for her to join him in Belgium.

On the day of the wedding all the public rooms on the first floor were thrown open for the use of the wedding guests, including the yellow salon where Lord Granbrooke had detained Elizabeth. There was a pianoforte there, and Elizabeth had been coaxed into playing for them while Charles Warmington turned the music for her. Elizabeth's singing voice was low and pleasant, and she played well. She sang a Highland love song, and the words were both tender and touching.

Everyone seemed to be enjoying the day with the exception of Lord Stanton. The more lighthearted and gay the wedding guests became, the more his spirits suffered, until finally Charlotte spoke to him in rare confidence, bringing his growing unrest to a head and making him feel that if he did not escape the house immediately, he would be suffocated by high spirits and goodwill.

Seated beside the viscount at the side of the room, Charlotte stared down at the engagement ring on her hand and said impulsively, "What did you think of the wedding ceremony, my lord?"

He had almost said that he found it much like any other wedding he had ever attended but fortunately realized in time how inappropriate such a comment would be and said instead, "It was quite exceptional . . . very moving."

"Yes," she agreed. "So I thought. My lord, we have not spoken about our own marriage." She continued to look down at her hands, and he turned to study her profile as she continued. "When I accepted your proposal, I did so because I, like you, thought we were well suited. During the past weeks I have come to know you better, and I wish you to know that I think you an admirable person, and I will do everything in my power to be a proper wife."

Stanton was stunned into silence. I wonder how admirable you would think me, Miss Sherwood, he thought, if you knew I had offered for you as the result of a drunken wager and for the promise of eighty-thousand pounds from my godmother?

He reached to take her hand, and she raised her eyes to his. He could think of nothing to say but managed to smile. It was enough for her. She returned his smile and relapsed into silence.

Stanton realized that Charlotte would not normally have spoken so to him. She was caught up in the elation of her brother's wedding day. She was relaxed, confident, and secure among her family, and he knew these feelings had prompted her pretty speech. But he wished she had not made it, for it brought home to him the enormous impropriety of offering for her in the way he had. This girl was both young and lovely. She was possessed of a gentleness and sweetness of nature that any man would find hard to resist. But just as clearly as he assessed Charlotte's character did he know his own. He did not love her and thought he never would. His nature was not constant, and even though he was attracted to her now, he knew that in less than a year he would undoubtedly make her miserable.

Somehow he managed to get through the remainder of that interminable day, and that evening, alone in the library of his home, he finally admitted to himself that he could not continue the farce. Richard had been right. It had been a matter for conscience—and conscience had been victorious.

The following morning Sir Hugh Broughton and Lord Stanton were riding in Hyde Park when the viscount startled his friend by saying suddenly, "I cannot marry Miss Sherwood, Hugh."

"Eh?" his friend replied, not sure he had heard aright.

"I said that I cannot marry Miss Sherwood. It wouldn't serve. I never should have asked her."

"You had to ask her. Swore you wouldn't renege on your wager, remember?"

"Yes. I remember only too well, and I am afraid I will have to settle with you some other way, Hugh, for I find I must go back on my word. I cannot continue with this engagement."

"Well, as to that, there is no question of going back on your word," Sir Hugh said reasonably. "The wager was that you should *offer* for the lady, which you have done, and the debt is satisfied. Whether you ever marry the girl is beside the point."

Stanton smiled at his friend's fine understanding of the gambling ethic. "Well, I will not marry her, of that much I am certain."

"Thing is, Julian, I don't rightly see how you can avoid it now. A gentleman can't cry off from an engagement."

"No," Stanton agreed. "But the lady can."

"True enough, but why should she wish to? She accepted you readily and seems well-disposed toward you. Don't seem to me that she would be likely to cry off."

"Under normal circumstances I would agree with you. But I have been thinking that perhaps the lady could be *induced* to do so."

"Induced?"

"Yes, my dear Hugh," his lordship answered grimly. "Induced."

Having determined to end his engagement to Miss Sherwood and having decided upon the method that would best achieve this end, Lord Stanton waited only for the opportunity to put his method to the test. He met Charlotte several times during the days immediately following Jonathan's wedding and on each occasion his manner toward her was reserved, almost austere. On the fourth day, when they were both invited to the Suttons' ball, he knew his opportunity was at hand.

One entire side of the ballroom was lined with tall windows hung with golden brocade draperies. With the hangings closed as they were this evening, each window provided a small enclosure, large enough for a couple to stand in with ease and be, for all intents and purposes, hidden from the eyes of the assembly. Young girls were traditionally warned to avoid such window embrasures, for it was not unheard of for a gentleman to steal a kiss after whisking a girl into this secluded place. No one seemed to notice, however, if on occasion a married or betrothed couple disappeared for a few moments for a tête-à-tête.

Lord Stanton and Charlotte were dancing, and as the music ended they found themselves near the ballroom windows. Taking her hand, Stanton drew Charlotte quickly through the draperies and pulled her to him, his arms about her waist.

"I have had no opportunity to be alone with you for three full days," he said. "Nor have I found opportunity to tell you how lovely you are tonight." His eyes dropped boldly to her low-cut gown, and she blushed and wished she had worn something less décolleté. He touched her face gently, and she looked up to meet his eyes in the dim light.

Surprised by this abrupt change in his recent manner toward her, Charlotte stood stiffly, vividly aware that his fingers were tracing the fine line of her jaw, then the side of her neck, and then down onto her shoulder. His fingers hesitated briefly as they came to rest against the neckline of her gown, and then very deliberately began to move again, following the neckline of her dress across her breast.

She gasped audibly and pulled away sharply. "My lord . . . please! You have been drinking, I think, and I also think—"

"And you also think I should not be permitted to sample the wares before the wedding night," he interrupted. "But I don't agree, dear Charlotte." He pulled her roughly into his arms and brought his mouth down on hers. Her lips were rigid and unresponsive, and for one fleeting moment he thought it would be amusing to coax her into yielding herself to him. But remembering that his purpose was to repel and disgust, he pressed his kiss ruthlessly upon her, bruising her mouth with his own.

Charlotte was profoundly shocked by his actions but felt that impassive behavior on her part would be the most effective way to damp his ardor. But when after a few moments he showed no inclination to desist, she struggled to free herself. He released her instantly, an amused chuckle escaping as he held her at arm's length.

"I see that there is a great deal I must teach you about love-making, my dear. I think I shall enjoy the task," he said consideringly.

Charlotte did not speak but wrenched herself free from his hold. He gave her a slight mocking bow and then held the drapery aside for her to step back into the ballroom. Conscious of the fact that someone might be watching them, she turned to face him and forced herself to say, "Thank you for the dance, my lord." He noted the tears in her eyes with regret, but only bowed formally and then turned and strolled away.

Charlotte did not see Lord Stanton again that evening and concluded that he had either left the ball immediately following their encounter or given up dancing in favor of the card room. Her evening was ruined. She forced herself to behave as normally as possible, and although her act may have convinced others, Elizabeth wasn't deceived. She saw at once that something was wrong, but Charlotte refused to discuss it. By the time they arrived home in the early hours of the morning, Charlotte pled fatigue and retired to bed, leaving her sister in suspense.

During his habitual early-morning ride in the park, Viscount Stanton pondered the possible repercussions of his behavior on the previous evening. As he considered the matter dispassionately, he concluded that he could expect one of three possible responses.

The first and most desirable of these would be for Charlotte herself to call, or perhaps her father, to inform him that she no longer wished for the match. If Charlotte employed her father, Stanton was relatively certain that she would not disclose her reasons but simply inform him of her wishes.

The second alternative was that Charlotte would choose to ignore the incident and take no action of any kind. Perhaps she would be willing to forgive what she considered behavior resulting from the influence of wine. Or, if she confided in another female, she would perhaps be assured that such behavior was normal and must be expected and tolerated. If this proved to be the case, then he would be forced to employ even stronger measures to repel her, and the idea was repugnant to him. Therefore he sincerely hoped that Charlotte would *not* choose to forgive him.

Finally, he considered that Charlotte may have gone to her brother. There was some safety in that fact that he and Charlotte were actually engaged, for within the engagement he was permitted intimacies that outside that agreement would be considered gross impropriety. If Charlotte went to Richard, Stanton could only hope that Richard's fine intuition would see and understand that although the viscount's method may have been a bit reprehensible, his motive had been pure. Charlotte would be safely out of the engagement, pride intact, and none the worse for a stolen caress.

Returning from his ride, Stanton settled himself in his library, intending to spend the day there. If any member of the Sherwood family wished to call upon him, he preferred that they find him at home.

When Elizabeth and Charlotte descended to breakfast at ten o'clock, they found Richard and their father already finished, and their mother not yet down. Elizabeth barely waited for the footman who had served them to close the door before she blurted out, "All right, Charlotte, I won't wait a moment longer for an explanation of what happened between you and Lord Stanton last night. One minute you were dancing with him, happy as a grig, and the next time I saw you, you were regularly blue-deviled, for all you tried to hide it. What's going on?"

"I have decided that Lord Stanton and I should not suit after all, Lizzie," Charlotte replied.

"Why ever not?"

"I think his nature is too passionate."

"Most men are passionate. Mama told us that!"

"Yes, perhaps. But Lizzie . . . I am afraid of him!"

"I daresay you feel that way because you are not in love

93

with him," Elizabeth said sensibly. "I think passion would be much easier to deal with if there were some love to accompany it."

"But men and women frequently marry without love," Charlotte said irritably.

"Of course they do. And so shall you and Lord Stanton. And I am sure you will deal admirably together," Elizabeth replied bracingly.

"Well, you're wrong," Charlotte contradicted, "for I will not marry Lord Stanton, not after his behavior last night!"

"For heaven's sake, Charlotte, what did he do?"

"He took me into one of the window embrasures, and he held me, and kissed me, and he . . . he . . . oh, Lizzie, I can't tell you!"

"Charlotte!" Elizabeth exclaimed. "Never tell me that his lordship compromised you! I don't know precisely what that is," she added thoughtfully, "but surely it cannot happen in a window embrasure!"

Charlotte smiled and turned watery eyes upon her sister. "Oh, Lizzie, you goose! Of course he has not compromised me, but I am beginning to think that you are right after all, and that I should not marry where I do not love, or at least feel some affection."

"You will not tell me what he did to distress you?"

"He had been drinking," Charlotte said, "and behaved, I am convinced, as no true gentleman would." Tears came at the memory, and Elizabeth impulsively took her sister's hand as Charlotte continued. "I can only regret that I did not have enough presence of mind to give him the set-down he so richly deserved! I am disappointed in him, Lizzie, and afraid of him, and I will not marry him! I had all night to consider my decision, and I will not change my mind." She looked down at the engagement ring on her finger and in one swift movement pulled it over the knuckle and dropped it on the table. "I am going to the drawing room this instant to write him a letter. I will enclose his ring with it, and I will politely but firmly inform his lordship that our engagement is at an end.

Shortly after midday Lord Stanton received a note and a small package, brought round by hand from Mount Street. He opened the package first, and his engagement ring dropped onto the desk. No more than he expected, after all. The note was also as expected: *I think we will not suit. . . . I am returning your ring. . . . I will not change my mind. . . . I am sorry for any inconvenience. . . . Please send the proper notices. . . . Yours, etc.* He wished she hadn't apologized, for the fault was entirely his.

He sat for some time in contemplation of Charlotte's note and then crumpled it into a ball and pitched it into the fire. He opened a drawer of his desk and dropped the ring inside. What did one do with *used* engagement rings, he wondered. How could he have been mad enough to involve himself in this whole business? It was so sordid. Mentally consigning his godmother's eighty-thousand pounds and her matchmaking schemes to perdition, he rose from the desk, deciding to go to White's and find some diversion there to take his mind from his broken engagement, but at that moment the library door opened and his butler appeared.

"Miss Sherwood has called to see you, my lord."

"That would be my fiancée, Woodly," he said, with a fine disregard for the truth. "You may show her in."

"Very good, my lord."

Stanton turned and walked irritably to the fireplace. No escape quite yet, he thought, and, ignoring the damage to his gleaming Hessians, viciously kicked the end of a log protruding onto the hearthstones, thereby sending a shower of sparks up the chimney.

The door opened behind him, and he turned as the butler announced: "Miss Sherwood, my lord."

Stanton started and then stared when he saw that it was

not Charlotte but Elizabeth who entered the room. She stopped just inside the door, and he remained standing before the fire until they were alone. He made no attempt to greet her.

"You misled my butler in the matter of your name, Miss Elizabeth."

"Yes, my lord. I was afraid you would deny me if I gave the correct name."

"And so I would have," he said grimly. "Why have you come here, ma'am? You must know that it is most improper for you to do so."

"I have brought my maid along. She is waiting in the hall. And you are engaged to my sister," she offered.

"I *was* engaged to your sister. That engagement is now at an end."

"You have had Charlotte's letter, then?"

"Yes, I have had her letter. But what is all this to you?"

"I watched Charlotte write that letter, Lord Stanton. You have made her very unhappy, and I don't understand why you should wish to do so. She would make you a good wife, if you would not press her and give her more time to become accustomed to you."

Oh, my God, he thought. The little sister has come to help us mend our fences. We cannot have this!

"Your sister is much too good to be saddled with a husband such as I would be," he said. "You may consider her well out of any connection with me."

"That's what Richard thinks, but I am not sure that I agree."

"You should, for he probably understands me better than I understand myself. What exactly did he say, if you don't think he would mind your repeating it?"

"He said he couldn't think that any woman would be happy married to you."

"And he's exactly right," he approved. "And do you know why? Because I am not long content with one woman.
96

I estimate that a month of your lovely sister would be enough for me, and then I would be looking elsewhere."

"I don't believe you, sir," she answered quietly.

"Don't you, Miss Elizabeth?" he asked mockingly, advancing toward her. "Do you desire proof? Very well, you shall have it. My engagement to your sister has been broken for perhaps half an hour, and already I am prepared to take an interest in the woman at hand—and a very pretty woman she is!"

Elizabeth felt her color rising. "I don't understand you, my lord."

"Oh, I think you do. Any female bold enough to call at a bachelor establishment and demand a private interview cannot be ignorant of the consequences she may expect."

"I am convinced that you would not offer me any insult, Lord Stanton," she said boldly, believing her words as she spoke them and then doubting as she saw the gleam in his eyes.

"Your confidence is misplaced, ma'am," he said grimly. Then, before she could think or move, one of his hands went around her waist and pulled her to him, while the other cupped her chin and turned her face up to his. Even as she contemplated escape his lips found hers, and she was startled into complete immobility, for she had never been kissed before, and a barrage of totally new and strangely stimulating sensations swept over her. Elizabeth stood surprisingly relaxed in his arms, and although she did not actually respond to his kiss, her lips were soft and receptive.

Stanton had intended to deal her the same treatment he had dealt her sister, but when he met with no resistance and only the tenderness and innocence of inexperience, he found he had no wish to hurt her. His lips moved gently on hers, seeking a response.

Recovering, albeit belatedly, from her initial shock, the impropriety of the situation rushed in upon Elizabeth, and she pushed herself free from Stanton's embrace. Never having lacked for courage, Elizabeth did not have the slightest inclination to flee as had Charlotte. Instead she was outraged and allowed this feeling to manifest itself in a resounding slap, dealt to his lordship with the full force of her arm behind it.

He smiled at her attack, resisting an impulse to rub his smarting cheek. "I suppose I deserved that."

"You may consider it payment from both my sister and myself," she snapped.

He pretended to give the matter some thought and then said, "From your sister, I will accept it, but from you, no, I don't think I shall, for I have the impression that you enjoyed the moment quite as much as I."

Her eyes flashed with indignation at his suggestion, and she drew back her hand to slap him again, but he caught her wrist and held it tightly.

"No, no, my little wildcat," he said. "I will not let you hit me again. You have revenged your sister admirably with the first blow."

"You are the most despicable, detestable man!" she hissed. "Richard was right. You would have made Charlotte miserable. You will be made to pay for this behavior, my lord, I promise you!"

"Intending to run to big brother with the tale of your woes, Miss Elizabeth?" he mocked.

"You are contemptible, sir! First you insult me, and then say you expect me to encourage Richard to meet a man who has proven himself to be unsurpassed in the use of pistols."

"Richard will not meet me, Miss Elizabeth, but not for the reasons you suppose."

"No. He certainly will not, for I have no intention of mentioning this incident to him. I am perfectly capable of fighting my own battles, my lord."

"Are you indeed?"

She became suddenly aware that he still held her wrist in a hard grasp, and she wrenched it away. "You are a hateful villain. If I had a pistol, I would not hesitate to shoot you myself!"

He regarded at her with interest. "Really, ma'am? Well, you're in luck, for I just happen to have one to hand. And loaded, too," he added as an afterthought. He stepped to his desk as he spoke and produced a handsome silver-mounted pistol from the top drawer. He cheerfully held it out to her on his open palm. She stared at the pistol, and then up at his laughing, mocking face; then, sensing that frustrated tears were only moments away, she moved to the door and, flinging it open, swept from the room, the echoes of his malicious laughter following her down the hall.

Stanton abandoned his plans to go to the club and instead returned to the fire and flung himself down in an armchair. The situation was going from bad to worse. He had succeeded in breaking his engagement, but making an enemy of Elizabeth Sherwood had not been part of his plan. He realized that he should have sent her away immediately, and under no circumstances should he have discussed his engagement with her. But somehow she seemed to sense that his behavior toward Charlotte had been a feint. He knew that she lacked the experience to be a worthy opponent, but he couldn't resist the temptation to outrage her. Now he regretted it, for he admired her spirit and her loyalty to her family and would have preferred her not to think ill of him.

Elizabeth returned to Mount Street in a vile mood, with righteous indignation at Lord Stanton's improper behavior warring with self-recrimination for her own crass stupidity in putting herself in his power. She wanted nothing more than to seek the privacy of her bedchamber and soothe her wounded pride by imagining any other ending to their interview than the one that had actually taken place. If only she had had the courage to take the pistol and put a bullet through him! That would have taken the smirk from his face!

11

The Sherwood family had varied reactions to Charlotte's announcement that she and Lord Stanton had decided that they should not suit after all. Elizabeth was puzzled when Richard showed little inclination to question Charlotte closer on the subject, but she was at the same time relieved, for the fewer questions Richard asked, the less likely it was that he would discover Lord Stanton's behavior toward Charlotte and Elizabeth's own improper interference in her sister's affairs.

Several days later, the Sherwoods received an invitation from Lord and Lady Kemp to join their party at Vauxhall Gardens on the following Friday evening. Lord and Lady Sherwood and Charlotte were already engaged to attend the theater with Harriet, who had been back in town only a few days and was impatient to join her husband on the Continent. Elizabeth had not committed herself to the play that evening and expressed a wish to visit Vauxhall.

"I was promised to Charles Warmington on Friday," Richard said, "but we haven't made definite plans. Shall we escort you, Lizzie?"

"Yes, please," she replied. "I shall write at once to Lady Kemp and accept for the three of us. That is, if you are sure Mr. Warmington will wish to go?"

Personally, Richard thought that Charles would rather

go to the play, or indeed anywhere where he might expect to find Charlotte. But as it was impossible to say this, he only replied, "I'm sure he'll be delighted."

On Friday evening, Charlotte and her parents left the house first, and when Elizabeth descended, she found that Mr. Warmington had arrived and was with her brother in the salon. She entered the room to find him engrossed in an animated recounting of the curricle race that had taken place that morning between Lord Granbrooke and Viscount Stanton. He paused to greet her and then at her insistence continued his narrative.

Elizabeth had forgotten that the race was to be run that day, although in contemplating it before the event, she had thought that nothing would be more pleasant than for the two contestants to entangle their racing carriages and somehow manage to break each other's necks, for two such odious, abominable men deserved no better end. But to her disappointment, there seemed to have been no such satisfactory conclusion to the race. Lord Stanton's pair had won by a good margin.

"It isn't that Granbrooke didn't have good cattle," Charles was saying. "They were fine-looking beasts— showy, but plenty of substance. The man's an excellent whip, too, but Julian has always had the edge on him. This is the fifth time they've raced, and the fifth time Granbrooke has been beaten. I personally think that it's Julian's method of conditioning his grays that gives him the deciding edge. Always knows how to bring them along just right for a big race."

At that moment their carriage was announced and they rose to leave, but Elizabeth was sure that she had not heard the last of the race. No doubt it would be one of the major topics of conversation among the gentlemen that evening.

They arrived at the gardens in good time and soon found the box that Lord Kemp's party had taken for the evening. Mrs. Ellis and Miss Ellis were both present, and Lady

Kemp was grateful to Miss Elizabeth for bringing two gentlemen as escorts, thereby somewhat evening their numbers. Dancing had already begun in the pavilion, and Mr. Warmington soon asked Miss Ellis to take the floor. Not many minutes had passed before Lord Kemp asked Richard if he had heard about the race between Granbrooke and Stanton, and with the men well launched on this subject, the women settled into a comfortable coze.

Richard later danced with Mrs. Ellis, and Elizabeth stood up with Mr. Warmington before they all enjoyed a delicious supper. Just as they were finishing, Elizabeth's enjoyment of the evening came to an abrupt end as Viscount Stanton and Sir Hugh Broughton came strolling past the box, stopped to exchange a few words, and were invited by Lady Kemp to join her party.

When the viscount greeted Elizabeth, she reluctantly placed her hand in his and then flushed indignantly as he held it overlong. A few moments later one of Miss Ellis's London cousins came to collect her for a stroll in the gardens, and after she had gone Sir Hugh suggested that the rest of the party go for a walk as well.

Lady Kemp demurred. "No, no. You young people go ahead. His lordship and I are much too sedentary for such exercise."

Richard made a point of taking Elizabeth's arm and strolled off with her down one of the lantern-lighted walkways through the gardens. Mrs. Ellis, in high spirits, found herself with no less than three escorts and laughingly took the arms of two of them as they followed along the same path. She insisted that the viscount give them a personal account of his race that morning, and she asked so charmingly that he could not resist her. His story-telling style was amusing, and since both his cousin, Charles, and his friend, Sir Hugh, had failed to get him to enlarge much upon the race, they hung upon his words quite as much as Mrs. Ellis did.

Some distance ahead, Richard was taxing his sister on the manner in which she had greeted the viscount. "Don't be rude to Stanton just because of this situation with Charlotte, Lizzie," he said. "She's well out of any connection with him."

"That is what he said," she responded without thinking.

He looked at her sharply. "You spoke with him about this? You should not have done so. It is none of your concern."

They were walking quickly and had outdistanced the rest of their party. As they came round a bend and continued down a long stretch of deserted pathway, Elizabeth realized that the conversation was taking a dangerous turn. She had not intended to mention her meeting with Lord Stanton, and if she didn't change the subject quickly, more likely than not Richard would have the whole story from her. There was no mistaking the disapproval in his voice, and on top of her humiliating treatment at Lord Stanton's hands, she didn't think she could bear a lecture from Richard.

Even as she tried to think of an answer that would direct them to a safer topic, there was a rustle in the shrubbery to their right as two burly men leaped from the bushes and hurled themselves at Richard. Elizabeth opened her mouth to scream but was suddenly grabbed from behind as her mouth and most of her face were covered by a large foul-smelling glove. Large man that he was, Captain Sherwood nevertheless had his hands full with two heavy opponents, so he never saw the fourth man who approached from behind and dealt him a stunning blow to the head. Elizabeth did not see her brother fall, for she was already being dragged off through the shrubbery, held fast in an iron grip.

When the rest of the party rounded the corner a few moments later, they were shocked by the sight of Captain Sherwood struggling to his knees on the path before them. Of Miss Elizabeth there was no sign. Mrs. Ellis uttered an exclamation as Stanton broke into a run. He reached Richard in seconds and knelt beside him.

"Richard, what happened? Where is your sister?"

Richard tried to speak and then closed his eyes as he fought to overcome a shuddering wave of nausea. As the rest of the party came up the viscount said, "There was no shot, so he must have been struck down." He ran his hand carefully over the back of Richard's head, and it came away covered with blood. Taking a large handkerchief from his pocket, he placed it over the wound.

"Should we help him up, Lord Stanton?" Mrs. Ellis asked, reaching to hold the cloth in place.

"No, ma'am. We'll leave him as he is for the present and allow him to overcome the dizziness. Richard, you've got a nasty bump, but you *mustn't* pass out. Did you recognize any of them?"

"Julian . . ." Richard finally managed. "Lizzie . . ."

"Yes," Stanton encouraged. "Someone has taken Elizabeth. But who? Did you recognize them?"

"No," Richard answered more clearly. "There were three . . . no . . . four, but it had to be Granbrooke."

"Granbrooke?" the viscount asked in astonishment. "Surely not!"

"Indeed, my lord," Mrs. Ellis confirmed. "Elizabeth refused his offer of marriage several weeks ago, and at the Sherwood ball he so forgot himself that Captain Sherwood asked him to leave the house."

Sir Hugh now joined in the conversation. "His losing that race to you this morning probably put him over the edge, Julian. He's rolled up; probably decided this was the only way."

As Stanton rose to his feet, Richard grasped his wrist. "It had to be Granbrooke. He needs a rich wife . . . and Julian . . . he'll give her no choice."

"I know," Stanton replied gravely. "I'll find them, Richard. Trust me."

Richard only nodded, but the effort made his head throb.

Stanton turned his attention to his friends. "Charles, you must get him to a doctor as quickly as possible. And Hugh, if you could stay with Mrs. Ellis and make our excuses to the Kemps. Tell them that Miss Elizabeth was taken ill and Richard and Charles have taken her home. Dispose of me any way you please." He turned on the words and was gone into the night.

Stanton was crossing the river to Westminster in a matter of minutes but then swore impatiently as he had to wait more than five minutes for his coach to be called up. As the carriage stopped before him and the footman jumped down, Stanton handed him some coins. "Take a hackney home immediately, Tim. Have the strongest coach team harnessed to the light traveling-chaise. Take the chaise immediately to St. James Square and await me there." As Tim turned and jogged off to the hackney stand, Stanton ordered his coachman to Lord Granbrooke's residence in St. James Square, but even as he drove, he knew he would not find Granbrooke at home. The question was: Where *would* he find him?

Within five minutes of the viscount's departure, Captain Sherwood was assisted to his feet, leaning heavily on Charles and Sir Hugh. Mrs. Ellis accompanied them to a scull and across the river, and there she and Sir Hugh saw Richard safely off to the doctor in Charles's care. They then recrossed to the gardens and strolled back to the boxes. Mrs. Ellis marveled at the ease with which Sir Hugh delivered his fabricated excuses.

"I am sorry to say, Lady Kemp, that our party has been greatly depleted. Miss Elizabeth became suddenly unwell, and Captain Sherwood and Mr. Warmington thought it best to convey her home."

"Ah, the poor child," Lady Kemp sympathized. "It was probably those shrimp. I, myself, never eat seafood away from home, for you never know when it might not be quite fresh. But what of Lord Stanton, Sir Hugh? Have we lost him as well?"

"Alas, I fear so, my lady. We came upon his brother, Henry, and he was dragged off to recount the story of his race yet once again."

"Poor Lord Stanton," her ladyship replied. "I think that before the night is over he may regret that he ever ran that race."

"Indeed, ma'am," Sir Hugh replied, "I am beginning to think that he regrets it already."

Mrs. Ellis regarded Sir Hugh critically but couldn't decide whether he had intended his words to have a double meaning. During the remainder of the evening she tried to assume a normal mien, but it was difficult, and she could only be thankful that neither Lord nor Lady Kemp was particularly perceptive.

Once, while they were dancing, Sir Hugh taxed her with her demeanor. "Come, Mrs. Ellis, smile! To look at you, people will think that it pains you to dance with me."

"I am sorry, Sir Hugh. Indeed I am. It is just that I consider both Captain Sherwood and his sister my friends, and I am worried and feel useless dancing here. I would rather be anywhere else, doing something to help."

"We are helping by keeping up an appearance of normalcy. Julian was right, you know. If we had all left suddenly, it would have presented a very strange appearance and would perhaps have given rise to speculation. As it is, I don't think anyone will be the wiser. As far as Miss Elizabeth is concerned, if anything can be done, Julian will do it. And as for Richard, he has taken many knocks harder than that one. He has a hard head—he will be fine, depend upon it."

At Granbrooke's house in St. James Square, Stanton was informed that his lordship was not at home, which was nothing more than he expected. When he offered to leave his card, the footman told him that his lordship had gone out of town. Not wishing to arouse suspicion, Stanton said no more but retired to his coach and instructed his man to drive round to the mews. Here he alighted and casually walked into the stables. There were several grooms working there, and Stanton was relieved to recognize one of them. He walked directly to the man who paused in his work to say, "Good evening, m'lord."

"Good evening. . . . Riddle, isn't it?"

"Indeed it is, m'lord," the man said, flattered that his lordship should remember him.

"Well, Riddle, I came by to see the bays. After I raced them this morning, I couldn't stop thinking what a fine pair they are, and I asked your master if I could come by and take another look at them. I have a similar bay pair, and I've been considering whether they might be made to go together as a team."

"Aye, I know your bays, m'lord, and mayhap you're right, 'twould be an impressive team." The man's eyes were sparkling at the thought, and Stanton knew that he was off guard.

They went together to the boxes to inspect the horses, and conversation progressed easily enough, for they were indeed a handsome pair of animals.

"Well, that's it, then," Stanton said decisively. "I must have them. Your master may name his price." Stanton was smiling openly at Riddle by this time, and the man felt favored to be sharing confidences with one of the most noted whips in the city. "Where is he now, Riddle? Do you know? He is usually at Watier's at this time of night, isn't he?" He turned to hurry away. "I'll make him an offer yet tonight."

"Wait, m'lord! I'm afraid you'll not find his lordship at the club, for he's gone out of town."

Stanton's face registered immediate disappointment, and he had to bite his tongue to keep from screaming—*where?* But he was immediately rewarded for his patience when

108

Riddle said bracingly, "But I don't think he intends a long stay at Epsom, m'lord, and should return in a few days time. I will tell him you called about the horses."

"Yes, please do, Riddle. And tell him to call on me. I will be impatiently waiting to hear from him." Stanton turned and moved without apparent haste back to his waiting coach. He proceeded to the end of the street, and then turning again into St. James Square, his town coach with two horses pulled up beside his traveling-chaise and four. As Stanton stepped down from the coach, he nodded for his coachman to come down as well. "Come along, Sweet, we're for Epsom, and I'll put my money on you to get me there as fast as any man can."

Sweet grinned as he jumped down from the box and quickly climbed up onto the chaise. "We've almost a full moon, my lord; that will help. And a fair road. Should be no problem to make good time."

"Let's be off, then. We'll make a change at Merton and stop at the King's Arms in Epsom for information."

Stanton ordered his town coach home, and without further ado, mounted into the chaise and set out. He was aware that he had lost valuable time in inspecting the horses in Granbrooke's stable, but it couldn't be helped. He must make the time up elsewhere. Epsom was no more than a twelve-mile journey and could be accomplished in one stage. Stanton was hoping that Granbrooke would take one team the entire distance. By changing horses himself at the halfway point, the viscount planned to finish the journey with a fresh team while Granbrooke continued with a tiring one.

The change at Merton was accomplished quickly, but more importantly, they learned that a chaise had passed through perhaps thirty minutes earlier, traveling south. To Stanton's relief, no change of horses had been made. From this point, with a fresh team, they should be able to gain on Granbrooke's coach.

Stanton found himself increasingly concerned with what was happening in the coach ahead. If Granbrooke had employed ruffians to overpower Richard, he would not need their services once he had the girl safely away. It was most likely that he and Elizabeth were traveling alone, and the viscount found the thought disturbing. With a man of Granbrooke's temperament there was no predicting how he would behave. Having laid such careful plans to abduct the girl and keep her hidden for a few days, he could certainly be patient enough to delay his seduction until he found himself in a more comfortable place than a rocking, bouncing carriage.

If Granbrooke did make some attempt in the carriage, Stanton had no doubt that Elizabeth would make an effort to defend herself. She had a good right arm! He smiled at the memory of the day she had slapped him. She had plenty of courage, Richard's little sister! But slowly, as the miles passed, the viscount's smile faded, and an irrepressible rage began to take its place.

At the King's Arms the proprietor knew Lord Granbrooke well and gave them simple directions to his house, less than a mile away.

12

Stanton would have suffered less anxiety had he known that Lord Granbrooke did indeed choose to curtail his advances until he and his "guest" reached the privacy of his secluded Epsom home. Having decided on this extreme course of action, it seemed to him the perfect place to take Elizabeth until she should agree to marry him. Few people knew of his house outside London, as he had kept it very close, retiring there on more than one occasion when his debts had made the town too hot for him.

"What is the meaning of this, my lord?" Elizabeth snapped, as she fixed her captor with a cold, furious stare. "Where are you taking me?"

"Somewhere where we can be alone together without fear of interruption, my dear."

"You're a fool, sir, if you think Richard will not follow me!"

"I am sure he will try. But from what my hirelings tell me, he will be incapable of doing so for some time at least, and by then I fear he may experience some difficulty in finding us. It was considerate of the two of you to walk off alone like that. You made my job so much easier."

"What have you done to Richard?"

"Nothing more than a slight knock on the head, I assure

you. You can't think that I should wish any permanent injury to my future brother-in-law.''

The meaning of these words could not be misunderstood, and the image they produced sickened her. "I will never marry you, Lord Granbrooke. You cannot force me to do so.''

"Can't I, my dear? I rather think you are wrong. You may be opposed to such an alliance tonight, but I think that in the morning you will have very different feelings in the matter.''

"Why are you doing this to me?''

"Because you have a handsome marriage portion, Elizabeth, and I am in desperate need of it. If I could have been victorious over Stanton this morning, things might have been different. But the fellow has the devil's own luck, so you are my last hope. I never cared much for the idea of marriage, but I must say I can almost countenance it to a morsel as choice as you.'' He reached forward to fondle a curl that had escaped and hung loose by her face, and she shrank from him.

He laughed. It was not a pleasant sound. Elizabeth did not answer him, and when she made no response to the next several comments he addressed to her, he relapsed into silence and didn't speak for more than an hour until the Epsom house was reached and the coach rolled to a stop.

Elizabeth had by then had time to consider the seriousness of her situation. She was anxious for Richard and prayed that he was not badly injured. She knew that the rest of the party were close behind, and Richard would not have been long without help. Had any of that party rounded the bend in time to see her dragged away? The attack took place so quickly that she thought it unlikely. Perhaps one or more of the other gentlemen would try to come after her. But how could they, she reasoned, when they had no way of knowing who had taken her, or where? She decided

112

she could not depend upon outside help and must discover a way to deal with Lord Granbrooke herself. There were no pistols in the coach holsters, and she wondered if he carried one upon his person.

Arriving at their destination, Granbrooke descended from the coach and waited for Elizabeth to alight. When she hesitated, he said imperatively, "You may walk into the house under your own power, ma'am, or if you prefer these men shall carry you."

One look at the stocky footmen at his side convinced her that they would not hesitate to obey him, so reluctantly she descended and entered the house. She knew she had no hope of prevailing against three men. She must bide her time until she had his lordship alone and then apply all her efforts to thwart him. She forced herself to remain calm. She must think. If there was a way to escape, she would find it.

Once inside, they ascended the stairway to a salon on the first floor. Elizabeth watched as Granbrooke closed the double doors behind them, locked them, and placed the key in his pocket. Her eyes swept the room quickly. There was only the one door, and the windows would all be too high from the ground to offer any possible escape. Food and wine had been set upon a sideboard, and a large fire crackled on the hearth. There was a small table and several chairs scattered about the room and a large sofa standing against one wall. Granbrooke went to pour himself some wine, and Elizabeth pretended to warm her hands at the fire. It had occurred to her that a poker might make a formidable weapon, but she saw to her dismay that there were no fireplace tools.

She turned suddenly to find his lordship directly behind her, and as she tried to move away he put his free arm around her and pulled her close, attempting to kiss her. She jerked away sharply, knocking the wineglass from his hand and spilling its contents over them both. He swore beneath his breath and, as she spun away, caught her right hand in his and crushed it ruthlessly. The pain stayed her momentarily, and as her eyes met his he said, "You would do much better to face the inevitable with dignity, my dear. I do not wish to hurt you, but if you fight me, I may be forced to do so."

With superhuman strength, Elizabeth pulled her hand free and tried to turn away, but he grabbed for her, catching her by the shoulders, and as she struggled wildly to free herself the shoulder of her gown came away in his hand. She tried to slap him, but he caught both arms, pinning them to her sides and forcing her relentlessly back upon the sofa. She felt his great weight descent on her, and as his face came close, she turned her head to avoid him, but his hand was in her hair, viciously twisting her head, forcing her face to meet his. He pressed his wet mouth to hers, crushing her lips cruelly against her teeth, and then she felt his hand at her breast and thought she must faint. She fought against a growing cloud of dizziness and continued feebly to struggle, even though she knew she was no match for him and in the end he would have his way.

Stanton's greatest concern upon arriving at Granbrooke's house was that he would be denied entrance at the front door. If it wasn't opened to him willingly, he doubted if he would be able to gain entry by force. He removed a pair of pistols from the interior of the carriage and, putting one of them into his pocket, handed the other to Sweet. The undergroom remained on the box, holding the team.

Stanton sounded the knocker and was immeasurably relieved when the door was opened almost immediately by a footman. "Viscount Stanton to see Lord Granbrooke," Stanton announced, stepping into the hall.

"Lord Granbrooke is not in residence, my lord," the man replied, and then took an involuntary step backward as the viscount produced his pistol and leveled it.

"Isn't he? Well, I hope you won't mind if I take a look for myself."

Sweet now entered the hall in his master's wake and closed the door behind them. Stanton glanced at the various doors around the hall and at the stairs ahead and demanded impatiently, "Where are they, man? Tell me now, if you value your life!" Sweet raised his own weapon threateningly, and the cowed footman nodded to the stairs.

"First door on the right, at the top."

Dropping the pistol into his pocket, Stanton took the stairs three at a time and then hesitated outside the double doors. He could hear no sound from within. He gently tried the handle and found it locked. Mentally preparing himself for what he might find, he took a step backward and then, raising his booted foot, planted a violent kick just below the handles. The wood splintered as the lock and the latch gave way and the doors flew wide.

Lord Granbrooke leaped from the sofa and turned furiously toward the door. When he saw who stood there, he was bereft of speech. Stanton's gaze alighted only briefly on Elizabeth, but even so took in her torn dress and her bruised, bleeding lips.

As Stanton continued to stand rigidly in the doorway, Granbrooke mastered his surprise and shouted, "You will explain yourself, sir! By what right do you force your way into my home? Your presence here is unwelcome!"

"To you, sir, no doubt it is, but perhaps the lady feels differently."

"What the lady and I choose to do is none of your affair, Stanton!"

"True enough, Granbrooke, if the lady accompanied you freely. Did you do so, Miss Elizabeth?"

"No, sir," she answered breathlessly. "His lordship brought me here against my will."

Stanton nodded in assent. "Just so, ma'am—as I thought."

"Get out of my house, Stanton," Granbrooke shouted wrathfully. "None of this is any concern of yours!"

"But I am making it my concern, my lord. I thought I had already made that clear." He advanced slowly on Granbrooke as he spoke and stopped a few feet short of him. "You know, Granbrooke," he said thoughtfully, "during all the years of our acquaintance I have always fancied that there was a smell of the barnyard about you, but it is only tonight that I have discovered why that is." Granbrooke stiffened at the words, and unveiled hatred gleamed in his eyes, but the viscount continued calmly. "Your manners would offend a pigsty."

Granbrooke started forward, then stopped again, clearly needing every effort of will to restrain himself. "You will meet me for this, my lord," he growled, between clenched teeth.

"Certainly," the viscount answered amiably. "When and where you please. Sir Hugh Broughton will act for me. You may send your man to call upon him in the morning." Then, deliberately turning his back on Lord Granbrooke, Stanton took Elizabeth's cloak from where it lay on the floor and put it gently about her shoulders as she rose from the sofa. He handed her her reticule and, without another look at Granbrooke, escorted her from the room, down the stairs, and into his waiting carriage. The door closed behind them, the horses were set in motion, and the lights of the house faded into the distance.

If Elizabeth had been able to speak, she would have been unable to think of anything to say. Her first reaction to the viscount's violent eruption into the room had been gratitude that her fervent prayer had been answered and that she had been delivered from Lord Granbrooke's evil plan for her. This feeling was quickly replaced by acute embarrassment at being discovered in such a compromising situation, with Granbrooke lying on her, and with her dress torn and her person disheveled. But nothing could equal her shock when

116

she realized that Stanton was purposely forcing a quarrel on Lord Granbrooke. The very man who less than three days ago had insulted her himself was now challenging Lord Granbrooke to a duel to defend her honor! How could she expect a man she despised to defend her? It was ludicrous! Unthinkable!

She started violently as Stanton laid his hand on hers, and as he quickly withdrew it, she looked up to meet his eyes in the dim light cast by the coach lantern. He was seated opposite her, with his back to the horses.

"Elizabeth," he said softly. "Please say something. You are frightening me."

I am frightening *you*, she thought. It should be Lord Granbrooke who frightens you. He is the one who will take a pistol and shoot at you in a few days time. But she said nothing and only continued to stare at him. Then suddenly she remembered her brother and found her voice. "How is Richard?"

"He has a nasty lump on the head, but I think he'll be all right. The others were seeing to him as I left."

"Thank God," she whispered.

Impulsively he leaned forward to examine her more closely. "Elizabeth, I *was* in time, wasn't I? He didn't hurt you?" Even as she nodded and assured him that she was fine, he saw that she was shaking, and, pulling his evening mantle from his shoulders, he moved across to her side of the coach to put it round her. She instinctively shrank from him, and he suddenly remembered the last time they had been alone together and could understand her anxiety. In her mind, she had only been conveyed from the arms of one scoundrel into the hands of another.

In an attempt to reassure her, he said, "You have nothing to fear from me, Miss Elizabeth. I followed you at Richard's request, and I would not betray his trust. You are shivering. Please, put this on." She leaned forward off the squabs as he drew the mantle around her. He then pulled

117

one of the carriage rugs over her legs, and although he remained seated at her side, he did not speak again until they reached Merton.

"We left my carriage team here," he explained, "and will stop to collect them. I think we should make some attempt to set you to rights, ma'am, for if I return you to your family as you are, I think they will be more concerned than necessary."

Elizabeth was struck by the sense of his words and raised a hand to her disheveled hair but, beyond nodding her agreement, made no other response.

Stanton left his coachman in charge of the change and escorted Elizabeth into the inn, where he demanded a private parlor. "We were involved in a carriage accident, and the lady has been slightly injured," he explained to the curious landlord. "We would like some brandy, and a cloth and some water, and a hairbrush if you have one."

The landlord soon produced the things they required and left them alone. Elizabeth seated herself at a small table, and Stanton pulled up a chair beside her. She watched him abstractedly as he dampened a cloth in water and turned to her.

"Look at me," he commanded, and she did so. "Your mouth is cut and bleeding," he said. "Let me see to it." He took her chin in his hand as he spoke, gently dabbing the blood away. Elizabeth steadily regarded his eyes as he concentrated on his work, forcing herself to remain still, willing herself not to pull away from his touch or to flinch at the discomfort he was causing her. "There," he said as he finished, "now hold this cloth to the split, and perhaps the bleeding will stop. Now for your hand." He picked up her right hand as he spoke, and she stared in astonishment, for several of the fingers were covered with dried blood. She hadn't even noticed. She watched as he washed the blood away, and realized that it was the hand that Lord Granbrooke had crushed so cruelly.

118

Stanton was tentatively turning the diamond ring on her third finger. "This is what caused the damage," he said. "The stone and the setting have both cut deeply into your fingers, here, and here. I am afraid it must come off. It may hurt a little." He pulled the ring over her knuckle as he spoke, and although it did hurt, it was over in a moment. He dropped the ring into the pocket of his evening coat and soon finished cleaning the wound. "I think that shall do. Can you manage your hair by yourself? I'm sure I can't help you there."

He held out the brush, and she took it from him and moved to a small looking glass on the far wall. She saw that her mouth was indeed swollen and discolored. She pulled the pins from her hair, and it fell in dark glossy waves to her waist. The viscount, pouring brandy at the table, watched her silently as she ran the brush through the long strands section by section. When she had finished, she gathered it up, and with several clever twists and turns of the wrist, piled it neatly on her head and began to secure it with pins. When she finished, she returned to the table, and he handed her a glass of brandy.

"I have no doubt this will burn your split lip abominably, but try to drink some just the same."

Stanton was uncomfortable with this silent and brooding Elizabeth. Always before he had known her to be ebullient, frank to a fault, full of infectious good humor, or, at the very least, outspoken anger. During the past hour, she had hardly spoken at all, and he was finding himself at a loss to know how to revive her spirits.

They soon returned to the coach and continued their journey. For some miles Elizabeth remained silent, and when she finally spoke, her tone was stilted and sounded rehearsed. "I would like to thank you, my lord, for coming to my assistance tonight. You were very kind to—"

"Nonsense," he interrupted rudely. "You do not consider me in the least kind. If you have forgotten the terms

119

you used to describe me only a few days ago, believe me, I have not. Let me see . . . despicable, hateful, contemptible. . . . I'm sure I've missed a few."

"Can you blame me, sir?" she was stung into retorting. "Your behavior was deserving of no better description!"

"You cannot have considered, ma'am, that you would not have been subjected to my behavior if you had not insinuated yourself into my home and into my affairs."

There was a slight pause before Elizabeth continued. "Is that why you behaved so to me?" she asked quietly, "to punish me for interfering between you and Charlotte?"

"Perhaps."

Elizabeth was silenced. She was still at a loss to understand what insane motive had caused Lord Stanton to force a quarrel upon Lord Granbrooke, but some instinct warned her that she should not introduce the subject. Had she done so, she would have found the viscount unwilling to discuss it.

It was close on two o'clock in the morning when Lord Stanton's carriage drew up outside the Sherwood residence in Mount Street. Williams alone of the servants had been taken into the family's confidence, and he waited patiently by the front door as the hours dragged by. Relief was clearly written on his face when he opened the door to admit his young mistress and Lord Stanton.

"The family is waiting in the small sitting room, my lord."

"Thank you. We'll go right up to them."

Charlotte had retired to bed soon after returning from the theater that evening, so was unaware of Elizabeth's abduction. Therefore, only Elizabeth's parents and her brother sat impatiently and impotently in the sitting room, praying for some word from either Elizabeth or Lord Stanton. They rose as one as the door opened, and there was a collective sigh of relief when they saw Elizabeth standing there. Richard was closest, and he received his sister against his

120

chest gratefully, wrapping one arm tightly around her and extending the other to the viscount.

Their eyes met over Elizabeth's head, and Richard's look spoke volumes, but he said only, "I knew I could count on you, Julian. I can't thank you enough."

Stanton turned to Lady Sherwood as she held out her hands to him. "Indeed, my lord, we owe you a debt of gratitude we can never repay."

"Seeing Miss Elizabeth home safely is payment enough, Lady Sherwood." As she surveyed her daughter with a worried frown, he took her aside and said quietly, "She has had a good scare, ma'am, and a little rough handling, but otherwise no harm has come to her. She would be better for a good night's rest."

Soon afterward, Lady Sherwood took her daughter off to bed, and Lord Sherwood also retired, gruffly informing his son that concussion could benefit from bed rest.

"Concussion, is it?" Stanton asked when the door had closed behind his lordship.

"So the doctor says. My parents have been plaguing me for two hours past to go on to bed, but I couldn't rest until I had some word of Lizzie."

"He took her to a house he keeps in Epsom," Stanton supplied. "I had the information from a talkative groom at his London stables. I took my traveling-chaise and four horses, changed to a fresh team at Merton, and made up some of the time I had lost."

"Is Lizzie really all right?"

"She assures me that she is. When I broke in on them, he hadn't gotten past the kissing, if you could call it that, and mauling stage. My God, Richard, the man is an animal! It was all I could do to keep from strangling him on the spot."

"Oh, no, my friend," Richard returned. "That pleasure shall be all mine. If Granbrooke thinks to get away with this, he'll learn his mistake before he's much older!"

"Well, I'm afraid your revenge must wait upon mine, for he is promised to meet me at the earliest convenience."

"What?" Richard thundered. "Julian, you didn't call him out?"

"Well, no, not exactly, but I did say that his manners reeked of the barnyard."

"Oh, Julian, that was not well done of you! You should have left this matter to me."

"That I should not have! You've a concussion, man! You're in no condition to be fighting a duel! I had already decided to bring the fellow to book while I was chasing him, but even if I hadn't, one look at your sister would have decided the matter instantly. Her dress was torn, her mouth bleeding, and the look of horror in her eyes I will not soon forget. It was more than any man could bear. Besides, I think I shall thoroughly enjoy putting a bullet through Granbrooke's ignoble person."

"You can't mean to kill him?"

"No. Unfortunately, that would create too much embarrassment for all of us, and I wouldn't like to be forced to flee the country. But I must tell you that I fear Granbrooke may plan to leave very soon himself. He lost a thousand pounds to me yesterday, and I'm sure that he cannot pay it. Now that he has failed with your sister, he will probably be hounded out of the country. I daresay he wouldn't hesitate to shoot to kill either one of us."

"If what you say is true, then you are placing yourself in considerable danger, Julian, for Granbrooke is accounted no mean shot."

"Very true, Richard, but you will perhaps recall that I am accounted an excellent shot, and if I fire first and place my ball in Granbrooke's shooting arm, I think that his aim will not be so good."

"Perhaps. But are you sure you can do it?"

The viscount smiled at him. "I wouldn't wager against it, my friend. I wouldn't wager against it."

122

13

The following morning, when Sir Hugh Broughton entered the gates of Hyde Park, he found the viscount awaiting him at their normal rendezvous. "I wasn't sure I would find you here this morning, Julian. What happened last night?"

The viscount briefly sketched the previous evening's events for his friend, as he had done for Richard, but leaving out such personal items as the condition in which he found Miss Elizabeth. He said only that she had been unhurt and safely returned to her family.

"Mrs. Ellis and I found little enjoyment in the evening after you left," Sir Hugh said. "She was particularly concerned for Miss Elizabeth's safety, and I had the devil's own time trying to cheer her up. Unlike me, she has no intimate knowledge of your resourcefulness, Julian, and therefore couldn't place as much confidence upon the success of your mission as I could. Shall we call on her when we finish our ride and set her mind at ease concerning the Sherwoods?"

"I shall call on her, if you like," the viscount answered, "but I should like you to stay home this morning, Hugh, if you would. I am expecting Lord Granbrooke's friend to call upon you."

Sir Hugh turned to him in surprise. "The devil you are!"

"Indeed, I am, and please spare me any lecture. I have already had one from Richard, thank you. Granbrooke is a blackguard, and clearly must be dealt with, and as Richard is in no condition to settle the matter himself, I am the logical person. Besides, the impulse to insult Granbrooke last night was irresistible, I promise you."

"Very well," his friend answered resignedly. "I will stay home to await his second."

"And, Hugh," the viscount added, "make it soon, tomorrow morning, if possible."

Mrs. Ellis spent a restless night, her mind in a flurry of concern in almost equal parts for Captain Sherwood and his sister. Her anxiety brought her at an early hour to the Sherwood residence. When she inquired for Elizabeth, she was informed that Miss Elizabeth was ill and would not be receiving visitors. Sarah then asked to see Lady Sherwood and was informed that her ladyship was still breakfasting. Sarah was about to leave her card and go away, when Captain Sherwood appeared through a door at the back of the hall.

"Good morning, Mrs. Ellis."

"Good morning, Captain. I have called to see your mother."

"She is just finishing her breakfast and will be with us directly," he replied smoothly. "Shall we await her in the salon?" He offered his arm to escort her upstairs.

No sooner were they inside the room than she turned to confront him. "Surely you should be in your bed, Captain, after the blow you sustained last night?"

He smiled at the concern in her eyes. "I'm well enough, ma'am, believe me."

She looked unconvinced but continued quickly. "And Elizabeth?"

"Safe and sound, thanks to Stanton."

"Thank God," she said with relief, sinking onto a sofa.

"Sir Hugh said that it would be so, but I could not be easy. I have been sick with anxiety all the night, worrying about you both."

"Both?" he asked quizzically.

"Certainly, both," she affirmed.

"You had no need to concern yourself for me, ma'am."

"Oh, really?" she said scornfully, rising once again to her feet. "You were unconscious when we put you into the coach, sir, and it was your blood on my hands!" She held out her hands in a gesture to reinforce her statement.

Richard grimaced apologetically and, stepping forward, took both her hands in his. "I'm sorry," he said. "It must have been dreadful for you."

"Dreadful for *me*!" she exclaimed. "Don't be ridiculous, Captain! You are the one who was injured, and I cannot believe that you escaped as easily as you pretend from that encounter."

"I have some slight concussion, Mrs. Ellis, nothing more," he insisted.

"If you have concussion, you should be in bed," she said acidly.

"Perhaps. But I have a great dislike of pampering myself."

"You are foolish beyond permission, sir."

"I daresay I am."

"And stubborn and willful."

"So I have been told," he agreed.

"And you will not get round me by being so agreeable, sir," she declared.

"Won't I?" He smiled charmingly at her then, and she could not resist the appeal in his eyes.

She smiled back at him despite herself and said quietly, "Well, perhaps this time." Their eyes held for a long moment, and then he dropped her hands as the door opened behind them and Lady Sherwood entered the room.

"Here is my mother now. I must go. Will you tell Jim-

125

my, ma'am, that I cannot take him out today, but that I shall call for him tomorrow at the usual time?''

"I'm so sorry, Captain Sherwood," she said sweetly. "Jimmy will be unable to accompany you for several days, *at least*. He is not feeling quite the thing, you see, and knows better than to *foolishly overtax his strength*."

"I did not imagine you capable of such underhanded tactics, ma'am."

"Didn't you, Captain? Ah, well, I daresay it's not the first time you underestimated an opponent," she said archly as she held out her hand to him.

He took it briefly in his own but only said, "Your round, ma'am, but we shall meet again." He turned and left on the words, and Mrs. Ellis sat down with Lady Sherwood. For the next half hour they discussed Elizabeth and the best ways of helping her to forget the unpleasant experiences of the previous evening.

Elizabeth slept until midday but woke feeling unrested and ill at ease. Her sleep had been troubled by dreams, most of them unpleasant. She moved to her dressing table and sat down despondently, gazing in the mirror at her swollen and discolored lips. Now she understood why young girls were continuously warned about men and the passions that ruled them. But certainly no warning any girl could receive would prepare her for the situation Elizabeth had found herself in last night.

She sighed. Things were happening too quickly in her life. Just two years ago, she had lived quietly in the country, never imagining that such violence would ever enter her world. Her father and brothers represented her total experience of men. They were passionate, yes, and intense; but they were also compassionate, and principled, and, above all—loving. She had been warned that there were evil men in the world, and she believed this to be true. But anything she had imagined or read about such

126

men could not prepare her for the shock of Lord Stanton's assault on her several days ago or the terror she had experienced during Lord Granbrooke's demonstration of unbridled, lustful passion.

Even as Elizabeth considered both men in the same light, she found herself comparing their behavior, or rather, the differences in their behavior and her own reactions. Lord Granbrooke wanted to possess her, and, in attempting that possession, he had not hesitated to physically abuse her. If Lord Stanton was to be believed, he meant only to punish her for meddling. And yet, even though his attack was also physical, he did not hurt her, nor frighten her, but only succeeded in arousing her fury.

For a moment she allowed herself to remember his kiss—the softness, the intimacy, her total inability to think or move because her entire being had been caught up in the touch of his lips on hers. In that moment of memory, Elizabeth sensed that Lord Stanton, even given the opportunity, would not have used her as Lord Granbrooke had, and therein lay the difference between them. Lord Stanton, Richard's friend, had acted for Richard on the previous evening, and had, in fact, conducted himself much as she supposed Richard would have. Lord Stanton's only intention had been to find her; his only motive, to protect her. He had treated her with consideration, kindness, and concern. And what had she done? She had been sullen and uncommunicative, distrustful and ungrateful, and when she finally did force herself to thank him, she expressed herself so clumsily that any fool could see that she wasn't sincere.

What must he think of her? He had rendered her supreme service, and had even challenged a man to a duel for her sake, and she had left it to others to thank him. Her behavior could be described as nothing less than rudely discourteous and ill-bred, and she couldn't think how she would bring herself to meet him again.

She slept again in the afternoon and by evening felt well

127

enough to join the family for dinner. Afterward she sat with Richard over a game of cards and found an opportunity to ask him about the duel. "Is Lord Stanton still determined to meet Lord Granbrooke, Richard?"

"It is not something for you to be thinking about, Lizzie."

"Well, I can't help thinking about it, and I will worry less if I know what is happening."

"They will be meeting at dawn tomorrow."

"I wish he knew that I appreciate everything he has done for me," she said miserably.

"He knows, Lizzie."

"No, he doesn't. I know it sounds terrible, and I am ashamed to admit it, but I never thanked him for helping me."

Richard was startled. "Why not?"

"It's hard to explain. We haven't been on the best of terms."

"Yes, I noticed that last night when Hugh and Julian first came up to our box at Vauxhall. In fact, we were discussing that very thing when we were set upon."

"Yes, we were, but I didn't wish to discuss it then, and even less do I wish to discuss it now." She rose agitatedly from the card table. "If you don't mind, Richard, I think I should like to go and read for a while." He nodded his dismissal, and Elizabeth excused herself to her parents and left the room.

In Park Lane, Viscount Stanton dined that evening with his brother, Henry, and Sir Hugh Broughton. After dinner, Stanton declined an invitation to accompany the other two men to Watier's, saying that he was promised to Richard Sherwood for a game of billiards.

Stanton lingered over his wine when the others had left, and at one point glanced up to see his valet standing just

128

inside the dining room door waiting to be noticed. "Yes, what is it, Peplow?"

"Excuse me, my lord, but I found this ring in the coat you wore last night and was wondering what you would have me do with it. It appears to be a fine stone but seems a bit loose in the setting." He walked to the table as he spoke and placed the ring into Stanton's outstretched hand.

"Thank you, Peplow. I will see that it is returned to its owner."

Stanton stared at the ring for some time and then slowly turned it in his fingers. Surely her hands couldn't be so small? And yet he had drawn the ring from her finger himself. There were no traces of the blood that had been there the night before; no doubt his meticulous Peplow had cleaned it thoroughly.

He wondered how Miss Elizabeth was recovering from her adventure of the previous evening. From the moment he came up with Richard on the pathway, until the moment he kicked in the door of Granbrooke's salon, he was driven by one thought, and one thought only—to find Richard's sister, and to find her quickly. It was only when he had her safely in the coach that he took time to think that she might not consider herself safe with him. Her silence and withdrawal showed him plainly enough that she had neither forgotten nor forgiven his previous behavior, and she was not prepared to accept him in the role of knight-errant. He could see she was badly frightened, and he wanted nothing more than to take her in his arms and soothe away her fears, as he was sure Richard would have done. But he was not Richard, and she did not trust him. It was a sobering thought.

Stanton rose from the table, Elizabeth's ring in his hand. He decided he would see to having the stone tightened. Before he left the house to keep his appointment with Richard Sherwood, he left the ring with his secretary, along with his instructions concerning it.

Elizabeth sat in her father's book-room, trying to read but constantly finding herself at the bottom of a page remembering nothing. She decided that the sonnets of Shakespeare, which she usually enjoyed, were too intense for her mood. Perhaps a novel could more easily hold her attention. She was about to replace the sonnets upon the shelf when the door opened behind her and a quiet voice said, "Richard said I should find you here reading, but I didn't know if I should believe him. Never tell me you're a bluestocking, ma'am."

Elizabeth turned quickly and observed Lord Stanton enter the room, close the door, and slowly cross toward her. She took in the elegance of his well-cut, blue cloth coat, his tight-fitting, buff-colored pantaloons, and his gleaming Hessians, but not one word would form itself in her brain, and so she spoke none but stood still, regarding him.

"I daresay you're wondering why I'm here," he continued. "I was engaged to Richard this evening for billiards. He just told me that earlier you had expressed a desire to speak with me. Do you still wish to do so?"

Elizabeth had dreaded this meeting, but she had not thought to face it so soon, and she was not prepared for the extreme embarrassment, the chagrin, and the shame as she remembered her behavior toward him when last they met. She shook her head in the negative, and he recognized it not only as an answer to his last question, but as a rejection of his very presence in the room. Silently Elizabeth laid down her book and started quickly for the door. When he realized she intended to leave him without a word, he took a step toward her as she passed him, and caught her hand, and held it.

"Elizabeth, please . . . wait. If you have nothing to say, then I would beg of you to listen, at least, for I have something I would say to you."

She looked down at her hand where he held it but made no attempt to draw it away as he continued.

"I would like to apologize for my behavior when you came to my house. You've been having some unusually bad luck with men lately, and for that I am partially to blame. What I am trying to say is, don't judge all your acquaintance by Granbrooke and myself. Believe me, we are the exception rather than the rule."

"Don't compare yourself to him, my lord," she said vehemently. "You are not at all alike."

"We are alike in that we both grossly offended you," he insisted.

"But you meant me no harm, Lord Stanton," she returned.

"No," he agreed. "But that alone does not excuse me. My behavior led you to mistrust me, and that mistrust rendered my service last night next to useless."

She had been staring at their hands all this time, but as he spoke these last words, her eyes came up to meet his as she exclaimed, "Your service next to useless? I was never so terrified in my life as I was last night! That horrible man—kissing me—touching me!" She shivered at the memory. "I was ready to die when you came through that door! I was so frightened at the time that I can barely remember what I was thinking. In the back of my mind, I knew that I disliked you, but I was numb—incredulous that someone had come in time to help me. But I have had time to consider the matter since; time to realize that I treated you disgracefully, my lord."

He stood quietly looking down at her and watched as tears gathered in her eyes. With each word her voice lost more control. "You came after me when you had no obligation to do so. You are determined to meet Lord Granbrooke because of the way he treated me. You tried to comfort me in the coach, and I treated you wretchedly . . . and I never even thanked you . . . and I am so ashamed!"

131

Her voice broke on a sob, and his hand tightened on hers and pulled her to him. She came willingly and buried her face in his shoulder as he held her close.

How long he held her he couldn't guess, but if anyone had told him that he would be comfortable holding a weeping female in his arms, he would have been aghast at the very idea. It was a new experience for him, and he found it strangely exhilarating. He had known many women, and without exception they had made demands upon him, and whether they were demands on his time, his wealth, or his person, they were all similar in the method of payment— he met all demands based on some feeling of responsibility, inclination, or desire. But here was Elizabeth feeling guilty and miserable, asking for no more than comfort, and he willing to give it, not for his own sake, but for hers.

Elizabeth had not shed a single tear during the entire course of her abduction and rescue, nor in the hours since her safe return home. But now, more than twenty hours of pent-up emotion would not be denied, and she found herself weeping bitterly in the arms of, strangely enough, Lord Stanton. It seemed natural for her to be there. As his arms went around her, she was reminded of the first time he had held her so, and although the situation was different, the touch of his hands was the same and seemed almost familiar. She couldn't understand why she should feel so secure in his arms, but she didn't question it. She recognized his embrace for what it was—an offer of comfort, and an acceptance of her unorthodox apology.

After a time, Elizabeth's tears subsided, and as she lifted her head, the viscount handed her a large handkerchief. She wiped her eyes and unceremoniously blew her nose, a childlike gesture that made him smile tenderly at her.

"Why did you try to make me think you were a terrible person?" she asked with brutal frankness.

"Because I didn't want you to encourage a reconciliation

between your sister and myself,'' he answered with equal honesty.

''You never really wanted to marry Charlotte, did you?''

''No, not really.'' *The girl is as intuitive as her brother,* he thought.

''Then, why did you offer for her?''

''Because of a dislike of being continuously plagued by my godmother to marry, and because of some misguided sense of what is due to my family.'' *Because of a drunken wager. Because I was promised an eighty-thousand pound inheritance. Impossible to say these things, of course,* but she seemed to accept his first two reasons as explanation enough.

''Did Richard ask you to stand away from Charlotte?''

''No. He simply told me that the question of Charlotte's happiness should be a matter for my conscience.''

''So he knows then why the engagement was ended.''

''I'm sure he suspects.''

''Then that explains why he didn't seem surprised when Charlotte said she no longer wished for the connection. Wouldn't it have been easier for everyone involved if you had simply told Charlotte that you wished to be freed from your obligation to her?''

''I considered that possibility,'' he said, ''but I couldn't think of any explanation to give her that would not be offensive, and I wanted to leave her pride intact.''

Elizabeth could see the wisdom of this. He could hardly say ''I offered for you because my godmother wanted me to, and now I have changed my mind because I realize I don't really wish to be married to you.''

''Well, I must say that your method worked admirably, my lord,'' Elizabeth said now. ''Charlotte said you frightened her, and that was enough to make her cry off, although I couldn't understand it myself. Your behavior did not frighten me in the least. It only made me angry.''

''Did Charlotte tell you what passed between us?''

"No," she answered quickly. "And I don't wish to know. It is not my concern."

"Do you intend to tell Charlotte what you have learned of my part in this?"

"No, I don't think I shall. I think her experience with you has been beneficial, for it has made her think that she should not marry where she cannot first feel some affection."

"And that's good?"

"Of course it's good. Despite what she says, I don't think she would be happy without love in her marriage."

"Personally, I feel that love would be catastrophic in marriage—at least in my marriage."

She looked at him strangely. "Then, I am glad you will not be marrying Charlotte, my lord."

"Yes, and so am I," he agreed amiably, and then added conspiratorially, "but we shall never let her know it. Tell me, Miss Elizabeth, are we ready to put all the misunderstandings of the past few weeks behind us and begin our relationship anew? I think we could be friends if we tried." He took her chin in his hand, turning her face up to his as he spoke and was rewarded by a warm smile.

"I should be pleased to think that you considered me your friend, my lord."

"Good. Then come with me, and you will observe the game as I soundly beat your brother at billiards. And then, when we decide that his concussion has had enough abuse for one day, you can lend me your support as I send him off to bed."

He turned as he spoke and offered his arm to escort her from the room. When they reached the door, she paused. "My lord," she said, "there is one thing more."

He saw that the worried frown was back on her face as he asked, "Yes, what is it?"

"Tomorrow morning. Promise you will be careful."

"I promise."

They went on to the billiards room, where they found Richard awaiting them. No further mention was made of the duel during the remainder of the evening, and of the three of them, the one who was about to fight it thought of it the least. Elizabeth could not keep it from her mind, and that Richard was thinking of it as well was evident when Stanton finally suggested that they call it a night. Richard made no objection to retiring early and said that he expected Stanton to do the same, since he could not help but benefit from being clearheaded and well rested when the dawn arrived.

Elizabeth tossed and turned for hours and then finally drifted off some time before dawn. She was shocked when she awoke to see her maid opening the curtains to bright morning sun. Her clock showed half past ten! The duel had taken place hours ago! Why hadn't Richard come to waken her? As the light from the windows fell across the table at her bedside, she saw a note lying beside her morning chocolate. It was Richard's hand. She plucked it quickly from the tray and tore it open.

Lizzie,
There has been no meeting, as Granbrooke failed to appear at the appointed time and place. It seems the man's effrontery is equaled only by his cowardice. Julian is mad as fire. I'll be home for luncheon, and we will talk then.

R.

Thank God was all she could think. It didn't matter to her that Lord Granbrooke was guilty of an unforgivable breach of honor. She cared only that no one had been hurt or killed because of her.

This unexpected turn of events acted as such balm to Elizabeth's spirit that she appeared at the breakfast table in

135

the best of humors, entertained her parents and sister with a flow of lively conversation, and dragged Charlotte off shortly afterward on a shopping expedition. She left her parents with little doubt that their sensible Lizzie had taken control of her feelings once again and had already put her experience with Lord Granbrooke behind her.

"There is no one like Lizzie when it comes to bouncing back after rough weather," her father said proudly.

"Yes," Lady Sherwood agreed. "I think we were justified in allowing her that private conversation with Lord Stanton last evening. Richard was convinced that it would help her, and I believe he was right, for she seemed more herself after she had spoken with his lordship. And this morning, I must admit that I see little amiss with her."

"Our Lizzie is a fighter, my dear," her husband replied. "She's not one to let anything keep her down for long."

14

The following morning Harriet called at Mount Street to share the news of her imminent departure for Belgium. "Jonathan has made arrangements for me to join him," she said joyfully. "I sail in four days' time."

"We shall certainly miss you, my dear," Lady Sherwood said, "but you may be home again sooner than you think, for Jon has promised to try for a short furlough in the new year."

"I am sure he will do his best to get leave," Harriet said. "I know he misses you all a great deal, even though he likes the army."

In a few days time, Harriet departed London to join her husband, and the remainder of the Sherwood family continued to enjoy the Season. Charlotte had expected to experience some awkwardness in meeting Lord Stanton following their broken engagement, but she found that it was not to be so. His manner toward her was easy and relaxed, and the obvious friendship that existed between his lordship and both Richard and Elizabeth had no little influence in reestablishing Charlotte's comfort in Stanton's presence. They never spoke of the previous relationship between them, and Charlotte never regretted ending it.

After his failure to appear on the morning of the duel, nothing further was heard of Lord Granbrooke. There were rumors about town concerning his sudden disappearance, and the consensus of opinion seemed to be that he had fled the country to avoid his creditors. Only a handful of people knew that he had also fled to avoid a meeting with Stanton.

Lady Sherwood was planning another entertainment to take place in late October. She presented her husband with a guest list of nearly forty persons and proposed an evening of dancing and a buffet supper. His lordship gave his wholehearted approval to the plan, asked if he could keep the guest list for a short time (to see if there was anyone he should like to add to it), and later that evening spoke privately with Richard.

"Your mother has planned a party. Here is the guest list. What do you think?"

"It appears to include most of our closest friends in town, and a few of the girls' friends, and a number of their male admirers as well. I would say that it includes most of those persons who call here regularly."

"Do you think our information-seeker may be on it?" his lordship asked.

"Well, we are agreed, are we not, that if such a person desires to be invited here, he must cultivate the acquaintance of one of the family at least. Yes, I would say there is a good chance of his being on the list."

"Think carefully, Richard. Who has been calling? Who joins you when you ride with the girls in the park? Who dances with them frequently? Who pays the most court? If you think of anyone fitting that description who is not already on the list, then put them on. If we could encourage our meddler to enter my book-room in search of information on that evening, we could cut our list of suspects considerably. And if we are clever, perhaps we can catch him as well. I have considered taking one of the footmen into our confidence, someone who could sit by the keyhole of the salon across the hall from the book-room and keep watch, while we do what's proper by our guests. As long

138

as we are very visible in the drawing room, our traitor will feel himself safe in coming downstairs.''

"It sounds like a good idea. Who did you have in mind?''

"I thought James would do nicely. He has some military experience; he's young, strong, and, above all—we can trust him implicitly.''

Richard nodded. "Let's do it then. I'll get this list back to Mother as complete as I can make it, and we can speak with James tomorrow.''

"We shall continue to keep this to ourselves, Richard. The less your mother and sisters know, the safer they will be.''

On the night of the Sherwood party, Elizabeth wore a new gown, just delivered that day from the dressmaker. It was of white satin, with a delicate pattern of leaves and flowers finely embroidered in pale lime-green silk. The skirt opened at the front to reveal an underslip of matching green, and the low scooped neckline and short puffed sleeves set off her shoulders to perfection. She fastened a fine string of matched pearls around her neck, pulled on her long gloves, and her ensemble was complete.

Elizabeth had stopped wondering what had become of her diamond ring, which had been a gift from her father. She could vaguely remember the viscount taking it from her hand the evening of her abduction, but since he never mentioned it, she assumed it lost or left behind that night at the inn where they had stopped. It was such a trifling thing when compared to the great service he had rendered her that she was never able to bring herself to mention it to him. She gave herself one final look in the glass and then went down the hall to Charlotte's room to collect her and take her along to dinner.

Later that evening, Lord Stanton and Henry Ferris were among the first guests to arrive. Elizabeth greeted them as they entered the room, and Mr. Ferris insisted that she save a waltz for him. As he was by far her favorite dancing partner, she readily agreed.

"By the way, Miss Elizabeth," Mr. Ferris said. "I saw you in the park this afternoon with your sister and my cousin Warmington. Couldn't take my eyes off that bay mare he was riding! What is she? Welsh?"

"Yes, she is," Elizabeth confirmed, "and he is very proud of her. He says he was lucky that both you and your brother were out of town last week when she came up for sale, otherwise he would never have gotten her for the price he paid."

"Damn Charles, Julian. He is always doing this to me! Remember that brown gelding that he beat me out of last year while we were home for Public Days? Where is he? I must have a word with him." Muttering a hasty farewell, Henry went off to find his cousin, leaving Elizabeth alone with the viscount.

"You and your brother are not very alike, my lord," she said.

"So you have said before, Miss Elizabeth. But in this one matter actually, we do have a lot in common. We both have an excellent eye for a good horse, and neither of us often finds himself in possession of a bad one. Will you allow me to say that you look charmingly tonight, ma'am? That color becomes you."

"Thank you, sir. Let me tell you that I consider it a great victory to have my mother agree to so much green in this dress. She considers too much color unbecoming in a 'girl of my age,' particularly in an evening gown."

"I have something that belongs to you, Miss Elizabeth. I would have returned it sooner, but I had it sent to the jeweler to have the stone tightened. It was returned while I was out of town, and I have brought it tonight." He held out her ring as he spoke, and she looked at it with a happy smile.

"I thought it lost that night," she said. "I didn't expect to see it again."

"Would you like to put it on?"

"Yes, please. It fits tightly. I must take off my glove." This she promptly did and then held out her hand to him.

He took it in his and surveyed the fingers critically. The cut had healed perfectly, leaving no marks. He slipped on the ring and held up her hand for her inspection. "It looks as good as new," he said.

"What? The hand, or the ring?"

"Both."

The musicians were striking up for the first country dance, and the viscount asked Elizabeth to join him. "I cannot aspire to Henry's proficiency, but I think I can manage to avoid treading upon your toes." She went off happily on his arm and for the next hour never found herself without a partner.

The dance was a waltz, Elizabeth's partner, the incomparable Mr. Ferris, and as the orchestra reached the last bars of the piece, he swung her round with a flourish and brought her up breathlessly at the edge of the floor. She was smiling and radiant and thanked him prettily.

As she stood catching her breath, she allowed her gaze to roam over the room. Lord Stanton had danced the same waltz with Charlotte, and Elizabeth saw them now, standing only a few yards away, engaged in earnest conversation. She was pleased to see that they were comfortable together. She unfurled her fan and was raising it to her flushed face when her gaze was arrested by a man standing in the shadow of the draperies in a bay window not far from where they stood. She laid her hand impulsively on Mr. Ferris's arm and said in an urgent undertone, "Mr. Ferris. Look! 'Tis Lord Granbrooke!" He followed her gaze but was unable to understand her tone, for to him

Granbrooke was only a debtor gone to ground to avoid his creditors.

To Elizabeth, however, he was much more, and she sensed instinctively that he had an evil purpose. As she watched him, he stood motionless, staring unwaveringly at Lord Stanton. She wondered fleetingly how he came to be there and then realized that a man of his athleticism would have little difficulty climbing one of the rose trellises that extended from the garden below to the balcony outside the window where he stood. As she hesitated, wondering what to do, she saw Lord Granbrooke bring his hand from behind the drapery and was stunned to see that he held a pistol. Not for an instant did she doubt his intention.

Even as Granbrooke raised his arm, Elizabeth threw herself across the space that separated her from Lord Stanton, crying his name. Hearing his name half shouted and strident, Stanton turned his eyes from Charlotte to encounter Elizabeth's face, close at hand. He had time only to register the terror in her eyes when a deafening report sounded in the room, a stab of fire tore his chest, and he slipped almost immediately into darkness and oblivion.

The room was an immediate scene of chaos. Several women were screaming. The three gentlemen closest to Lord Granbrooke leaped upon him as one man, searched his person for further weapons, and dragged him from the room. Charlotte stood for an instant frozen with shock, staring down where both Lizzie and Lord Stanton lay in a heap at her feet. Then she dropped to her knees beside them, feeling helpless yet wanting desperately to help. Richard was there, tearing the cravat from around his neck and folding it into a thick pad. He laid it over a fast-spreading stain on Elizabeth's shoulder, and when he said, "Charlotte, hold this!" she didn't think, she only obeyed him.

Henry Ferris was reaching inside his brother's coat, where an already blood-soaked waistcoat and shirt gave evidence that he had been seriously injured. Sir Hugh Broughton was endeavoring to clear the room. Lord Sherwood knelt, and as he surveyed the scene, his words were more a statement than a question: "The one ball has injured them both?"

"Yes, sir," Richard answered. "It has passed through Lizzie's shoulder and taken Stanton in the chest." Turning to Mr. Ferris, he said, "Henry, get us a surgeon quickly. Two if you can manage it. We will see to Julian. Go on!" Mr. Ferris rose and left the room immediately, and within a very short space of time, both Elizabeth and Lord Stanton were carried abovestairs to await the administrations of the surgeon.

The remainder of the guests were encouraged to go down to supper, but they did so reluctantly, their enjoyment of the evening at an end.

When the first surgeon arrived, Richard directed him to his own room, where Lord Stanton had been taken. "My sister has a shoulder wound, Doctor, but we have managed to stop the bleeding. The ball is lodged in his lordship. . . . The wound is directly over the heart." The doctor frowned and shook his head forebodingly but went away with Sir Hugh to the viscount's room.

When the second doctor arrived, he was led immediately to Elizabeth. He dismissed everyone from the room, with the exception of Mrs. Ellis, who had offered to assist him. Richard and Lord Sherwood found themselves banished to the corridor, where Richard took his father aside. "I wonder that shot didn't bring James to the drawing room."

"His instructions were to sit tight and guard that room, but we should let him know what's been happening here."

"I'll go," Richard offered. He went quickly downstairs and, pausing outside the book-room door, glanced about to be sure no one was in sight and then entered the salon directly opposite. He was surprised to find the room empty. He stepped back into the hallway and cautiously turned the handle of the book-room door. He opened it slowly and then nearly fell over James's body as he stepped inside. A quick sweeping glance showed him that they were alone, and he closed the door before turning his attention to the footman. He rolled the young man over on his back, and almost immediately James groaned and began to regain consciousness. As far as Richard could tell, he had received no more than a sharp blow to the head. How long he had lain there unconscious there could be no way of knowing.

"James! James! What happened?"

James struggled with the effort of memory. "I heard a shot fired somewhere in the house," he replied, "but decided to stay put as I was told. Some time after that, a gentleman came down the hall and made himself free of m'lord's book-room. Couldn't see anything but his back through that hole, but it was a man, definitely, and dressed in evening clothes. Well, I give him a few minutes to get his fingers well into m'lord's papers, and then I carefully opened the door to surprise him like. But when I looked in, there weren't no one in the room, and when I stepped in to see if perhaps he had left through a window, I must have been struck from behind, for I saw no one, and remember naught else."

Richard shook his head with understanding. "Our friend was evidently expecting to be followed or observed. He was very clever. He simply waited behind the door in the event anyone attempted to come after him. Then, once he had laid you low, he could peruse my father's papers at his leisure. He knows now that we suspect him; he will not be so careless again."

"I was a fool to fall into such a trap, sir, and it's that foolish I feel."

"Don't concern yourself. He found nothing in those files that will profit him."

144

"But what was the shot I heard, Captain? I wondered but dared not budge."

"The shot was fired by Lord Granbrooke, James," Richard answered grimly. "Tonight he attempted to murder Lord Stanton."

15

Viscount Stanton opened his eyes to a strange room and a strange bed. For a moment he couldn't think where he was or why. He felt tired, and listless, and his chest ached as if there were a huge rock sitting upon it. He brought his hand up to see if this were indeed so, and this slight motion brought his valet, Peplow, to the bedside. Stanton looked at him questioningly—at least his face was familiar. Peplow glanced anxiously at his master and then quickly left the room saying, "I will fetch the doctor, my lord."

Evidently this worthy was not far to seek, for in a very few moments he had returned with the valet and approached the bedside. "Please, my lord, you must endeavor to lie still. You have suffered a bullet wound. . . ." Memory came flooding back. Elizabeth calling his name, and the report of a gun.

"Who shot me?"

"I am given to understand that it was Lord Granbrooke who fired the pistol, my lord."

"What?" he shouted, and then regretted the way he had wrenched his body as a sickening pain spread over him.

"Please, my lord, you must lie still. The ball was lodged in the wall of the heart muscle itself. There has been considerable damage. I cannot be responsible for the consequences if you refuse to take care."

Stanton's face registered his disbelief as he brought his hand up gingerly to feel where the heaviest bandages lay on his chest. "Are you serious, man? If what you say is true, I should be dead!"

"I said the ball lodged in the *wall* of the heart, my lord. It did not enter the heart itself, and I was able to extract it without doing any further damage."

"I appreciate your effort, Doctor, but I don't understand how a ball could strike me in such a place and fail to enter the heart. Was it deflected?"

"No, my lord. By the time the ball reached you, it was nearly spent."

"Nearly spent? You are making no sense, sir!"

"Lord Stanton," the doctor said with finality, "I can tell you no more than that. My advice to you is to rest and allow your body to heal. You have a strong constitution, but you cannot afford to aggravate such a serious wound."

As the doctor walked away, Stanton frowned after him and then spoke to his valet. "What time is it, Peplow?"

"Two o'clock in the afternoon, my lord."

"Two o'clock! I've been out for nearly twelve hours? Is this the Sherwood house?"

"Yes, my lord."

"So I thought. Find Captain Sherwood, and tell him that I would speak with him immediately."

This was soon done, and within a few minutes Richard entered the room, greatly relieved to see his friend returned to consciousness. "Julian, you can't know how good it is to have you with us today! For I must tell you—when I saw where you had taken that ball last night, I thought you'd surely had your notice to quit."

"That crazy sawbones is trying to tell me that the ball didn't do more damage because it was spent."

"He's right. I had begun to suspect as much myself when several minutes had passed and you were still with us, for I knew that if the ball had entered the heart you would have been dead within seconds after the shot was fired."

"You are being no clearer than he was, Richard," Stanton said in exasperation.

"He was only trying to protect you from anxiety, but I can see that it won't serve. The ball was spent because it struck Elizabeth first. It passed through her shoulder and then hit you, but didn't have enough momentum to cause a fatal wound."

The viscount stared for a moment in disbelief, and then asked quietly, "How is she?"

"She's in considerable pain, and the doctor expects there will be some high fever." Stanton moved restlessly, and Richard added, "He also predicts the same for you if you don't behave."

"She must have seen him there," Stanton said thoughtfully, "and she was trying to warn me."

"Yes. I think she was."

"Richard, you must believe I would give anything not to have had this happen to her."

"You would have given your life, my friend. There is no doubt that Granbrooke meant to kill you, and would have done so if Lizzie hadn't stepped in the way."

"Your sister is mad, Richard! Why should she endanger herself to protect me?"

"How can you ask that, Julian? You know that she feels under an incredible obligation to you for rescuing her from Granbrooke. When she saw him last night, she had to know that he was after you because of her. She was only repaying the debt when she tried to warn you."

"But, my God, Richard, she could have been killed doing such a foolish thing!"

"Yes, she could have. And you could have been, too. But you weren't, and with any luck you'll both come through this with flying colors. You should know by now that Lizzie thinks with her heart. Believe me, if given the choice again, she would much sooner accept the wound she now has than the picture of herself standing safely out of harm's way, watching you die. If I were you, I should be thanking God right now for the brave, quick-thinking foolishness of my little sister.''

The doctor returned soon afterward and insisted that the captain leave so that the viscount could rest. Stanton did eventually sleep again but not before another thought had come unbidden into his mind and would not be dismissed. Perhaps Elizabeth's motive was only to warn him, and she had accidentally gotten in the way. But what if it hadn't been an accident? What if she had purposely placed herself in what she knew to be the direct line of fire? What if she had intentionally used her body to protect his? He could think of only one reason why she should wish to do so, and that thought would haunt his dreams and disturb his waking moments for many weeks to come.

He passed the better part of that day and the next night and day as well, sleeping. He knew the doctor was keeping him sedated, and he didn't much care, but on the fourth evening he declined any offer of laudanum.

"You will not sleep without it, my lord," the doctor objected.

"I shall sleep well enough. The worst of the pain is past, and I would prefer to have my wits about me. I can deal with some discomfort, I assure you."

The doctor went away but confided later to Captain Sherwood that Lord Stanton would in a few days' time prove an impossible patient. "He already speaks of removing to his own home, insisting that he is a burden on your household."

"I will speak with him," Richard promised.

As the doctor had predicted, Elizabeth had a bout with fever lasting a night and a day. Then on the second night it had suddenly receded. After spending many hours in exhausting delirium, she had woken to recognize her mother and sister, and then almost immediately drifted off into a deep, restful sleep.

During the next several days, Elizabeth's condition continued to improve and Stanton greeted this news with profound relief. He demanded to be assisted to sit up in bed while he talked with Richard, and although Richard complied with this request, he found an opening to discuss the viscount's behavior. "The doctor says that you are becoming a difficult patient."

"Well, I hope you don't intend to lecture me. I believe it was you who not so long ago chose to ignore your doctor's instructions concerning a certain concussion."

"The situations are hardly the same, Julian. You mustn't think of removing to your own house. Your valet has taken full responsibility for you. He has left very little to the hands of others, believe me. When the doctor gives his permission, I will convey you home myself. Meanwhile, I shall endeavor to keep you suitably occupied. In proof of that statement, I will tell you that Mrs. Ellis is belowstairs at this very moment and has offered to give you a game of chess if you should desire it. But let me warn you—she is a formidable opponent."

"Help me into that infernal dressing gown, then, and send the lady up," the viscount said. "I am in the mood for a good challenge!"

Mrs. Ellis played chess with Lord Stanton until nearly ten o'clock, and as Richard had promised, she was an excellent player. She left him then, offering him a game of piquet on the following day.

With Peplow's help, Stanton was soon ready for bed, but he slept fitfully, and he dreamed. Once again he heard Elizabeth call his name, heard the report of the gun, saw the terror in her eyes . . . and suddenly he woke, her eyes still burningly visible in waking. That was what had been eluding him these past days! That look in her eyes. It was terror—blind terror. It had startled him then, and it startled him now in memory. It could have been terror of Lord Granbrooke, but somehow he felt that it wasn't. Somehow he felt that that look of terror had been for him—fear for his safety.

Suddenly he had an overpowering desire to see Elizabeth. He carefully pulled himself up in bed, and, moving slowly to the edge, lowered his feet to the floor. He saw no slippers but couldn't be bothered. Slipping his arms into his dressing gown, he tied the sash at his waist and then rose to his feet. He felt no dizziness and only a little pain as he made his way cautiously to the door and through it. He knew that Elizabeth's room was only a few doors away. Two small tables had been placed in the hall for the use of servants carrying trays to and from the rooms. There was one outside his door, and another, three doors down, told him which room was Elizabeth's. He hesitated only a moment and then turned the handle. There was a young maid seated near the bed, and she rose as he entered. She was surprised to see him there but said nothing when he motioned for her to leave. She closed the door behind herself and took a chair in the hall. When the gentleman left, she would take up her post again.

Elizabeth was sleeping soundly, and he had no intention of waking her. He moved stiffly across the room and stood silently by the bed. She looked tired. Her face was very pale, with just the slightest tinge of color in her cheeks. She was tiny, he thought, in the big bed, her dark hair spreading over the pillow.

"Why that strange look of terror in your eyes, little Elizabeth?" he asked aloud. "Was it fear for me? And if it was, then you deliberately took a bullet intended for me. You place a higher value on my life than you do on your own." Even as he spoke these words, their implication acted upon him like a physical blow. "You cannot, must not, love me, Elizabeth. You would find no joy in loving me, for there can never be any future for us." He leaned

151

over the bed then and kissed her gently on the forehead. She didn't stir. He had no way of knowing how long he stayed there, but his feet were cold and his chest aching when he finally let himself out of the room and accepted the young maid's offer of her arm back to his own room and into bed. It was a long time before he slept again.

It was nearly two weeks before Lord Stanton was permitted to remove to his own home, and four days later he made a call at Mount Street to ask after Elizabeth. During the days that followed, he called each day to inquire after her health, and on one occasion, when Richard asked if he would like to come up to her room to see for himself how well she was mending, he declined the invitation, saying he would rather not intrude. Richard did not press him. The situation was an unusual one, to say the least, and there would no doubt be some awkwardness when Elizabeth and Stanton met again.

It was soon decided that Elizabeth should be moved to Sherwood Manor, where the relative quiet of the country and the decidedly fresher air would speed her recovery. Mrs. Ellis offered to cut short her own stay in London by two weeks in order to accompany Elizabeth on the journey and to keep her company once they arrived in Surrey.

"I can come over as often as you like," she said. "Perhaps your brother could take us driving. And then, when you feel stronger, we can go for long walks."

It was Richard, in fact, who had suggested that Elizabeth come to the country with him. He had been intending to return himself the day after the party, but the shooting had made it impossible for him to leave as planned.

Miss Virginia Ellis had her father's permission to extend her own stay in London under the chaperonage of Lady Kemp, and Elizabeth was secretly relieved that it was to be so, for as much as she liked Sarah, she couldn't bring herself to enjoy the company of Virginia, who simpered, she thought, and giggled a great deal.

The journey south was accomplished with relative ease, Sarah keeping Elizabeth company in the chaise while Richard took Jimmy up with him as before. Elizabeth had her shoulder well supported with pillows, and the coachman had been instructed to take particular care when they neared Dorking and the rougher roads beyond.

Jimmy was destined to enjoy this trip more than any he had ever taken, for he had persuaded Richard to allow his team to gallop for a time, something they were seldom permitted in London. The boy's enthusiasm was so great that Richard had to smile, and it occurred to him that he was missing a great deal in not having children of his own. Until he had met Jimmy, children had not often come in his way. Being the eldest, his mother had teased him good-naturedly about settling down and supplying her with grandchildren. Well, the pressure was off him now, he thought, for surely Lizzie or Charlotte would marry before long, and with Jon already wed, no doubt Lady Sherwood would have a grandchild or two in the near future.

Their first days in the country passed pleasantly. The weather was cool but remained clear. Sarah came each morning to Sherwood Manor and stayed throughout the day. She and Elizabeth would talk, sew, read, or try to increase their skill at piquet. They were fast becoming close friends. Jimmy spent each morning with his tutor but came every afternoon to the Manor. He accompanied Captain Sherwood on visits to the village or the tenants and even sat in on several meetings between the captain and his agent. Sometimes he employed himself running errands for his mother and more than once he offered to entertain Miss Elizabeth.

Late in the afternoon on the third day after their arrival, Sarah left Elizabeth to take a nap, and coming downstairs she found Jimmy and the captain in the hall, just returned from the village.

Richard handed her a small parcel. "Here is the blue silk you needed, ma'am." Then he added impulsively, "Why not come out for a walk with me, Mrs. Ellis? You have been with Lizzie almost continuously since we arrived. I am sure the exercise will benefit you."

"I doubt if Elizabeth will sleep longer than an hour, Captain," she objected.

"Go with Captain Sherwood, Mama," Jimmy encouraged. "I will stay to keep Miss Elizabeth company when she wakes. I can read to her, or give her a game of piquet if she prefers."

Sarah smiled proudly at her son, thinking how mature he was, and how generous. "Very well," she said, "I will go for a walk. I must admit it sounds tempting." She went upstairs to change her light shoes for serviceable half boots and to collect a warm pelisse. She had brought these things with her only today and planned to leave them at Sherwood Manor against the day Elizabeth decided she would like to venture out of the house herself. Sarah soon joined the captain in the hall and they strolled out together to enjoy the crisp November day.

They walked for some time in silence, westward along the floor of the valley in which the Manor was situated. Tree-covered ridges rose on both left and right, and although there were a number of pines, there were several deciduous varieties as well, and the leaves they had recently shed carpeted the ground beneath their feet. The rustling of the leaves and the occasional call of a bird were the only sounds to disturb the silence.

"Captain Sherwood," Sarah began, "I have a great deal for which to thank you."

"I was just about to say the same thing to you, ma'am! You have been a trooper these past weeks, helping me to entertain Lord Stanton, with no thought for the inconveni-

154

ence to yourself; and giving your assistance to Elizabeth, first as a nurse, and now as a companion."

"I was more than happy to do it, Captain, and I have enjoyed the time I spent with them both. The gratitude I feel toward you concerns my son. It has been two months since the day you brought Jimmy home in the rain, and from that day to this I have seen a steady change in him. I had thought myself to be doing a good job in rearing him, but I have been brought to see that I was doing far less than I should have been."

He started to object, but she forestalled him. "Please, Captain, allow me to finish. Jimmy was always a considerate, thoughtful child, but I have never known him as animated as he has been since meeting you. He takes so much more interest in life, and in the people about him. He has been growing up in many ways that I never realized, and he seems to me years older since knowing you. I have seen his self-esteem grow considerably. He is more courteous than before, and seems to be so naturally, and not through any conscious effort. He shoulders responsibility capably and readily, and is willing to take on even more than I feel his age requires. I know that all this is due to your influence, and I am truly grateful."

"You give me too much credit, Mrs. Ellis," Richard objected, "and yourself not nearly enough. Jimmy is a fine boy, but his friendly good humor, his notion of what is fair or unjust, his honesty, his sense of responsibility, his pride in his family and his country, these are all things that he was taught long ago—taught by you. If you have noticed a change in him, then it is only a matter of his personality flowering under what I hope is a good influence."

"You may call it a flowering if you like, Captain, but it has happened because you have taken a special interest in my son."

"I have grown very fond of Jimmy," Richard admitted,

155

"and yet I felt in the beginning that you did not welcome my interest in him."

"That is true," she admitted. "I have been jealous of letting anyone influence him. I have particularly dreaded Sir Winston taking an interest in him."

"Why?"

"Because Sir Winston is not a man after which I would like to have my son model himself."

"And I am?"

"Yes. Most definitely," she said frankly. "You are not like any man I have ever known. Please don't misunderstand me when I say this, Captain, but I find your personality more like that of a woman than a man."

He stopped, startled, and stared down at her. "If you were a man, ma'am, I think I would be forced to call you out for that!"

She smiled. "I asked you not to misunderstand, and I do not mean it as an insult, sir, but as a compliment. You are gentle, tender—you do not threaten a woman with your manner."

"But certainly these can be male traits, ma'am?"

"Perhaps, but I have never seen them in any male of my acquaintance."

"Then I think you have been singularly unfortunate in your male acquaintance, Mrs. Ellis."

"Maybe so, and I suppose by some standards I have not known many men. I had cousins when I was young, but I didn't know them well. I was certainly well acquainted with my father, however, and my husband, James, and, of course, Sir Winston. They were, and are, all quite different from you, sir, I assure you. Many men in society are polite to women, and their manners are polished to just that end. Your manner with women is something you have not practiced, I think, but something that is part of your nature. I don't mean to imply that there is anything feminine about you, Captain. Quite the opposite, in fact. I find you commanding . . . athletic . . . ." They had come to a stile, and he offered her his hand to come over. As she came to the ground, he retained her hand in a hard clasp. ". . . and you are strong," she said, looking pointedly at his fingers where they held hers. Keeping his hold, he drew her closer, and she brought her free hand up to lay it flat against his chest. ". . . and you are very attractive," she finished, as she brought her eyes up to meet his.

"You don't know how relieved I am to hear you say so, ma'am," he murmured. His next intent was clear. Mastering her will, Sarah pulled her hand away and quickly turned to continue walking. Richard frowned but fell instantly into step beside her, and after a few moments, he said, "Let me understand you, ma'am. You find me attractive, but you do not welcome my attentions. Have I that correctly?"

"I wasn't saying these things to encourage a demonstration, Captain Sherwood. I was simply trying to make a point."

"I see."

She stopped once again to look at him. "Please, let us not spoil our friendship. I value it highly, and I would wish for it to continue."

Richard was puzzled and hurt by her behavior, but he couldn't resist the appeal in her voice. He held out his hand, palm up, and she hesitantly placed her own in it. His strong fingers closed around hers and then lifted her hand to his lips. "Friends, then, Mrs. Ellis—if you insist. But if you wish me to believe that you enjoy your time with my sister, then you must believe that I enjoy the time I spend with your son. Let there be an end to any feeling of obligation between us, for friends do not question a gift or the motive in giving."

16

In early December, Lord and Lady Sherwood and Charlotte arrived in Surrey, intending to remain in the country for some months. During the weeks preceding their arrival, Sarah continued to call daily at Sherwood Manor, but Richard made no attempt to advance their relationship beyond the limits of friendship she had prescribed. This he did partly because he knew it was what she desired and partly because it would be improper for him to take advantage of her presence in his house. There were numerous instances during those weeks when they found themselves alone together, sometimes for a few minutes, other times for several hours, but he allowed no repetition of his behavior on the day of their first walk.

More than once, Sarah had puzzled over her own behavior that day. She had told him she was not trying to encourage his advances, and yet, if she were entirely honest with herself, she had to admit that she did encourage him. She had begun her description of him simply to explain herself. But as she realized the effect her words were having on him, and when he held her hand in that possessive manner, she added her last comment deliberately, wondering what kind of reaction it might bring. Then, when he had responded, she pulled away, suddenly realizing that the very last thing she wanted was an emotional involvement with Captain Sherwood. Having suffered five years of domination by her husband, and another five since his death under the thumb of her father-in-law, she was not eager to give any man power over her. She knew better than anyone that she must continue to bend to Sir Winston's will while he lived, but what little freedom of choice and will her widowhood gave her, she was determined to keep to herself—completely to herself.

Less than a week after Lord and Lady Sherwood's return, Lord Stanton and his cousin, Charles Warmington, arrived for a week of shooting. Having been invited by Richard, Stanton considered that although he did not wish to encourage any tender feelings in Elizabeth, he could offer no plausible reason for refusing the invitation. And, if he was honest, he had to admit to a strong desire to see Elizabeth again. He had not seen her since the night he had stood in her room, watching her sleep, more than six weeks ago. He had never thanked her for saving his life, and although he suspected that she had done it purposely and not accidentally, to admit as much would be to admit that he guessed how she felt about him. He shuddered as he realized the kind of uncomfortable situation that would create! He couldn't imagine what he could possibly say to her when they met, so he tried not to think about it but just to let it happen.

He and Charles arrived early in the afternoon, but there was no opportunity for private conversation with Elizabeth until after dinner that evening. When the gentlemen joined the ladies in the parlor, she was sitting alone near the fire reading, and as he came to sit beside her, she put her book aside.

"I meant what I said earlier," he said. "It is good to see you looking so well."

"You had a serious wound, too, my lord, and you also look fit."

"I've had all these weeks to think of an adequate way

159

to thank you for what you did, Miss Elizabeth, but it hasn't served. There is no way to properly thank someone for saving your life."

"There is no need to thank me, my lord. If I rendered you a service, you may consider it repayment of a debt I owed you. For if my being wounded delivered you from death, you may be sure that I feel your action for me, on an earlier occasion, delivered me from a fate that I considered worse than death."

"Richard said that you would probably view the situation in this light, but still, it was an insane thing to do. Courage is a good thing, but it can be carried too far."

"I don't know that courage had much to do with it," she said. "I wanted to warn you, and I didn't stop to think about anything else. I daresay I didn't expect Lord Granbrooke to fire unless he had a clear shot."

Richard soon joined them, and the conversation turned to other subjects. Stanton had to admit to himself that seeing Elizabeth again had brought him no closer to understanding her actions. Her conversation seemed to indicate that gratitude had been her only motive, and yet he sensed that there was more to it than that. Either Elizabeth intended to be very careful to hide her feelings from him, or (and this was a totally new thought to him) she didn't realize herself why she had protected him. If she was in love with him and didn't know it herself, he had no intention of doing anything to enlighten her.

The intricacies of the situation were beginning to make his head ache, and he decided that the best course would be to put it all out of his mind and try to enjoy a good week of shooting. He and Elizabeth traveled in the same social circle, and he was destined to meet her. He would neither encourage her nor avoid her, and let the chips fall where they would.

The following evening the Ellises were invited to dine at Sherwood Manor. The presence of Sir Winston, Sarah, and Virginia swelled the number of the dinner party to ten and even gave Lady Sherwood the satisfaction of having her numbers equal. Lord Sherwood viewed the bluff Sir Winston with tolerance, and if Lady Sherwood didn't quite cherish Miss Ellis, she had nothing but praise for Mrs. Ellis, who had proved herself indispensable in the days and weeks following Elizabeth's injury.

After dinner, Elizabeth played and sang for them, and she even coaxed Charles into joining her for a few songs of the sea that her father had taught her and that Charles also knew. Richard slipped away after a time and went to the library, where he was surprised to find Sarah.

"I thought you went to fetch a shawl for my mother?" he asked.

"Yes, I did," she said, indicating the shawl over her arm. "I just stopped here to pick up a book that I was reading several weeks ago and that I wanted to discuss with your father. It was some kind of a log from one of his ships. Here it is." She pulled the volume from the shelf and turned to find Richard close behind her. She raised her eyes to his. Taking the book from her hands, he laid it on the edge of the desk and then disposed of the shawl in the same manner. He pulled her into his arms, and she came rigidly. Clearly feeling her reluctance, he bent his head anyway and covered her mouth with his own.

Sarah braced herself for the bruising, possessive kiss that had been her husband's sole technique, and then was startled by the touch of Richard's lips. Soft, so soft, and yielding, yet strangely compelling. If this was a kiss—surely she had never been kissed before! The shock and the newness kept her from responding, and even as he released her, she felt a rising desire to do so, but the moment was lost, and they stood apart. She stood staring at him for a few moments in silence. This time there could be no mistaking his confusion and the pain of rejection in his eyes.

161

She deliberately picked up the shawl and the book from where he had laid them and walked silently from the room.

From that evening, Sarah noticed a distinct change in Richard's attitude toward her. When they met, he was polite and civil as always, but gone was the light of humor in his eyes. He seemed restrained, controlled, unnatural. During the remainder of Lord Stanton and Mr. Warmington's visit, she saw little of him, for he was occupied with entertaining his friends, and she was busy with some new thoughts of her own, for Sir Winston had shared with her his plans for moving the family to Jamaica in the spring.

The idea was not a new one, for Sir Winston had for many years had business concerns there and had considered a move. Now it seemed his enterprises were flourishing and would benefit even more from his personal supervision. Sarah wasn't sure how she should greet this news. Her first reaction was that she should not like to leave England permanently. She had never yearned for travel, and a primitive island thousands of miles away held little attraction for her. But she was practical enough to realize that if Sir Winston wanted her to go, she would have little to say in the matter.

Several days after the departure of his friends, Richard arrived unexpectedly one morning at Ellis End and asked to speak with Sarah. She made her way to the salon nervously and tried not to show the anxiety she felt as she held out her hand in greeting. He took it as briefly as possible, she thought.

"There is something I wish to discuss with you, Mrs. Ellis. It concerns Jimmy."

"Yes, certainly, Captain."

"I was wondering if you would object to my taking the boy out shooting with me. He has several times asked if he could come along. There are some fine birds to be had, but I know that some people have strong feelings about guns, and that others are opposed to killing of any kind."

162

"I am not opposed to taking game birds for food, Captain Sherwood."

"Jimmy would be along only to observe, of course. He is a bit young to take a gun out himself. I promise you he will come to no harm."

"I have never been concerned for Jimmy's safety when he is with you, Captain. Surely you must know that."

"Perhaps he would like to come out tomorrow, then."

"You may ask him yourself before you leave, but I think we both know what his answer will be. And thank you for asking me before you said anything to him."

"I would never approach Jimmy without consulting you first, ma'am. It would be most improper for me to encourage him in any activity that ran counter to your wishes. I will see him then, before I leave. Good day, Mrs. Ellis."

Sarah could have wept at the cold formality of his words. The warmth and closeness they had shared just a few days ago seemed to belong to another lifetime. As he turned to leave, she took an impulsive step toward him. "Captain Sherwood . . . must there be such tension between us?" He turned to look at her, noting the uneasy frown and the sadness in her eyes. "I know that what happened the other evening has changed things for us, and I am so sorry—"

"No. Don't apologize, ma'am," he interrupted. "There is no blame attached to you in this. The problem is mine, and I shall deal with it . . . if I can." He turned and left on the words, and she stood pondering the last part of his sentence.

"And if you can't deal with it, Captain," she said to the empty air, "then I shall have lost a dear friend."

Richard *was* trying to deal with his feelings for Sarah Ellis, but he was finding it a difficult task. The lady wanted him simply as a friend, and he knew that such a relationship would never be enough for him. He had been attracted to her from the moment of their first meeting, even when he had thought her a married woman. Their acquaintance

163

had not progressed far at all before his interest in her had far exceeded that of mere friendship.

He was intrigued by her behavior at the stile and thoroughly confounded by her reaction in the library, for although she said she wanted only friendship from him, surely he saw the promise of more than that for them. Apparently he saw something that wasn't there, or perhaps he was seeing only what he wished to see. At any rate, the lady made it clear that she wanted none of him. Easy enough to say it. Much harder to accept it.

Never before in his life had Richard known such a one-sided affection. Always when he had given love, it had been returned. It was a pain, he decided, worse than any other he had experienced, for it carried with it an overwhelming sadness and hopelessness that permeated the fiber of each thought and every action. It was a pain that dulled the bright side of the spectrum in everything he did, taking the joy from laughter, the glitter from the stars, the glory from the sunset.

The final days of December passed, and Richard found himself eagerly awaiting the diversion that would be created by the arrival of Jonathan and Harriet for the New Year. He didn't avoid meeting Sarah, for it made little difference whether he saw her or not; she was constantly on his mind, within his sight or out of it. Throughout the month of December he had taken Jimmy out shooting with him or driving when the weather permitted, and his relationship with the boy thrived. But with the mother he could find no solid ground for creating a comfortable bond between them, and their friendship floundered.

One afternoon, just four days after Christmas, while Richard was sitting in the parlor reading the newspaper, and Elizabeth and Charlotte were chatting idly nearby, Charlotte said something that turned his thoughts in a new direction.

"Do you remember Jessica Roth?" Charlotte asked

164

Elizabeth. "Lord Burridge showed a decided interest in her, but you can be sure that it wasn't marriage that he had in mind!"

" 'It wasn't marriage that he had in mind.' " Richard repeated the words in his head and found himself wondering if Mrs. Ellis had questioned *his* intention. He had never considered offering her anything less than marriage, but he had never made his intentions clear to her. Could she think that he was interested in her only as his mistress? Surely a widowed woman could be forgiven for having such a thought, for it was not that unusual after all. And if she did think so, was that why she had repulsed him? Would she perhaps show him a different front if she understood that it was marriage he was offering?

By the same time next day, Richard had decided that he must speak with Mrs. Ellis and make his intentions absolutely plain, even at the possible cost of the additional wound to his pride should she continue to reject him. So when he found her sitting in the parlor with Elizabeth, he did not hesitate to ask if she would care to step to the library for a few moments, as he had something of a private nature to discuss with her and they were less likely to be disturbed there. She went with him willingly, thinking he wished to discuss Jimmy, so it was with some surprise that she listened as he began to speak.

"Mrs. Ellis, it has occurred to me quite recently, yesterday, in fact, that you may have thought, perhaps still do think, that my interest in you is something less than honorable. If that has been the case, then I beg of you to banish the thought, for nothing could be further from the truth. I have had only one intention where you are concerned. I want you as my wife, nothing less, and I—"

"No, please," she interrupted. "Please don't say any more. I cannot!"

"Why?"

"I do not wish to marry again, Captain."

165

"You don't wish to marry? Or you don't wish to marry me?"

"I don't wish to marry anyone." She walked to the windows and stood looking out, her back to him. "I will not marry again."

"I know you haven't given me any encouragement," he continued, "and yet—I can't explain it—I have sometimes felt that you are not indifferent to me. . . . I love you, Sarah, with all my heart, and I think that you care for me."

She turned to face him then, and as he stepped closer and took her by the shoulders, she brought her hands up to his chest. She was shaking her head no, but her eyes were trapped by his and she could not pull them away. She knew he was about to kiss her again, and all she could think was: Would it be that same tender touch? . . . It was the same, and she felt herself responding as if she were another person. Her mouth softened and moved on his. She began to tremble violently, and strong arms pulled her close. She felt as if his kiss were consuming her, and she was spinning, falling, forgetting all she thought she had ever known about love. Surely the winter sun must be shining into the room, beating on her head, heating her through, for she felt on fire. The kiss went on and on, sensual, intimate, and then, again with a strange abstraction, she realized Richard would misunderstand, and she pulled away. She was amazed to find herself capable of speech.

"Please, Captain, you must stop. This is not seemly!"

"Say you will marry me, and we need not concern ourselves with the proprieties."

"I have already told you that I cannot marry you."

"Cannot? Or will not?"

"Both."

"How can you say that to me now, after what has just passed between us?"

"A kiss has passed between us, Captain, nothing more. You place too much significance upon it."

166

"No. I don't think I do," he said thoughtfully as he reached for her once more. She avoided him and made her way to the door, but he was there before her and blocked her exit. She hesitated, lifting her eyes to his, and they held steadily for some moments, his questioning and speculative, hers defiant.

"You have made your request, and you have had your answer, Captain Sherwood," she said formally. "I beg you to let there be an end to this subject between us."

He moved out of her way then, and she was distressed to see that her hand shook as she reached for the door handle, but she soon had it open and was gone.

Lady Sherwood had her wish, and the entire Sherwood family spent the beginning of the new year together, a time made even more special this year by the addition of a new daughter. Everyone was in spirits, except for Richard, who Elizabeth thought looked rather more melancholy than festive. The whole family was aware of his regard for Mrs. Ellis, and they could see that the relationship was not prospering, but they did not plague him with their concerns. Richard preferred to keep his affairs private, and they respected that, knowing that if he desired advice from any of them, he would seek it. Elizabeth was the only one Richard ever permitted to trespass on forbidden ground, and she did so now, as they sat alone in the parlor after dinner.

"Your private conversation with Sarah the other day—it didn't prosper?" she asked.

"No. I'm afraid not. I asked her to marry me, Lizzie, and she has refused."

"You love her a great deal, don't you?" He didn't answer her, and she didn't seem to expect him to as she continued, "It must be terrible for you. I love her, too, but not, of course, in the way you do. I find it hard to believe

167

she doesn't love you, for to me you are quite the easiest person to love.''

He smiled and, putting an arm about her shoulders, drew her close to him on the sofa. "I don't think she is indifferent to me, Lizzie, but she insists she won't have me just the same. Says she won't marry again.''

"Maybe she just can't like the idea of marriage, like Lord Stanton. You know—the vows of faithfulness to one person, the lifelong commitment, the responsibility. He finds all those things foreign to his nature. Perhaps she feels the same.''

"Oh, come now, Lizzie, you know that those are only words when love is involved. Love doesn't fear faithfulness, or responsibility, or commitment. Look at Mama and Papa if you need proof of that.''

"I agree with you," she said, "but there are many who don't. Perhaps you should ask her why she doesn't wish to be married again.''

"No, Lizzie, I can't force myself on her further. I've already pushed her so far that there is only the thread of a relationship between us. And I will honestly admit that I have had enough rejection in the past two months to last me a lifetime. I have been thinking about Charles Warmington's invitation to Leicestershire. Do you still wish to go?''

"Yes, of course, but you said you couldn't leave until the end of January.''

"Well, I've changed my mind. We'll not stay a moment longer than Jon does. When he returns to Belgium, we'll be off to the hunt. Stanton and his brothers will be there, and perhaps Sir Hugh. It will be an excellent house party. I will write to the countess today and let her know when to expect us, and I will make arrangements to send the horses ahead in plenty of time.''

When the time came for Harriet and Jonathan to leave, it was not a sad occasion, for this was a family well accustomed to the farewells and long separations imposed by life in the military. Every time Lord Sherwood had sailed they had missed him dreadfully, and each time he returned home he was somewhat older but the same loving, caring father they remembered. And so it had been with Richard in the army, and now with Jonathan. The leave-taking was lighthearted and tearless. Harriet promised to write, as indeed she had done faithfully since her marriage, and they all looked forward to the next furlough and the next reunion.

Two days after Jonathan's departure, Richard and his sisters journeyed to Leicestershire, and Lady Sherwood stood on the front steps of the Manor, watching their coach disappear down the drive, and pondering the strange parting words of her youngest daughter. Elizabeth had kissed her mother good-bye and then startled her by whispering close to her ear, "If you see Sarah while we are away, Mama, try to discover why she doesn't wish to marry again, for Richard's happiness may depend upon it."

No matter how Lady Sherwood tried to interpret this remark, each time she came to the same conclusion. Richard had apparently asked Mrs. Ellis to be his wife and had been rejected, and Elizabeth seemed determined to take a hand in the affair and to involve her mother as well.

17

Viscount Stanton's major seat was a large rambling Tudor mansion in Hampshire, but as he and his brothers had no other family, they habitually spent Christmas and the hunting season in Leicestershire with the Earl and Countess of Haigh. The countess and Stanton's father were brother and sister, and although Lady Haigh had never held a high opinion of her brother during his lifetime, she was fond of all three of her nephews and always made them welcome in her home. She had three sons and two daughters of her own and seemed most content when her house was overflowing with young people.

The Sherwoods arrived in the early afternoon, and Elizabeth found herself confronted by a roomful of people, half of whom she did not know. She had previously met Charles Warmington's parents, the earl and countess, and greeted them first, thanking them for their kind invitation. Next Charles introduced her to his sisters, Lady Mary and Lady Sophia; then to his eldest brother, Lord Flint, and his wife; and his second brother, the Honorable Stephen Warmington, and his wife. Elizabeth, of course, knew Sir Hugh Broughton, Lord Stanton, and Henry Ferris, but Charles made her known to Giles Ferris, Stanton's youngest brother. Finally she greeted Mrs. Polk, a widowed cousin of the earl, and Miss Templeton, daughter of Lord Templeton, a near neighbor.

Elizabeth thought that between them, she and Charlotte should be able to remember everyone, and all in all it seemed a pleasant group. They sat down eighteen to dinner that evening, and the talk was all of hunting, for they planned a meeting the next day, weather permitting.

Elizabeth was seated at dinner between the Honorable Stephen Warmington and Mr. Giles Ferris. She found Charles's brother to be a warm and intelligent gentleman, but it was Mr. Ferris who intrigued her. She remembered that Mr. Henry Ferris had told her that his youngest brother was twenty, just one year older than she. It did not take her long to decide that Giles was by far the handsomest, and perhaps the most engaging, of the three brothers. Later in the evening, after the gentlemen had left their port to join the ladies in the salon, Elizabeth found herself again near Giles Ferris.

"What do you think of this style of tying a cravat, Miss Elizabeth?" he asked hopefully. "It is all the crack at Queens."

Before she could think of an appropriate answer, she heard the viscount's voice close behind her. "I would rather call it a massacre than a style," he said dampingly.

"Oh, Julian, the devil fly away with you!" Giles objected. "You know I will never aspire to your splendor." His eyes lingered jealously on the splendid effect created by his brother's neckcloth, and he said wickedly, "You have had so many more years to practice than I, and then, of course, you have the incomparable Peplow."

"Peplow should receive no credit for my accomplishments. What you see is the work of my hands alone," Stanton returned.

"So you have always said," Giles countered, "but you will never allow anyone in the room while you are tying your neckcloth, so you cannot prove that the skill is only yours.''

''I can understand that his lordship should wish to be alone at such a time, Mr. Ferris,'' Elizabeth said. ''My brother Richard insists that a more delicate operation does not exist, and it is imperative that there be nothing to break the concentration, and although he *has* allowed me in the room, he will *never* allow me to speak until he is quite satisfied with his effort.''

''Spoken like a sensible woman,'' the viscount approved. ''But I'll tell you what, Giles. Rather than have you continue to disgrace the family with your appearance, I will break my hard and fast rule. Come to me in the morning, and I will permit you to observe a master at work.'' He raised a finger as Giles would have spoken. ''But . . . you must abide by the same rule that governs Miss Elizabeth. You must watch and listen only and not speak. If you are an apt pupil, you may return to Oxford with a style all your own.''

There was no question but that Giles was flattered by this offer, and Elizabeth thought that despite his bantering tone, Giles Ferris viewed his eldest brother with considerable respect.

Stanton soon left them, and they spoke of other things. Elizabeth had dreaded the thought that someone would mention the shooting incident of last October and was relieved when several days passed and no one introduced the subject. She knew it had caused a considerable stir in London. The story told was that Lord Granbrooke, angry with Stanton after loosing the race and half-crazy with worry over his debts, including his debt to Stanton, had tried to kill the viscount, and Miss Sherwood had accidentally stepped into the way. The exact nature of the wounds was never disclosed, so it was not general knowledge that Stanton was alive only because of the providential placement of Miss Sherwood between himself and the bullet. Such a story would have been sensationalized beyond all bearing, and so the facts were closely guarded. Elizabeth was certain that the silence of this house party on the matter stemmed from a wish not to remind her, or Lord Stanton, for that matter, of a time that was painful for them both.

The first day's hunting was excellent, the weather clear and bright, and the exercise exhilarating. As they rode home, Elizabeth found herself beside Henry Ferris.

"Lady Flint tells me that you and your brothers have been here since before Christmas, Mr. Ferris," she said.

"Yes, we have. We have been spending Christmas at Haigh Court for, oh, it must be seven years now since our father's death. I fear the winter would be long and dreary if the three of us spent it alone at Stanton Castle."

"But surely your mother—"

"Our mother no longer lives in England, Miss Elizabeth. She returned to France soon after our father died. She is French, you know, and she was never happy here."

"Yes, Richard said she was French, but I didn't know that she had left the country. Surely that was hard for you?"

"Not really. I was nineteen and Julian twenty-one at the time. We were old enough to accept her decision. If anyone really suffered, it was Giles, for he was only thirteen."

"Certainly very young to lose both parents at once," Elizabeth sympathized.

"My mother wanted to take Giles with her to France, Miss Elizabeth. You musn't think that she wished to desert him."

"Then why did she?"

The question was out before she could consider that he might view it as an impertinence, but he raised no objection and answered without hesitation. "Because Julian refused to allow her to take the boy with her, and she had no say in the matter, for by my father's will, Julian was our guardian until we came of age."

If Elizabeth thought twenty-one a young guardian to

nineteen and thirteen, she didn't say as much, but asked instead, "How did your brother manage his military service abroad and his guardianship at home at the same time?"

"That's where the countess helped us the most," Henry replied. "I daresay Giles feels this is more his home than is Stanton Castle, for he spent his vacations here while Julian and I were in the army. I served only two years with the regiment and then took a position in the Foreign Office, so Giles was able to come to me when he wasn't at school. I'm sure that if Julian hadn't had our aunt to rely upon in those early years, he would never himself have joined. As it is, I think things have worked out for the best, for Giles has become the most civilized of the three of us. He never gets into trouble at school, or, at least, very little," he amended.

"And you and Lord Stanton did?"

"Lord, yes! But don't tell Julian I admitted it!"

Two evenings later, Lord and Lady Haigh held a hunt ball, which for a country affair was very grand, with more than eighty persons in attendance. Elizabeth, who always loved to dance, and who especially enjoyed a party where she had the opportunity to take the floor with the light-footed Mr. Ferris, had a delightful time. She danced the quadrille with Sir Hugh Broughton, a country dance with Henry Ferris, and was pleased when Lord Stanton requested her hand for the waltz. Charles Warmington and Charlotte stood up for the same dance, and Stanton remarked conversationally, "My cousin Charles and your sister make a charming couple."

"Yes. I have often thought so," Elizabeth agreed. "I think he shows a decided preference for her company, and I know she thinks highly of him."

"It is not perhaps a connection you should encourage, however, Miss Elizabeth."

"Why not?" she asked, surprised by his remark.

"It would be rather an uneven match, ma'am, don't you think?"

"It surprises me that you should say such a thing of your own cousin, my lord, for certainly his birth and breeding are unexceptionable."

"I do not dispute his birth, Miss Elizabeth, which is actually better than my own, but there is the matter of fortune to consider. Charles is a younger son, and his injury some years ago curtailed any career he may have had in the army. He has a small property in Kent, but aside from that, he will have little to offer a wife."

"But you are forgetting that Charlotte has a fortune of her own, my lord!"

"I am not forgetting it, Miss Elizabeth, but I think your sister's fortune will do more to hinder such a match than promote it."

Elizabeth frowned, but as the dance was ending she had no opportunity to pursue the conversation. Stanton did not ask her to dance again, and she found that perplexing, for it had not been uncommon for them to dance two, and occasionally three, times during the course of an evening.

From the moment Lord Stanton had discovered that Elizabeth was to be a member of the hunting party that season, he had determined to limit the time he spent with her, not enough to arouse any suspicion but enough to reduce the risk of any further intimacy between them. He had underestimated Elizabeth's sensitivity. Fewer than four days had passed since her arrival in Leicestershire, and already she sensed the change.

She watched him now as he danced with Miss Templeton, and gritted her teeth as the girl's shrill laughter rose above the strains of the music. Miss Templeton was the only member of the house party whom Elizabeth had taken in almost immediate dislike. She was a pixyish blonde, with angelic features and a tiny, perfect figure, but Elizabeth thought her giddy and considered her boldness and continuous flirting unseemly.

Elizabeth watched as the viscount flirted, in his turn, with Miss Templeton and was puzzled at the change in his behavior. In the past, they had such an easy, friendly comradeship, and now he seemed to be holding her at arm's length. He seldom sought her out, never seemed to have flattering things to say about her appearance, and rarely asked her to dance. She knew he had no romantic interest in her and that he had no desire to marry, and she didn't think he would be concerned about what others thought of their friendship. She was aware that the shooting incident had changed things between them, but she was at a loss to understand why, and was hurt by his rejection.

So blithely unaware was she of her growing attraction for him that she allowed herself on the following day to fall into an embarrassing, uncomfortable scene. Elizabeth, Miss Templeton, Charles Warmington, and Lord Stanton made up a riding party early in the afternoon of the day following the ball. There was no meeting planned for that day, and most of the ladies preferred to remain at the house, recovering from the rigors of the previous evening. The four had ridden far, and when they came to a small brook, Miss Templeton expressed a desire for a drink.

"We have no cup, Miss Templeton," Lord Stanton said, "but if you would not object to my hands, ma'am, I will endeavor to make them into a cup for you."

"I am sure water could never taste sweeter than from your hands, my lord," she replied.

Since this was just one in a string of similar comments that she had been uttering for the past hour, Elizabeth rolled her eyes in disgust and, catching Mr. Warmington's eye, nearly laughed aloud at the barely suppressed grimace on his face.

Meanwhile, the viscount dismounted and took hold of Miss Templeton's horse as she began to dismount. Somehow she seemed to tangle her feet in her skirts, and she half slid and half fell from her horse. As she staggered against him, the viscount clasped her to his chest to keep her from falling. Stanton was smiling, Miss Templeton was laughing, and to Elizabeth's eye, the viscount held her much longer than was necessary.

As Elizabeth realized that Charles was waiting for her to dismount, she said suddenly, "No, thank you, Mr. Warmington. I don't think I will stop after all. I shall meet you all back at the house." Wheeling her horse on the words, she cantered away. The viscount spun around at Elizabeth's uncharacteristic tone, and Charles called after her, but she paid no heed.

"See to Miss Templeton's drink, Charles, if you would," Stanton said to his cousin. "I'll go after her." He caught his horse's bridle as he spoke and set off after Elizabeth, already a goodly distance away and covering ground rapidly.

Elizabeth rode recklessly, blinded by tears and shaking with a rage she could not understand. She was rapidly approaching a pasture hedge, started to pull her horse up to turn off from it, and then at the last instant decided to take it anyway. Her horse was confused and uncollected. He took the jump off stride, caught his hind legs as he went over, and stumbled on the uneven ground as he landed. Elizabeth was pitched forward over his head, landing unceremoniously in a pile of rocks and wind-blown winter leaves. Her horse scrambled to his feet and trotted a few paces away. She regarded him critically. No harm to you, old fellow, she thought with some relief, as she began to brush leaves and twigs from her dark red riding habit.

Moments later she heard the sound of hoofbeats approaching on the hard ground and looked up angrily as Stanton pulled his horse up beside her and dismounted. "What kind of mad stunt was that?" he asked wrathfully, hoping his anger would hide the concern he felt. "Are you all right?" He knelt beside her and took hold of her arm as he spoke, but she shook him off resentfully.

"Save your assistance for Miss Templeton, my lord. I assure you she has more need of it than I!"

He saw instantly that her tears were emotional and not physical, and that she had no thought for the nasty fall she had just taken. He seated himself on a large rock no more than two feet from where she had landed, thinking that she was fortunate to have missed it. "Would you like to tell me what all this is about?" He spoke in a calm, matter-of-fact voice that seemed to have the desired effect, for when she answered she was less angry and more civil.

"I'm sorry. I just couldn't remain another instant in that girl's company. If I had stayed, I would have said something unforgivable to her. And *you*, my lord," she said accusingly, "*you* encourage her, hugging her as you did!"

"I was not *hugging* her," he objected. "I simply tried to keep her from falling."

Elizabeth struck a pose and batted her eyelashes as she gave a creditable impersonation of Miss Templeton. " 'I am sure water could never taste sweeter than from your hands, my lord.' Ugh! How can you listen to such rubbish? It's disgusting. And don't laugh at me! I'm not trying to entertain you!"

He had found her performance delightful, but he suppressed his laughter as he answered. "I see that you have strong feelings about Miss Templeton, but was it worth making a scene?"

"I didn't mean to make a scene," she said, "but I can't bear the way she throws herself at you."

Stanton thought Elizabeth had reacted from simple jealousy, but she didn't seem to realize it, and he prayed she wouldn't. "Tell me, Elizabeth," he said carefully, "even if Miss Templeton continues to 'throw herself at me,' as you so colorfully put it, do you think it likely to profit her?"

178

"I couldn't say. Only you know the answer to that question."

"Miss Templeton is an extremely silly, entertaining chit, who happens to be a first-rate horsewoman, and that is as far as my interest in her goes or ever will go. She is no threat to our friendship, believe me." He had come to his feet as he spoke, and now he smiled warmly at her and held out his hand. "If you're sure you're not hurt, I think we should be getting back."

Elizabeth found it curious, as she had on other occasions, that he used her Christian name so easily when they were alone together. It didn't seem at all inappropriate to her, but rather more a manifestation of the closeness they sometimes shared. He dried her eyes, helped her brush the leaves from her skirts, and then caught her horse. He helped her to mount then, and they rode back to the house in relative silence, good-will having been reestablished between them.

The viscount's mind was in turmoil. Surely this uncharacteristic outburst from Elizabeth supported his theory that her feelings for him far exceeded those permitted by friendship. And while it warmed his heart to have this further proof of her affection, he chided himself for being pleased by her jealousy. He could not afford to encourage her, and yet, when she put her small hand in his, it had taken every ounce of will power not to take her into his arms. How would she react if he kissed her now? He was hopeful that she would not slap him again. But would she welcome his embrace? Would she return it? This situation must not be permitted to continue, he thought, mentally shaking himself. I cannot be continuously in her company without causing more outbreaks of a similar nature, and sooner or later I'm bound to give myself away. He decided during that ride back to Haigh Court that he must leave Leicestershire as soon as he could reasonably do so and thereafter take care to avoid meeting Miss Elizabeth Sherwood.

179

Miss Templeton, deeply mortified when the viscount had turned his back on her and ridden off after Miss Elizabeth, had, for whatever reason, chosen not to mention Elizabeth's strange behavior. But that evening, after dinner, she recommenced her fatuous attempts to attract the viscount, giving him so little peace from her constant inane prattle that by the time the tea tray was brought in he had had more than he could bear and dragged Richard and Giles off for a game of billiards. When he finally retired for the evening, he and Sir Hugh went upstairs together and settled in the viscount's bedchamber with an excellent bottle of cognac.

"How would you feel about loping off to London, Hugh?"

"I thought you intended to stay till the end of the month?"

"I did, but things here are getting damnably uncomfortable." He related to Sir Hugh the incident with Miss Templeton at the brook and Elizabeth's reaction to it.

"Sounds like jealousy to me. Has she made any effort to attach you?"

"No. There is no way I can be certain how she feels."

"You know, Julian, I think you are more than half in love with the girl yourself!" Sir Hugh accused.

"Much more than half," Stanton admitted.

Sir Hugh's eyes widened in surprise. "Well, now there is something I never thought I would live to hear! You admitting that you were in love with *any* woman!"

"You may believe me when I say I wish I weren't. It's a cursed position to be in. I very nearly gave myself away today. She frightened me half to death when she took that fall! She's so headstrong, Hugh—endangering herself in such a heedless manner!"

"Seems to me most of the danger she's been in lately is directly connected with you—the attempt by Granbrooke, and now this incident with Miss Templeton," Sir Hugh pointed out.

"Exactly, and that is why I feel I must remove myself from her vicinity. Every time I'm with her, or even near her, I am taking a great risk. Stay on if you like, but I think I shall leave for town, or perhaps Stanton Castle, by the end of the week."

"There is another solution to this problem that you are overlooking, Julian, and it is far simpler than running away. . . . You could ask her to marry you."

"No. That is the one thing I am determined not to do."

"Why not? What have you to lose?"

"For myself, not so much perhaps—but for her, if she accepted me, a great deal. I wouldn't wager a groat on a happy ending to any marriage with me, and I will not gamble with her happiness. It means too much to me."

"I would never have picked you as the man to fall in love with an unsophisticated innocent like Miss Elizabeth," Sir Hugh mused.

"Nor would I," Stanton agreed. "And yet, my friend, it appears that I have, and I can't tell you why. I won't deny that it shook me a great deal when she took that bullet for me. It's a humbling experience to realize that someone is willing to offer their life for yours. I had similar experiences in the war, but aside from Henry, or perhaps you, no soldier would risk his life for mine out of affection but rather duty, which is a very different thing. Elizabeth acted out of pure selfless instinct, and a motive of that nature is hard to comprehend. But even though that night made me question *her* feelings, I think *I* was attracted long before that—the night Granbrooke took her from Vauxhall, or perhaps even earlier." When I kissed her in my library, he thought. "I can't explain my feelings for her—they defy description."

"You needn't explain, Julian. I know what you mean. I've been there myself."

"Harriet Putnam?" the viscount asked. Sir Hugh nodded, and Stanton continued speaking as he refilled his friend's glass. "Did she ever know you cared for her?"

"No. She had no thought for anyone but Jonathan Sherwood. I think she was in love with him even before she came to London, for they were neighbors in Sussex."

"So, my dear Hugh, we are quite a pair, are we not? Here you are with the woman you love married to another man, and here I am, destined no doubt for the same fate, for I cannot think that Elizabeth will remain unmarried for long."

"I don't suppose that there is anything I could say that would make you reconsider your decision, Julian?"

"Absolutely nothing, my friend, so let us pour some more of this excellent brandy and toast the numerous benefits of bachelorhood."

18

Lord Stanton was wakened the following morning by the tittering sounds of Miss Templeton, her shrill voice echoing in the corridor outside his room. As her voice and that of her companion faded down the hall, he sat up in an attempt to shake off the drowsiness caused by too much brandy the previous night.

How could Elizabeth imagine for one instant that I could be attracted to that silly chatterbox? he asked himself. Just listening to that voice could drive one mad in a fortnight. As he swung his legs out of bed and rang for his valet, he wondered briefly if Elizabeth would be sore this morning after her tumble yesterday. Then he frowned, realizing that his waking thoughts were of Elizabeth Sherwood, and he had just sworn the previous evening to put her from his mind.

Determined to master his obsession with her and stick by his resolve to avoid her, he descended to the breakfast parlor sometime later, took a seat beside the earl's cousin, Mrs. Polk, and set about to please her. She was an attractive woman in her late twenties, who had been widowed for nearly two years. She had met the viscount socially on many occasions, but never had she known him to be so congenial. She responded to his conversation enthusiastically, and by the time they rose from the table had agreed to ride with him later in the day.

For her part, Elizabeth felt extremely foolish about her behavior at the brook on the previous day. What concern was it of hers if Miss Templeton wished to flirt with Viscount Stanton and he with her? She wasn't his keeper, and it wasn't her place to be either offended or incensed by his behavior. She was willing to admit that having his friendship meant a great deal to her and she had felt threatened by Miss Templeton, for it seemed to Elizabeth that the viscount preferred Miss Templeton's company to her own. She recognized that such jealousy was childish, and she resolved to overcome it.

Elizabeth kept herself busy for the next several days. She hunted every morning that a party went out. She spent her afternoons chatting with the other young ladies, or playing piquet with Giles Ferris, or learning billiards from Richard. She noticed that Lord Stanton was spending less time in the company of Miss Templeton and seemed to be seeking out Mrs. Polk. Elizabeth admired the older woman. She was quiet and circumspect, a restful companion when compared with Miss Templeton. Elizabeth's admiration for the widow Polk was not destined to last.

One evening Elizabeth was enjoying a game of piquet with Giles Ferris while at a table nearby, Lord and Lady Flint, Viscount Stanton, and Mrs. Polk made up a table of whist. Elizabeth glanced occasionally at the other table, noticing that the foursome seemed in high spirits. She and Giles played until it was quite late, but even so, Elizabeth found it hard to sleep after she had retired for the night. Each time she closed her eyes she would see either the viscount's amiable face or Mrs. Polk's smiling, pleasant countenance in her mind's eye.

She tossed and turned for nearly an hour and finally sat up and relit her candles. Elizabeth did not often suffer from insomnia, but when she did, she knew that the best way to tire her eyes was to read. She reached for the book at her bedside and then remembered she had left it behind in the library, where she had been reading earlier in the day. Pulling on her dressing gown and slippers, she left the room. The house was dark and quiet, the last of the guests having passed her door sometime earlier. By the light of her single candle she made her way to the ground floor. The door to the library was slightly ajar, the fire still burning high, its light flickering off the walls and furnishings. She padded silently to the door, pushed it open on well-oiled hinges, and then stood frozen on the threshold. Before the fire, locked in a passionate embrace, were Lord Stanton and Mrs. Polk. As the light from Elizabeth's candle fell upon them, they broke apart and turned to face her.

Elizabeth blushed and stammered, "Ex . . . Excuse me, my lord, ma'am." She sketched a curtsy and, turning quickly, fled down the hall and up the stairs. Slamming the door of her room, she leaned breathlessly upon it, shaking like a leaf, tears standing in her eyes. She closed her eyes, and the painful scene she had just witnessed came clearly to view. The viscount's handsome head bent over Mrs. Polk, her face turned up to his, their lips melting together with passion, his hands at the small of her back, holding her tightly against him.

Suddenly Elizabeth remembered that day in his library. He had held her as close, his mouth on hers, and she imagined herself responding as Mrs. Polk had. Slowly she bent her knees and slid down the door until she crouched against it. "Why can't he want me like that?" she whispered to herself. "Why not me?" She sat huddled against the door until she was cold and stiff, and then forced herself to go back to bed. She had found no satisfactory answer to her question, but one thing she did know. She wanted more than anything to put herself in Mrs. Polk's place, for what she felt for Lord Stanton was something much, much stronger than friendship.

Elizabeth slept poorly and made an excuse not to join the hunt the next morning. She kept to her room until early afternoon and then sought out Charlotte to see if she should like to walk to the village.

"I promised to tour the succession houses with Lady Sophia and Lady Mary," Charlotte answered. "Why don't you come with us?"

"No. Maybe another time. I would rather walk. I'll take my maid."

Charlotte looked doubtful. "Is something wrong, Lizzie? You don't look well."

Elizabeth shook her head. "It's nothing. I didn't sleep well last night, that's all. I need some exercise."

"Very well then, enjoy yourself, but don't be gone too long. Some of the gentlemen were saying at luncheon that it could snow before evening."

"I won't be long. I'll see you at dinner."

Elizabeth soon left the house with her maid and had walked nearly fifteen minutes before she became aware that her companion was sniffling almost continuously into a handkerchief. She stopped walking suddenly and stared at the girl. She had been so wrapped up in her own thoughts that she hadn't taken time to consider Molly.

"Molly, you have a cold."

"Yes, miss," the maid answered in surprise. "I have had it for the past week, as you know."

"Yes, I do know. How could I be so thoughtless? I should never have asked you to come with me! It is much too cold. Why, you could catch your death!"

"No, Miss Elizabeth. I shall be fine. 'Tis not so cold, and I can manage."

"I don't want you to manage! I want you home, and that is where you are going—instantly. And since I won't need you until it is time to dress for dinner, you may go to your room and rest until I ring for you upon my return."

"You intend to continue your walk alone, miss?"

"Surely; why not? We have walked to the village before. We have never met anyone who was not a member of the house party. I could be naught but safe on Lord Haigh's land."

"I don't know, miss," Molly said doubtfully. "The captain wouldn't approve of my leaving you on your own."

Elizabeth would not hear her objections. "Go home, Molly. You will be warm and comfortable in no time, and I will have my walk. I will go to the village and back, no farther, I promise, and I will stay to the private road."

When Molly was gone, Elizabeth was glad of the solitude. There was a post road that ran through the village and passed the gate house and the main drive into Haigh Court, but Elizabeth was following a cart track that ran from behind the stables along a winding route through the home wood and eventually to the village. She walked at a brisk pace, her mind working just as quickly.

What she had seen last night was not a bad dream, but the pain of heart she had felt during the long hours of darkness had vanished with the light of day. Now she chided herself for a fool. How could she ever have convinced herself that she admired the viscount as a friend, when in reality she had been attracted to him as a man almost from the very beginning of their acquaintance. She thought back again to the day he had kissed her in his library. She had been shocked by his behavior, but she had also been strangely attracted by it. Although she had vehemently denied it at the time, he had been right when he accused her of enjoying his embrace. She had enjoyed it. More than that, it had thrilled her. Frightened of such overwhelming feelings, and far beyond her experience with this worldly man, she had hidden her insecurities from him and from herself with an admirable show of anger. Then, on the night they had both apologized, and she had thanked him for rescuing her from Lord Granbrooke, and he had held her as she wept—that night, for the first time, she had

187

seen his humanity, and felt she could trust him. She could see now that from that moment her love had grown steadily, until his life had been threatened by Granbrooke, and she had moved instinctively to protect him, never counting the cost.

"You're a fool, Elizabeth Sherwood! He probably won't ever marry. And if he should, he would choose an experienced woman like Mrs. Polk, or at least an accomplished one like Charlotte, not an outspoken, impetuous schoolgirl like you!"

Eventually Elizabeth slowed her pace. Alone with her thoughts she had opportunity to dissect them, to look back over the events of the past several months. Most of what she remembered was not encouraging. When she reached the village, she made a few small purchases and was soon on her way home again. She had barely left the village behind when the snow began to fall in earnest.

When Lord Stanton drove his curricle up the drive in the late afternoon, he met Richard Sherwood coming out of the house. He handed the reins to his groom, stepped down from the carriage, and started up the broad stairway as Richard greeted him.

"Well met, Julian! I was just on my way to the stables. Will you loan me your carriage?"

"Gladly," Stanton responded, "but I would advise against going out in this weather. It's bound to be treacherous before long."

"I'm sure you're right, but Elizabeth walked to the village earlier and has not yet returned. I thought I would go out a little way to meet her."

"She hasn't gone alone, surely?"

"Yes, I'm afraid she did. She started out with her maid but then became concerned for the girl's cold and sent her back alone."

"That sounds like your sister," Stanton agreed.

"She's been gone quite a long time," Richard contin-

188

ued. "She's bound to turn up soon, but it's growing dark, and I won't be content until she is safely in for the night."

"Do you know which way she went?"

"Yes. Her maid said she took the old road through the home wood, the one that leads from the stables."

"Do you know it?" Stanton asked.

"No. I've never been that way."

"Let me go, then. I know it well."

"You don't mind?"

"Not at all. She can't be far. I'm sure we'll be back in no time."

Turning, Stanton mounted into his curricle again and dismissed his groom, curricles not being built to accommodate three persons comfortably. As he turned his carriage and headed toward the stables, he noted that the tracks he had made in the snow just a few minutes earlier were nearly covered, for the snow was falling heavily, obscuring the ground and making visibility impossible beyond several hundred feet.

When Elizabeth had covered nearly half the distance to Haigh Court she stopped and stood still in the road. The snow was falling faster now. There was no wind, so the large flakes fell straight down. It was deathly quiet, so quiet that if she listened carefully, it was possible to hear the hiss of the snow itself as it struck through the bare branches above and settled on the woodland floor. Newly awakened to love, everything looked different to her somehow. The snow had quickly turned her world white, and she felt tiny and insignificant, but at the same time very aware of the life that flowed within her. She moved to a large fallen log at the side of the road and sat down upon it, folding her hands in her lap. She sat motionless, imagining herself part of the landscape, allowing the snow to settle on her. Slowly her lap and arms turned white. She had been thinking of the viscount, so when she heard the jingle of harness and looked up to see him coming toward her, she decided she must be imagining him. She did not move but continued to sit as he brought his horses to a standstill beside her.

The steaming horses seemed very real, and his voice as he spoke was clearly concerned. "Miss Elizabeth, are you all right?"

"Yes, my lord, thank you."

"Are you resting, then?"

"Not really, just sitting, enjoying the snow."

He glanced around at the wooded scene before them and had to admit that it was appealing. Hundreds of branches both large and small were outlined by the damp, clinging snow, creating intricate networks of dark and light.

"May I offer you a ride back to the house, ma'am?"

Suddenly she saw him again with Mrs. Polk in his arms, and she resented his intrusion on her solitary walk. There was a militant look in her eye as she responded, "I am content to walk, my lord."

"Perhaps, but your brother is not content that you should. The snowfall is heavy, and it will soon be dark. I met him as he was coming in search of you, and I offered to come in his stead."

"How *galant* of you, my lord."

"He is not familiar with this road. I am," he said shortly.

"I am also familiar with it, sir. I have walked it several times."

"Come, Miss Elizabeth, let us not spar. Your brother is concerned for you. You cannot wish to worry him."

She rose then, shaking the snow from her skirts. His horses backed as she approached the carriage, but he quickly steadied them and then held one hand down to assist her into the curricle. Elizabeth watched with silent admiration as the viscount accomplished the difficult but seemingly effortless feat of turning his carriage and pair in a very restricted space.

She waited until he had set his horses in motion toward

the house and then spoke in a conventional tone. "I am sorry if my interruption last night spoiled your evening with Mrs. Polk, my lord."

"What?" he asked sharply.

"I said that I am sorry—"

"I heard what you said," he interrupted.

"Then why did you ask me to repeat myself?"

"Because I cannot believe that you said it! Who taught you your manners, Miss Elizabeth?"

She lifted her chin. "My mother, sir. But I am afraid in some areas she was not entirely successful."

"That, ma'am, is an understatement! In some areas she has failed totally! You begin conversations that are wholly inappropriate, you make comments that are, to use your own word, impertinent, and you have the most unsettling habit of intruding yourself into the private affairs of others!"

Elizabeth was well aware of her shortcomings, but somehow on his lips they seemed ten times more damning. A moment of silence followed his ringing speech, and then Elizabeth said quietly, "I know, my lord. That is why I wished to apologize."

Feeling he had been too harsh, he relented a little. "As far as last night is concerned, no apology is necessary. You spoiled nothing."

"Mrs. Polk does not share your opinion, Lord Stanton."

"She spoke to you about it?" he asked, his voice incredulous.

"I met her as I was leaving the house today. I believe she was angry with me."

"What did she say?"

"I would rather not repeat it, my lord."

"You started this conversation, Miss Elizabeth, and you shall finish it! Tell me what she said, word for word, as well as you remember it."

Elizabeth repeated the words for him, but she left out

191

the biting sarcasm that had laced the older woman's bitter comment. "She said, 'Such a good idea for you to take a walk, Miss Sherwood. If it is a long and tiring one, perhaps you will not find it necessary to wander the house at night.' "

The viscount was silent. It wasn't difficult for him to interpret this comment or to add the inflection Elizabeth had omitted. Clearly he had raised some hopes in the widow's breast with his recent attentions. He had been mildly amused by his flirtation with her, but if the truth were told, the kiss in the library had been more her idea than his. He was not opposed to a liaison with her and had been enjoying her skilled kiss when Elizabeth interrupted them. Elizabeth's face, briefly though he had seen it, had driven all desire for Mrs. Polk from his mind. She stood there only a moment, her face illuminated by her candle, but it was all there—first the surprise, then the shock, the disappointment, and finally the resignation—all there for him to read, as clearly as printed words upon a page. He had no intention of ever allowing Elizabeth Sherwood to play a major role in his life, but he admired her more than any woman he had ever known, and he valued her good opinion.

"Elizabeth, what you saw last night was nothing, it was less than nothing. . . ."

"Just another interesting interlude," she said flippantly; "a new woman each month." She shrugged her shoulders. "Variety adds spice, they say."

His eyes narrowed as he glanced briefly at her. "So it does. I believe I told you once that no woman can hold my attention for long."

"I didn't believe you."

"Perhaps you should." When she didn't answer, he continued solemnly. "Elizabeth, we have a strange friendship, you and I. We have shared a scrape with death, and that binds us in an unusual way. You saved my life, leaving me with a debt I can never repay. . . . We may always

192

be friends—I should like it if we could be—but we cannot use our friendship as an excuse to trespass in certain areas of each other's lives. We are very different people. You are traditional and romantic, and you believe that people are basically good. I, on the other hand, am . . ."

As he paused, searching for the proper word, Elizabeth supplied it. "Cynical."

He nodded in agreement. "All right, perhaps I am. It is true that I have little faith in my fellow man. I have no grand plans for the future. I live from day to day, and I worry about tomorrow, tomorrow. I welcome your friendship, but we cannot remain friends if you insist upon placing your values on me, and then are disappointed when I fail to live up to them."

"But I don't do that!"

"I think you do. You were scandalized when Charlotte announced that I had frightened her into breaking the engagement. In your ordered, well-regulated life, engagements, like marriages, are made in heaven, and not intended to be broken. You came to see me determined to set the world right again, and when I foiled your plans to do good, you were furious with me. Then when I kissed you, I spoiled your image of the ideal brother-in-law—wealthy, titled, the perfect gentleman—and you were angry at me for that, too. Deny it if you can."

"You're right," she admitted. You did take a perfect situation and spoil it, and I did resent you for it. But I have learned a great deal in the past months. I am not so naive as I was. But you are also right when you say it is not my place to judge you."

"Then you agree to accept me, just as I am?" he asked.

"Yes, I do." Then she smiled up at him, and when he responded in kind, she tucked her hand in his arm and leaned her shoulder against his as she thought, I love you just the way you are. I wouldn't change a thing.

* * *

The following day Lord Stanton received a letter from his steward at Stanton Castle, which he viewed as the hand of providence. It informed him that one of his race mares had foaled, and included a description of the foal, but he led his aunt to believe that the letter had a far more serious import, and that its content required that he leave immediately for Stanton Castle to attend to urgent business. The entire party expressed their regret that he must leave so soon. Giles decided to accompany his brother and spend the few remaining days of his vacation in Hampshire, and they made hasty arrangements to leave the following morning.

The Sherwoods remained at Haigh Court through the first week in February, and Elizabeth had numerous opportunities to observe her sister and Charles Warmington together. She no longer questioned Charlotte's attachment to Charles, and one evening taxed her with it.

"I think you have finally found the man you decided to wait for—the one for whom you could feel some affection?"

"More than affection, Lizzie," Charlotte confided. "I am afraid that I have fallen in love with him."

"Why afraid?" Elizabeth asked. "I think it's wonderful!"

"Do you think he cares for me, Lizzie?"

"I'm sure he must. His attentions have been most marked."

"I have certainly felt that he liked me a little, but he has said nothing."

"Nor should he! It would be most improper for him to speak to you before he had received Papa's permission."

"Are you sure that's all it is?" Charlotte asked doubtfully.

"Of course. What other reason could he have? Wait until we are in London again in the spring. I will be willing to bet that he calls upon Papa the moment we arrive in town."

Charlotte seemed reassured by Elizabeth's words, but even as she spoke, Elizabeth was remembering the viscount's comments concerning a match between his cousin and Charlotte, and she determined to discuss the matter with Richard at the earliest opportunity. She found her opportunity two days later when Richard offered to drive her to the village where she had engaged herself to run some errands for Lady Haigh.

"Richard, have you ever noticed that your friend Charles seems to have an interest in Charlotte?"

"Lord, yes. I noticed it years ago."

"Years ago!"

"Yes. One of the first times he ever came to Sussex. I had that shoulder wound, and he had already been invalided out, and came down to stay. Charlotte couldn't have been more than seventeen at the time, but he was instantly taken with her."

"Was it a serious interest, do you think?"

"I would say very serious."

"Then why did he never speak of it?"

"I daresay he intended to when she was older, but by the time Charlotte turned nineteen, Father had inherited and that changed things."

"His feelings for her changed because Papa inherited?"

"I don't think his feelings have changed at all, Lizzie, but when Father inherited, he settled a handsome fortune on Charlotte, and that, unfortunately, creates an obstacle for Charles."

"That's exactly what Lord Stanton said, but I don't see why it should change anything, except perhaps to make things better."

"I don't think Charles would offer for a woman whose fortune far exceeds his own," Richard explained.

"But, Richard, that's foolish. They are the same people

195

they were before Papa inherited! If he loved her then, and he still loves her now, he should not allow the money to influence him!"

"You may see it that way, but I assure you that Charles does not. He permits himself to enjoy Charlotte's company, but I don't think he has any intention of offering for her. I feel for him in this, for Charlotte will eventually marry, and I think it will be difficult for him."

"Do you think that Charles is right to give up so easily?" Elizabeth asked with spirit. "He seems to accept his unhappy plight tamely. Would he not be wiser to fight for Charlotte if he wants her?"

"I cannot advise him to do so, Lizzie. I can't say what I would do under similar circumstances, but I do know that a man cannot compromise his principles for the gratification of desire. Some obstacles are too great to overcome, even with the greatest will in the world."

She knew he was thinking of his own involvement with Sarah, and she hoped that her mother was taking advantage of their absence to encourage Sarah to confide in her. Elizabeth forced her thoughts back to the question of Charlotte.

"And what if Charlotte should return Charles's regard, Richard? What then?"

"Then I suppose it would be Charlotte's place to encourage him to overcome his scruples. But I wouldn't place any dependence on her being able to do so, for he feels very strongly in this matter, and I doubt if he will ever declare himself, even if he thought she cared for him."

"Then I am afraid that you will continue to have an unhappy friend, Richard, and we will have an equally unhappy sister, because Charlotte told me just two days since that she is in love with Mr. Warmington."

19

Something less than two weeks after she had seen her three children off to Leicestershire, Lady Sherwood found her first opportunity to act on Elizabeth's parting request. Lord Sherwood had offered to take Jimmy shooting in Richard's absence, and the enthusiastic hunters had just departed. The ladies sat alone in the parlor, occupied with their embroidery.

"That is a fine boy you have, Sarah," Lady Sherwood said. "You must be very proud of him."

"I am. He has been the only true joy in my life."

Lady Sherwood looked up from her work and regarded her companion critically. "Certainly your husband, Sarah?"

"I never loved my husband, Lady Sherwood. I know that must seem strange to you, for I can see that there is great tenderness between you and his lordship."

"It doesn't seem strange to me, my dear. Many marriages are not love matches. You were married very young, perhaps before you had time to meet a man you could care for."

"My marriage was arranged by my parents when I was seventeen. I was not consulted."

"And the man they chose for you—you disliked him?"

"It wasn't that I disliked him, for indeed, I barely knew

197

him. We had met only a few times before we became engaged, and the engagement lasted only one month."

"Then you were wed, in fact, to a stranger," Lady Sherwood said. "I imagine that must have been difficult for you, especially at so young an age."

"It *was* difficult, for I was very innocent, and had received no instruction concerning my duties as a wife. I wanted to be a good wife, and I wanted to please my husband." She paused for a moment while Lady Sherwood waited patiently. Finally Sarah continued in a harsh tone. "I must not bore you, ma'am, with the sad history of my marriage. All in all, it is not a pleasant story."

Lady Sherwood regarded Sarah sympathetically. It was easy to see how Richard could love this woman, but it was also easy to see that she was deeply troubled. "Nothing you could say would bore me, Sarah. Sometimes I think that if we have painful memories that we are accustomed to bearing alone, we can render them less painful if we share them with a sympathetic ear." Lady Sherwood paused for a moment, but when it became clear that Sarah had no intention of speaking, she continued mildly. "His lordship and I had a fifth child, another boy, born between Richard and Jonathan. When Richard was barely six, and Jon not yet a year old, young Thomas was taken from us by the fever. My grief was so great that I could not bear to mention the child's name or see anything that reminded me of him. I refused to allow Richard to speak of his dead brother, which I know now was not the proper way to help him deal with his own grief, which was, in its way, as profound as my own. Jarvis was at sea at the time, but when he came home nearly six months later, he wasted no time in encouraging me to speak of my loss, of our loss, and in that way I began to come to terms with the pain. These days, I am able to think back fondly on the three years I had with my second son, and my memories of him are pleasant ones."

"There was nothing pleasant about my marriage to James Ellis," Sarah said bluntly.

"You have Jimmy," Lady Sherwood argued. "Certainly he is a pleasant product of your marriage, however unhappy."

"Yes, you're right." Sarah admitted, "and Jimmy was my one anchor to some kind of sanity during those years. But my marriage was not unhappy, Lady Sherwood—my marriage was a nightmare."

"In what way?" Lady Sherwood asked gently. "I am willing to listen if you would like to tell me about it."

"James, my husband," Sarah began, "was domineering and autocratic. Many of his attributes I have seen in Sir Winston, and I think Lady Ellis was quite as unhappy as I in her own marriage. James had very definite notions about what I should do, and how and when I should do it. I was not expected, or even permitted, to have an opinion of my own. He thought mending a menial task, so I was not permitted it, even though I enjoy sewing. He did not consider it proper for women to be educated, so I was forbidden his books and his library. He felt that newspapers were printed for the exclusive use of men and were not for my eyes. He decided what I should wear, who my friends should be, how much exercise I should or shouldn't take while I was increasing, and what name my child should have. He considered that my sole responsibilities as his wife were to plan his entertainments, be the perfect hostess at his dinner table, and warm his bed."

Lady Sherwood listened to Sarah's story with growing incredulity, and the bitterness of the last words was not lost on her. She leaned forward sympathetically and laid a hand on Sarah's knee. "He didn't abuse you?" Her voice revealed her shock at the thought.

"I suppose that would depend on what you mean by the word *abuse*," Sarah answered. "He came to me on our wedding night and frightened me witless, for he offered me no reassurances or instruction and had no patience with my ignorance. For a full week I became nauseated at the thought of his touching me, and then, slowly, I began to accept what I could not change, as a blind man accepts the darkness. During the day, I could bear his behavior, for I learned to keep myself above it—I bent continually to his will, and I never fought back, so he never knew how much I despised him. But at night . . . at night he had everything his own way, for then he would strip from me every shred of dignity. I felt that I had no more worth than a piece of clothing, to be used and then cast aside. I had decided that I would rather be dead than married forever to this man, when I discovered I was to have a child.

"After Jimmy was born, things were better, for James didn't concern himself with the nursery, and I finally found one portion of my life that he did not control. He undoubtedly considered the rearing of children an unmasculine activity, and beneath him. He was just beginning to take an interest in Jimmy when he was killed. I had so dreaded his influence over my son, for I could not bear the thought that Jimmy would grow up like his father. Now I have Sir Winston to contend with, and although he has not yet tried to take control, I fear the day when he may decide that Jimmy could benefit from a man's influence in his affairs. I know he would not hesitate to order my son's life as he does mine. I also know that I would be powerless to prevent him from doing precisely as he wishes. He never seeks my opinion, and if I do happen to voice it, he invariably overrides me, and his will consistently prevails."

"Have you considered, Sarah, that if you were to marry again, you could remove both yourself and your son from the power of Sir Winston?"

"Yes, and place us once again in the power of a husband!" Sarah replied scathingly. "I have sworn I will never give a man that kind of control over me again."

"But certainly, if you were to choose the man yourself and not have him chosen for you . . . ?"

"I would not trust myself to make such a choice, Lady Sherwood. I have known many charming men during the past five years, and some of them seemed the type to make fine husbands. But I think there are many men who leave their charm outside the bedroom door! I would be a fool to take such a chance. Sir Winston has a great deal of control over my life, but my body is my own, and I intend for it to remain so."

"I understand the way you feel, my dear, but you may be missing a great deal of happiness in your life by pursuing such a course."

"Perhaps I am," Sarah agreed. "But I assure you, ma'am, that I would much rather do without the happiness than take a chance on the misery again."

Lady Sherwood had discovered what Elizabeth wished to know, but she had a sinking feeling that this information would do little to aid Richard's suit. Sarah carried deep scars, and the years of trauma that had put them there would not be easily forgotten. She was a woman of strong convictions, and having once known the feel of a strangle hold on her spirit, Lady Sherwood thought it unlikely that she would turn from her decision to keep herself free in the future.

Her heart went out to Richard, for she knew he was not one to commit himself lightly, and he would find the rejection hard to accept. The sad thing was that she felt certain her son would be the perfect man for Sarah. She also believed that Sarah held Richard in affection, for no woman who viewed the majority of men with mistrust would allow her son to spend time with a man whom she did not hold in considerable esteem.

Richard and his sisters arrived in Surrey on the tenth of February after a long, cold journey, for the winter was one of the hardest in anyone's memory, with heavy snowfalls and bitter winds. They were travel-weary, but spoke with enthusiasm of their stay in Leicestershire.

Two days later, Richard was driving his curricle home from the village when he met Sarah at the end of the drive to Sherwood Manor. He knew she was walking home, for she often did so, claiming that she enjoyed the exercise when the weather permitted. Richard pulled up his pair beside her. It was the first time they had met since his return home.

"Good day, Mrs. Ellis. You have been to the Manor?"

"Yes, Captain. I spent the morning with your mother and sisters. Did you enjoy the hunting?"

"Very much. We had some excellent meetings, and the company was congenial, but it is good to be home. May I offer you a ride to Ellis End?"

"I like to walk."

"I know you do, but I would enjoy the pleasure of your company." When she hesitated, he added, "I will not make things uncomfortable for you, I promise."

He had transferred the reins to his left hand and was reaching his right hand down to her, and in that moment she made her decision. She stepped up to the carriage, put her hand in his, and felt herself pulled easily up to sit beside him.

As he set his horses in motion she said, "I have never been driven by you, Captain. Jimmy says you are an excellent whip."

"Jimmy is biased. The next time we are in London I will have Lord Stanton take him up. One exhibition of Julian's skill will be enough to lower my meager talents in Jimmy's eyes."

He spoke in a light, bantering tone, but she answered in more serious accents. "You're wrong, Captain, for nothing could do that. I am almost certain that you have risen even above the Duke of Wellington in Jimmy's esteem."

He glanced at her quickly, suspecting her of mockery, but her face was grave. "I missed him while I was gone."

"He missed you, too, and is eager to see you. But I told him he must not present himself upon your threshold only moments after you had crossed it yourself."

They continued a light conversation until they were nearly arrived at the house, and then Richard said abruptly, "Mrs. Ellis, I have promised that I would not make this drive uncomfortable for you, and indeed, I do not wish to do so, but there is something I feel I must say. I have no wish to plague you with my attentions, for you have made it plain that you do not welcome them. But I wish you to know that my feelings are unchanged, and my offer stands. I promise that I will not mention this matter again if you will give me your assurance that you would inform me should there be any change in your sentiments."

I will never change my mind, she thought, but she said, "You have my promise, Captain. If you will give me your hand down, you need not see me in, for I know you will not care to leave your horses. Good-bye, Captain. Thank you for seeing me home."

Alighting from the carriage, Sarah entered the house and immediately summoned Jimmy. She had hoped that during his absence, Captain Sherwood would come to terms with her refusal and learn to accept it. After his words today, it was clear that he had no intention of doing anything of the kind. It was left to her, then, to bring to an end any hope for a future for them, so that he, at least, could forget her and get on with his life.

She thought once again of Sir Winston's intention to move the family to Jamaica. She had considered asking Sir Winston if she could stay on with Jimmy at Ellis End, promising to engage a companion if he balked at the idea of her living alone. But now, suddenly, Sarah began to think that Jamaica might be the answer to her problem, and as Jimmy entered the room in response to her summons she greeted him almost enthusiastically.

"Jimmy, I'm sure you've heard your grandfather speaking of his plans to move to Jamaica. What would you think of our going with him?"

"You mean to visit him there, Mama?"

"No, Jimmy. I mean to live there with him, permanently."

"Leave Ellis End! Leave England permanently?"

"Well, you would, of course, come back one day, my love, for this house will be yours when your grandfather is gone. But we must all hope that will be many years from now."

"Do you want to go, Mama?"

"Yes, I think I should like to go."

"But what about our friends?" he asked. "Won't you miss them?"

"Yes, of course we shall miss our friends, but there are times in our life when we must make changes, and sometimes that means leaving old friends behind. We will make new friends in our new home."

"And what of Captain Sherwood, Mama? Won't you miss him?"

"Yes, Jimmy, I shall miss him. Perhaps he would write to you." Obviously the boy found this suggestion unpalatable, for he stared stonily at her, saying nothing, and finally she continued, "Will it be so hard for you to leave him, then?"

"Yes, Mama, it will," he said with feeling, "for he has been more than a friend to me. He seems more like a father really. And it isn't that he spoils me, either, although he has been awfully generous. He can be quite strict, and demanding of perfection, yet at the same time he always makes allowances for my shortcomings, and never fails to encourage me."

"In your driving, you mean?"

"In that, and in everything, for we talk of many other things besides horses, Mama."

She looked at him in surprise, for she hadn't thought to wonder what they discussed during the many hours they spent together. "What do you talk about?" she asked curiously.

"Oh, he's told me about the time he spent in the army, and we have discussed politics. He has taught me a great deal about farming and estate management. And we've talked about people, and the relationships between people, and the value of things like integrity and honor." Sarah stared at her son in amazement as he continued. "And he's answered some questions I had about girls."

"Jimmy!"

"Well, why shouldn't I have questions?" he asked defensively. "I'm not a baby anymore, Mama. And you must know there are things a fellow would just as lief not ask his mother."

"I told you long ago, Jimmy, that I would willingly answer any question you had."

"I know you did, Mama, but you must see that it is ever so much easier to ask such things of a man than of a woman."

She had to admit the truth of this, but her head was spinning with all he had told her—estate management, integrity, politics! She had never imagined! "I had no idea you had grown so fond of the captain, Jimmy. I can see that it will be harder than I thought for you to leave him."

"I am not fond of him, Mama. I love him. And somehow, I thought you did, too."

Soon after their return to Surrey, Elizabeth asked her mother what she had been able to learn from Sarah. Lady Sherwood told her daughter that she had discovered nothing that she felt could help Richard's cause, and she strictly forbade Elizabeth to involve herself further in the matter.

Lady Sherwood could see little justification in revealing Sarah's confidences to her first-born, and she had absolutely no intention of sharing such revelations with her youngest and most innocent child. But one morning, nearly two weeks after their return, Charlotte came home from the village with two pieces of news, both of which the family found interesting, and one of which profoundly affected Richard and made Lady Sherwood reconsider her decision to keep Sarah's confidence.

Charlotte erupted into the parlor where Richard, Elizabeth, and Lady Sherwood had gathered before luncheon. "We have had a letter from Harriet, and it's the most wonderful news! She is increasing! You shall have your wish at last, Mama. You will be a grandmother by September!"

Clearly this was news to be exclaimed over, but since it was a subject soon exhausted, Charlotte recollected her other news and directed her question to her brother. "Did you know, Richard, that the Ellis family is planning a move to Jamaica? The vicar told me that the house is to let and has been on the market for nearly a week."

Lady Sherwood watched as her son turned noticeably pale, but he answered Charlotte's question easily. "No. I hadn't heard of it. I'm surprised that Jimmy said nothing. I was with him only yesterday."

"Evidently, they plan to leave quite soon. Sarah had mentioned that Sir Winston has property there, but I never imagined they would wish to live there. We will miss Sarah dreadfully, won't we, Lizzie? She has become much like one of the family."

Lord Sherwood joined them at that moment, and Charlotte turned the conversation back to her first item of news. Both Elizabeth and Lady Sherwood noticed Richard quietly leave the room, but when Elizabeth rose to follow him, Lady Sherwood took her arm and spoke quietly.

"Let me go to him, Lizzie. I think that perhaps it is time I tried to help—if I can." She caught up with her son in the front hall and asked if he would spare a moment for her.

"Could it wait until later, Mother?"

"It is about Sarah that I must speak with you, Richard, and no, I don't think that it can wait."

For a moment as he regarded her, she felt he was about to ask her, politely of course, not to interfere. But after a slight pause he said, "Very well, Mother. Shall we go into the library?"

Richard handed his mother to a sofa near the hearth and bent to add a few logs to the fire.

"Richard," Lady Sherwood began, "you know that I do not like to meddle in your private affairs, but it is not an easy thing for a mother to see her children unhappy. This is a subject that perhaps a mother should not speak of with her son, but if not I, then I cannot imagine who would speak. I think I know the kind of man my son is. I think I know that you value other people's feelings and their worth. I think I know that you would love and respect your wife, and do your best to make her happy and content. But if it is Sarah that you have set your heart upon, then there is something that you must know before you continue to pursue her."

"I suppose Lizzie told you that I asked Sarah to marry me?"

"Not in so many words, but she hinted as much."

"Then I suppose she also hinted that Sarah refused me, and offers me no hope."

"I know why Sarah refuses to hear your suit, Richard. She was unhappy in her first marriage and fears a similar experience should she marry again."

"I guessed as much," he said, "but I don't know what makes her think she would be unhappy with me. I know she cares for me."

"Sarah fears placing herself in a subservient and de-

207

fenseless position, and she also fears the physical relationship of marriage.''

''But, Mother, that's not possible! She was married for five years! She has a child!''

''Listen to me, my son. She was married five years to a man who did not cherish her, a man who allowed her no freedom either in thought or deed, a man who came to her bed with no word of love for her, a man who used her, and hurt her, and never brought her any pleasure. I think I need not tell you that this was not a marriage in which any woman could be happy. Sarah must never involve herself in a marriage that will not offer her the kind of freedom and contentment that your father and I have found. If you persist in wanting her, and if you succeed in having her agree to become your wife, then you must be willing to be patient. She must have time to feel your love for her, time to trust you, time to believe that selfish passion is not your motive in seeking her bed.'' Richard had turned away to gaze into the fire but, seeing the tenseness of his broad shoulders, Lady Sherwood could sense his disgust for a man he had never known and who was long dead. ''There is something else, Richard,'' she continued, ''that you must consider. There is the possibility that the scars her first husband left cannot be erased, and that they will cast a shadow over your own happiness. Yet I have reason to hope that it may not be so, for although I have seen some part of her pain, and know that the wounds are deep, I have also seen her love for her son, which knows no bounds. If she is capable of such love for her child, can we not assume that such a love for you could be possible as well?''

''We must hope it will be so, Mother, for I will not give up seeking her hand.''

''Even though you know she has a prejudice against your sex?''

''Especially now that I do know it.'' He turned and took

208

her hands in his. "Thank you, Mother. You can't know how much you have helped me. There is no worse feeling than to be unaware of your enemy's position or his strength. I have been fighting this battle with my hands tied. But now that I have some idea of what I'm up against, I have more confidence that I can gain a victory in the end. I promise you, I intend to put up one hell of a fight."

Lady Sherwood smiled. "I thought that was what you would say, and I am glad we had this talk. I would have all my children happy in life."

Richard bent his fair head and planted a kiss on her cheek. "And so we will be, if we continue to accept wise counsel."

Two days later, when Sir Winston drove Virginia over to visit with Charlotte, and Sir Winston himself disappeared into the library with Lord Sherwood, Richard had Sultry saddled immediately and rode to Ellis End, knowing that he would find Sarah alone.

A footman showed him into the salon, and when Sarah joined him a few moments later, he barely waited until the door was closed before he said, "Is it true that you plan to move to Jamaica?"

"Yes. Sir Winston has growing business concerns there. He plans to build a house, and he wants me to take charge of it for him."

"Let his daughter keep his house," Richard said bluntly. "Sarah, don't run away from me!"

"You promised that you would not bring this subject up again, sir," she objected.

"That was before you decided to go halfway round the world to avoid me. My God, Sarah! Do you think that putting an ocean between us will make me care for you less?"

"Perhaps not, but it will be easier—"

"Easier for whom? For you? For Jimmy? Sarah, don't

do this to us. You know that I love you, for I have told you so, and I have tried to show you in every way I know. You have tried to make me believe that you don't return my affection, but you haven't succeeded. You gave yourself away that day you kissed me, and I don't think you would feel the need to run away like this unless you cared for me. Do you have the courage to admit how you feel, or would you rather deny that you love me?" He took her by the shoulders as he spoke and turned her roughly to face him. She looked up at him, and as their eyes met he said, "Go on, Mrs. Ellis, deny that you love me, and try to make it convincing."

His hands gripped her painfully, but she was only dimly aware of it, for he was waiting for her answer and she could not will herself to speak against her heart. She felt tears stinging her eyes and said suddenly, almost angrily, "Oh, very well, I love you," and then repeated, in a whisper, "I love you."

"Will you marry me?'

"No."

"Sarah, not every man is like your first husband!" Her eyes flew to his face, and he read the question in them. "Yes, my mother told me that James Ellis was cruel to you, but I had guessed as much myself. If you truly think that I would be the same type of husband, acquit me, for my tastes don't run to sadistic abuse." He let go her shoulders and took her hands in his, his voice softening as he added, "We can be happy together, Sarah, I know we can, but you must trust me. Give me a chance to prove that life can be special for us. Please, say you will marry me."

She jerked her hands away and turned from him. "How many ways must I say no before you will understand? I have been married before. I do not wish to be married again."

"You have been married. You have never been loved. I

am offering both love and marriage, neither without the other."

"I want neither from you, can't you understand that?" she shouted at him. "I must be free! I will not endanger my freedom for any man, regardless of my feelings."

He had never heard her speak with such passion, and he stared at her incredulously. "What did that man do to you?" He spoke it more as a thought than as a question needing an answer, but even as he heard himself utter the words, he decided that perhaps it needed answering, so he repeated it. "What *did* he do to you, Sarah? Tell me!"

"Didn't your mother tell you?"

"She said he allowed you no personal freedom, that he didn't love you or even treat you kindly, that he wanted you for self-gratification and nothing more."

"Is that not specific enough for you?" she asked bitterly.

"And you refuse to marry again because you fear a revival of that kind of treatment?" He felt a subtle rage building as the implications of her rejection materialized. "And you are refusing to marry me because you think that I . . . you think that *I* could behave in such a manner? Good God," he said, his words disbelieving, "I have been deluding myself from the beginning. If you could believe such things of me, then you know *nothing* of me. To know that you would even consider me *capable* of such behavior is a thought more humiliating than a hundred rejections, and there can be no hope for us—no hope at all." As he finished speaking he turned and walked toward the door. He had thought it impossible for her to hurt him any more, and yet she had managed to do so. He was a fool to have given her the opportunity. When he reached to door, he stopped with his hand on the latch and spoke again, making no attempt to hide the anger and bitterness in his voice, "If I don't see you again before you sail—*Bon voyage*."

Even as he turned the handle, Sarah cast herself across

the room to him. "Richard!" she cried. "Please, please, don't go! Not like this." He turned to face her as she spoke his name, and now he found her anxiously grasping both his hands, unable to meet his eyes, mumbling a disjointed apology as her tears feel freely. "I'm sorry . . . please forgive me . . . you mustn't think . . . I didn't, I don't think you could be cruel . . . at least, perhaps once I did, but I don't now, not since I've come to know you. Oh, I'm not saying any of this properly! I love you, and I would like nothing better than to be with you always, *but I am afraid*!"

Richard pulled his hands from her grasp, and gathering her into his arms, held her close until she was calmer. And then, still without speaking, he tipped her face up to his and kissed the tears from her cheeks, and then kissed her trembling lips until her senses swam and she was limp and nearly swooning in his arms.

"Trust me enough to say you will marry me, Sarah Ellis, and when you have promised to be my wife, then I will tell you the kind of marriage we shall have."

"I will marry you, Richard, I promise," she whispered.

"Good, and now I will make you a promise." He led her to a sofa and sat with her in the circle of his arm. "Never, from this moment forward, will you have cause to be frightened, either of me or of any part of our life together. I think we will get on far better than you imagine, but if you have any fears or concerns, you need only voice them, and we shall deal with them, between us. You may have all the same freedom within our marriage that you now have, perhaps more, for you need not answer to Sir Winston for anything save his interest in his grandson. As far as Jimmy is concerned, I have no intention of ever bypassing your wishes. He is your son, and in all the months I have known you, I have never seen your judgment on matters concerning him to be anything but sound and sensible. I foresee no problems between us over him.

And *please*, my love, you must *never* see me as any kind of a physical threat to you. I would not willingly harm a single hair of your head, and I swear to you, on my honor, that I will never force you to do anything you do not wish. It will require nothing more than the simple word no to deter me from any course. Do you understand, Sarah?"

"Yes, I understand."

"If you will give me the right to take responsibility for your welfare, and for Jimmy's, and if you will give me the right only to call you wife—then all the rest can wait—for however long it takes."

They remained seated together on the sofa, heedless both of time and convention. It was there that Sir Winston found them almost thirty minutes later, and it was he who was first to receive the news of their engagement.

20

The following morning at breakfast, Richard apprised his family of his engagement, and there were mingled expressions of surprise and delight. His mother and sisters were full of questions like when, where, and how, but Richard laughingly fended them off, saying that he and Sarah hadn't discussed it but no doubt the wedding would be quite soon.

Lord Sherwood congratulated his son warmly and some time later left the breakfast parlor to go to his study, but he returned a few moments later with the London papers in his hand. "Bonaparte has escaped from Elba," he said simply.

No one had an adequate response to this news. They had all thought that with Napoleon's defeat by the Allies the previous spring and his abdication and retirement to Elba, Europe had seen the last of him. During the days that followed, even as Richard and Sarah made plans for their wedding, it was learned that Bonaparte had landed in the south of France, and was marching on Paris.

Lord Sherwood soon returned to London, promising that he would come down for the wedding even if it should be for only a day, and Lady Sherwood reluctantly separated from her husband, remaining behind in Surrey to supervise the preparations for the marriage of her eldest child, the date having been set for the twenty-fifth of March.

On the morning following Lord Sherwood's departure, Richard received, by special messenger, a confidential letter from his father. He was alone in the library when it arrived, and he opened it with curiosity, but the expectant look on his face faded to a deep frown as his eyes traveled down the page.

Richard,
I arrived in town today to find the house and the servants in an uproar. It seems that last night someone managed to break into my book-room from the outside. The place is a complete shambles. The intruder was not content with emptying all the desk drawers and files. Almost all the books were pulled from the shelves and scattered everywhere. God only knows what he thought he would find, but he left no possible hiding place unexplored. The carpets were taken up, pictures torn from the walls, sofa cushions slashed. Some documents are missing, of course. I will not be sure which ones until I have time to sort through the rubble. The most amazing thing is that none of the servants heard anything and were unaware of any problem until they opened the room this morning.

I feel I owe it to you to mention, in the strictest confidence, of course, that at a closed meeting at the War Office this afternoon, the name of your friend Charles Warmington was raised. It seems that he was in his cups several evenings ago at White's. That in itself is unusual for your friend, I think, but he was heard to say several less than respectful things about the army—his (your) regiment in particular. Most of them dealt with what he considered his unfair medical discharge. He insisted his present disability is not sufficient reason to bar him from his chosen profession. I need not tell you that in these troubled times such remarks do not always fall upon sympathetic ears. Mr. Warmington's comments do him no credit when there are several senior ministers suspecting spies under every rock.

Please understand that I make no accusation with my next words, but as memory serves me, Warmington was present at both functions where our spy made his intrusions, and the night of the shooting I cannot recall seeing him for some time after the shot was fired. He was not helping with either of the wounds initially, nor was he among those men who carried Elizabeth and Lord Stanton upstairs.

You must realize that under any other circumstances I would keep this information to myself, but as you were privy to the intrusions into my papers, and as Warmington is not only your best friend but soon to be your groomsman as well, I felt myself obliged to write. You may tell your mother and sisters about the break-in, as there will be no hiding it from them. The room will need to be redone, of course, and the servants will talk. I am letting it be called a robbery.

Yours, etc.
Your Father

Richard read the letter through again and then rose and walked to the fire. He tried to picture Charles selling information to the French, Charles rifling through his father's desk, Charles striking James down while his cousin lay seriously wounded and perhaps dying abovestairs.

Even as he bent to lay the parchment on the flames, he

216

reconsidered, and crossing to his desk, drew a fresh piece of paper forward. He wrote a short letter to his father, refusing to believe any ill of his friend, for disappointment over a lost career was a world away from treason. Then as he folded the letter he decided not to send it. He rang for Jepson instead and ordered the chaise. He departed for London within the hour and sat in conversation with his father by late afternoon.

Later that evening, Richard called at the Earl of Haigh's town residence and found Charles at home. He was alone in the library when Richard was admitted, and he smiled with pleasure when he saw his friend.

"Richard! I didn't know you were in London. Did you have my letter?"

"Yes, and I thank you for agreeing to stand up with me."

"Always pleased to lend my support to a friend. Can't say I was too surprised when you wrote me of your engagement. It's been easy enough to see these past months where your interest has been. Allow me to offer my congratulations in person. You and Mrs. Ellis are well matched. I hope you will be very happy together."

"Thank you, Charles."

"But you haven't said what brings you to town. Is it this news of Boney?"

"In part, yes. Charles—there is a matter I must discuss with you. It's . . . awkward."

Charles sobered instantly at his friend's serious tone. "What is it?"

"I received a letter this morning from my father, and it is that letter that has brought me to town. The letter concerns you, Charles."

"Me? In what way?"

"I would like you to read it for yourself, but before you do, there is something I must explain. There have been several instances since last fall, when my father's book-

217

room has been invaded by some unknown person. Once during our ball last September, again on the night Lizzie and Julian were shot, and most recently just two nights ago. Each time, delicate documents were taken."

"Military documents?"

"Yes."

"I fail to understand how this concerns me."

"Read the letter, Charles." Richard handed it over as he spoke, and Charles took it, moving to stand in the light of a candelabra on the mantel.

He began reading with interest, but as he continued down the page his face grew stern and then angry. When he finished, he looked across at Richard, and his eyes were both cold and bitter.

"Clearly Lord Sherwood believes me to be the spy he seeks."

"He thinks no such thing! In that letter he simply put some facts and possibilities before me and desired my opinion. Are they facts, Charles? Were you drunk and did you say those things?"

"Yes, I was drunk, and yes, I am sure I said those things your father credits me with a great deal more besides. Does it therefore follow that I am a damned traitor?"

"No. And so I have just told my father. But the scene he describes is hard to imagine."

"The things I said were innocent enough, but I suppose they could sound less than loyal to a dedicated flag-waver. But part of it is true. I am bitter about the army turning me off."

"And it's partly because of Charlotte, isn't it?"

"If I had stayed in, I may have had a majority by now. As it is—"

"Your feelings for Charlotte haven't changed, then?"

"No. She's the only woman I have ever had any serious interest in. I suspect it was Rayburn's prattling the other night that got me started drinking so heavily. He was sitting at the next table, discussing your sister's many fine qualities and his intention to try to fix his interest with her in the coming season. I tipped the bottle too often and took my frustrations out on the army. I never dreamt it would come to this." He slapped the letter as he spoke. "It won't happen again, Richard, you can assure your father of that."

"You have given up on Charlotte, then?"

"Your sister is not for me. There is too great a gulf between us. Nor can I think that Lord Sherwood would welcome me as a son-in-law after this." Once again he indicated the letter he held, and Richard twitched it from him and tossed it onto the fire.

"This is rubbish, and we both know it, and you wrong my father if you think he would judge a man based on suspicion alone. That letter was not meant to accuse, but to inform me of what was being said of you."

"Do you think your father meant you to show it to me?"

"I think he knew I would if I thought you innocent."

As the month of March wore on, everyone in the Sherwood household found themselves fully occupied, for in addition to preparing for the wedding, there were arrangements to be made for their removal to town for the Season soon afterward. Richard and Sarah would stay behind and begin their married life in the solitude of the country, but Lady Sherwood and her daughters were to leave for town soon after the wedding. In early March they made a short excursion to their favorite dressmaker in London to order new gowns. These arrived only five days before the wedding itself, and Mason, Lady Sherwood's dresser, had them unpacked immediately to be sure that no last-minute alterations were necessary.

Sarah arrived in Elizabeth's room that afternoon to find her stepping into a beautiful confection of white gauze over satin, and she exclaimed in delight as she saw the dress.

"Elizabeth! How lovely! You will quite cast me in the shade!"

Elizabeth smiled at her soon-to-be sister but only said, "It is pretty, isn't it? But you know very well, Sarah, that your dress is nothing short of exquisite. What Richard will say when he sees you in it I can't imagine."

Sarah smiled as she considered the thought herself. From the moment she had agreed to marry Richard, she had been inextricably swept along on the tide of his family's enthusiasm. Although the thought of marrying again filled her with trepidation, and she was more than once assailed by doubts, she was determined to be Richard's wife and joined wholeheartedly in the wedding preparations.

Jimmy had been overwhelmingly relieved to learn that he was not to leave the captain behind but was to gain him as a stepfather instead. Sir Winston did not seem to consider it surprising that Sarah should wish to marry again. If he had misgivings or objections to Sarah's plans, he did not voice them but merely said that his daughter-in-law was her own mistress and must please herself. A tenant had been found for Ellis End, and he and Virginia were set to sail on the first of April. Sir Winston graciously accepted Richard's offer to oversee his property during his extended absence from England.

Charlotte's abigail struck her head in at the door to ask if Miss Mason would step along to Miss Charlotte's room to assure herself that her dress would do. "Go on, Mason," Elizabeth said, "Mrs. Ellis will help me out of my gown—if you see nothing amiss?"

"No, nothing, miss. It looks perfect to me." She bustled off on the words, and Sarah helped Elizabeth out of the gown again.

"I would love to have a gown slightly off the shoulders as yours is, Sarah," Elizabeth said, "but even if I were old enough for such a daring cut, I shan't ever be able to wear it now." She plopped herself down in front of the dressing table mirror and pulled her chemise from her right shoulder, exposing the puckered scar left by Lord Granbrooke's bullet.

Sarah watched her sympathetically. Even though Elizabeth was not in the least vain, it could not be easy for a young girl to accept such a disfiguring scar.

"It has been five months now," Elizabeth continued, "I think it has finished with fading away. What do you think, Sarah?"

"I think that it will fade a bit more, Lizzie. You have such lovely shoulders, does it fret you a great deal, having that scar?" There was so much concern is Sarah's voice that Elizabeth met her eyes in the mirror in surprise.

"No, Sarah, truly," she assured her. "I seldom think of it. It was a small price to pay to protect him. I would have died willingly." She was still watching Sarah in the mirror and saw the startled, arrested look in her eyes.

Sarah stepped around in front of Elizabeth, meeting her gaze directly, and her next words were as much a statement as a question. "You are in love with him, aren't you?"

Elizabeth could see no reason to deny it as she answered in her typical truthful and straightforward manner. "Yes, I do love him, though I try not to think of it."

"But, Lizzie, surely—"

"Sarah," Elizabeth interrupted, "it can't signify. No doubt there are countless girls in love with him, for he is very eligible, you know."

"Countless girls who would risk their life for his? No. That I cannot believe!"

"Well, perhaps you're right, but it can make no difference, for he thinks of me only as a friend, and as his friend's little sister. He has no interest in me beyond that."

"Oh, Lizzie, are you sure?"

"Yes. I'm quite sure. He doesn't believe in love, you know, not the kind Mama and Papa share, and the kind you feel for Richard and he for you. He has told me that he has no desire to marry and is content that the title should pass on someday through Henry or Giles."

"The right woman might change his mind," Sarah insisted.

"Perhaps. But it won't be me. He likes me, I know, and he's been unfailingly kind, but he has shown no romantic interest in me, Sarah." When Sarah still looked doubtful, she added, "If he were to become passionate toward me, Sarah, I'm sure I would notice."

At that, Sarah burst out laughing. "Yes, Lizzie, I'm sure you would!"

Elizabeth leaned forward to take Sarah's hand and clasp it warmly. "You have made Richard so happy. I am pleased and proud that I shall have you for my sister."

As the days passed, the unrest in the country grew. There was now little doubt in anyone's mind that they would soon be at war again, and this time it seemed as if the Duke of Wellington and Bonaparte would meet at last on the same field of conflict. Napoleon had entered Paris on the twentieth of March to find that King Louis had fled the city and moved with his court to Ghent. The British Army had begun to muster in Belgium, and a letter from Jonathan made it clear that the army near Brussels expected action in the not-too-distant future, for he spoke of sending Harriet home if and when it became unsafe. Brussels, he wrote, was very gay, despite the French threat. Wellington was delayed at the Congress of Vienna, but they expected him in Brussels shortly, to take command of the Allied Forces.

Lord Sherwood was actively involved in commandeering ships wherever possible and arranging for transport of troops, horses, artillery, munitions, and supplies to Ostend. He was busy but wrote as often as possible with what news he could give. With little idea of how soon Napoleon would strike, it was imperative that Wellington have the troops and supplies he demanded as quickly as possible.

Just two days before the wedding, Richard and Sarah sat

together in the library at Sherwood Manor. Elizabeth was reading on the other side of the room. For the past few days, Sarah had been aware of a growing restlessness in Richard, and she now decided to say what was on her mind. "You're concerned about the coming conflict, aren't you?"

"Yes, I am. An Allied army, thrown together in great haste, will not be an easy force to command."

"But certainly if anyone can do so, it will be the Duke?"

"I am sure he will be equal to the task. It's just bad luck that our best infantry, almost all the Peninsular veterans, are in America. I don't see how they can hope to be back in time."

"But your father wrote that he felt the cavalry would be under orders soon. Surely once they are in Belgium we can be easier?" He didn't answer, and after a moment she asked, "Do you wish you were going with them? With your old regiment?"

"Yes . . . no . . . I don't know. I feel so useless here. I know many untried troops will be sent over. I could make myself useful."

"Richard, if you feel it is your duty to rejoin, then you must do so. I wouldn't like to think that any consideration for me would keep you from doing what you feel is right. You mustn't think of me. . . ."

"Of course I must think of you," he objected. "What would you have me do? Marry in two days, and take ship for Belgium in three?"

"Yes, if you feel you must!"

"If you keep this up," he said, "you will have me believing that you wish to be rid of me!"

"I wish for you to have the same freedom in our marriage that you have promised me."

"None of us will ever know any real freedom as long as Bonaparte threatens Europe. He must be stopped once and for all, if there is to be any lasting peace."

"So will you go?"

"Not for the present. I will await developments, and make a decision later. Come here, my love." His troubled frown lifted, and he smiled as he drew her into his arms. Sarah glanced anxiously at Elizabeth, but Elizabeth, deep in her book, or pretending to be, didn't even look up.

The twenty-fifth of March dawned cloudy and cool but with only a hint of rain in the air. Most of the wedding guests who were to stay at Sherwood Manor or Ellis End had arrived on the previous day. Lord Sherwood arrived late on the evening of the twenty-fourth, as he had promised, but could stay less than twenty-four hours. The wedding day itself was a cheerful, happy occasion, but at the back of everyone's mind was the gathering threat across the Channel.

Two months had passed since the hunting in Leicestershire, two months during which Elizabeth had examined and dealt with her feelings for Lord Stanton. But when he arrived on the afternoon preceding the wedding, she knew instantly that it had not been time enough. A large number of wedding guests were gathered in the parlor when the viscount and his cousin Charles were announced, and Elizabeth could only be grateful for the distraction that such a large group offered. She had thought herself prepared to meet him, but no sooner had she set eyes upon him than she found her pulse racing. How could she have gone all those months without realizing how she felt? She determined to greet him as normally as possible and then take care to avoid him for the duration of his visit. Certainly that should be easy enough with a houseful of guests, and with the large number of persons invited to the wedding on the following day.

When the viscount finally came around the room to where she stood, she had gathered her senses enough to greet him calmly. She then greeted Charles and introduced them both

224

to her mother's sister, Mrs. Wyeton-Smith, and then they passed on and she was able to breathe easier. She left the room soon afterward, making a quick stop at the dining room to be sure that she would be seated nowhere near the viscount at dinner. Somehow she managed to get through the evening, although she found her eyes often straying toward him when she knew he wasn't looking. How handsome he was, she thought . . . how dear . . . How foolish she had been to allow herself to love him.

The wedding ceremony was nearly unbearable for Elizabeth. She listened to Richard and Sarah exchange their vows with tears running unheeded down her face. Her mother handed her a handkerchief, but she didn't see why anyone should care. Everyone cried at weddings. It was expected. Everything was working out so perfectly for her brother and her friend. They loved each other, and they were getting married. Surely that was a simple enough thing to do. Not for the man you have chosen to love, Elizabeth Sherwood, she told herself. You have fallen in love with a man who has no use for marriage, so even if you could encourage him to care for you, it would lead nowhere.

Elizabeth had come to believe that Lord Stanton was a man who carefully guarded his heart, failing to believe that love could ever occupy any meaningful place in his life. In this weakness of his, she recognized her greatest strength. She understood love and knew its worth, but she also knew that her love alone would never be enough.

So she listened to Richard and Sarah pledge their love and faithfulness, and found herself jealous of their opportunity to do so. She returned her mother's handkerchief and dug in her reticule for one of her own. She withdrew a large man's handkerchief that had been in her possession since Stanton had lent it to her in the book room the night after her escape from Granbrooke. She had never wanted to give it back, not really knowing why, and now it was all she had that belonged to him. She smoothed the fine lawn under her hands, studying the delicate monogram skillfully embroidered across one corner, JWF, and wondering, not for the first time, for what name the W stood. In less than a week, they would be removing to London for the Season, and she would meet Lord Stanton often. She couldn't decide if she should view this prospect with pleasure or regret.

Elizabeth managed to avoid any private conversation with the viscount throughout the day of the wedding, and she excused herself early in the evening, determined to make no appearance the following morning until she was sure he had departed for London. Richard and Sarah took leave of their guests shortly after nine o'clock and retired to their private apartments in the east wing.

Richard kissed his wife good night at her door and went on to his own bedchamber, where his valet awaited him. He was soon ready for bed, but he did not retire. He sat instead before the fire, staring into the glowing embers. There had been so many hopelessly depressing weeks in the past few months when he had been convinced that Sarah would never be his. Now, knowing that she was finally his wife, he was overwhelmed by almost equal portions of elation and relief, and he promised himself that he would never allow her to regret marrying him. He rose suddenly, and walking to the communicating door to his wife's room, passed through it without knocking.

Sarah sat before her dressing table in her nightgown and wrapper, while her maid brushed out her hair. She turned her head as she heard her husband enter and then dismissed her maid. "You need not come in the morning until I ring for you, Betty. Good night." The woman left, closing the door softly, and as Richard crossed the room to his wife, she rose to her feet and turned to face him.

"I think I have wanted to see your hair down like this from the very first day we met. It's . . . indescribable." He swept the thick, auburn hair from her shoulders and let

226

his eyes travel down the gown she wore. "You are just as lovely in that, my dear, as you were in your wedding gown." He took her hands in his and brought them both to his lips. "My wife . . . I don't think I will ever tire of calling you that . . . my lovely, breathtaking wife." His voice was infinitely tender, his eyes smiling, and Sarah stared mutely up at him as he continued. "This is our wedding night, Sarah, and I do not wish to spend it alone. Can you understand that? Do you mind if I stay?"

She didn't know how to answer him, so she said nothing but went willingly into his embrace and raised her face for his kiss. They clung to each other as long minutes passed, and finally Richard put her from him and, taking her hands once again, said simply, "Come to bed." As he turned to lead her away, she hesitated, and he smiled indulgently. "You are too suspicious, my love. Just come to bed. It has been a long and tiring day, and we could both use some sleep."

She accompanied him to the edge of the bed, where he helped her out of her wrapper. As she got into bed he took off his own dressing gown, revealing his nightshirt beneath, snuffed the bedside candle, and climbed in beside her. He pulled his wife close, and she found the warmth and hardness of his body strangely comforting and restful. They lay together so, nearly motionless, for a long while. Neither spoke. After some time had passed, Sarah fancied that her husband's breathing had become more even and a bit deeper, and just as she decided he had fallen asleep, he said very quietly, "I wish that you were seventeen again, Sarah, and that this were your first wedding night. I would I had the opportunity to make your life over again, to erase the pain and the disillusionment. Dear God, if I could do that, I would ask nothing more from life." She felt his arm tighten convulsively about her, and she turned her face into his shoulder and felt his lips warm on her cheek, and so they lay, until they fell asleep.

Sarah woke as the pearly light of the new day streamed through a crack in the draperies, and was momentarily startled to find her husband sleeping beside her. James had never stayed the whole night in her bed but had, without exception, come to her early, taken his pleasure of her, and then left her sometime afterward for the comfort and privacy of his own room. She moved slowly so as not to disturb Richard and, raising herself on one elbow, stared down at his face. He lay on his back, his breathing quiet and even, a fine pale stubble clearly visible on his chin. Not since the birth of her child had she looked upon another human being with such love in her heart. She reached out and laid her hand softly on his chest, for she needed and wanted to touch him. Often during her first marriage, she had wondered what she had done to deserve such a narrow-minded, tyrannical husband. Now, as she looked at Richard, she couldn't help wondering what she had done to deserve having this gentle, loving man in her life.

Richard opened his eyes and, instantly aware of her beside him, turned his head to look at her, bringing his hand up to cover hers where it lay on his nightshirt. His eyes registered immediate concern as he saw the tears in hers, and he said, "What? Tears, my love?"

She reached out to smooth the frown from his brow. "Tears of joy, my Richard, only tears of joy."

21

Lady Sherwood and her daughters joined his lordship at their London town house in the early days of April, and by the time three days had passed, most of their London acquaintance had come to call. Charles Warmington came on the second day and made no attempt to hide his pleasure at seeing them in town again. But after five days passed with no sign of Lord Stanton, Elizabeth became curious enough to ask Charles if perhaps his cousin was out of town.

"As a matter of fact he is," Charles answered. "He's gone down to Stanton Castle. Said he had some things he must settle with his steward before he leaves."

"Before he leaves . . . ?"

"Yes. For Belgium." He could not fail to see the surprise this comment brought, and he added quickly, "Didn't he tell you? He has rejoined as a volunteer and is under orders to sail in about ten days."

"He has rejoined the army!" Elizabeth exclaimed, and found it impossible to hide the consternation in her voice. "But why?"

"He has a hankering to meet Boney at last, I suppose. Quite a few fellows are doing it, you know. And heaven only knows we will need good men with all the best troops in America. He feels confident that one of his old commanders will pick him up as a staff officer, but if not, he says he will be content just to see some action."

"What of Sir Hugh? Will he go back?"

"He says not, but I know he wishes he could. Thing is, he promised his mother when he sold out that he would stay out of the army. His younger brother was killed in Spain, and Hugh's the last of the line."

"I think Richard has thought about rejoining," Elizabeth said slowly, meeting her mother's eyes steadily across the room.

"Has he said as much, Lizzie?" her mother asked.

"He said that he feels he could be more useful there than here at home. I hope that he will decide to stay. It is enough to worry for Jonathan."

"And now for Lord Stanton, too," Charlotte added.

"Yes," Elizabeth repeated stiffly. "And now for Lord Stanton, too."

"Do you expect your cousin back in town before he ships out, Mr. Warmington?" Lady Sherwood asked.

"Yes, ma'am; as a matter of fact he should be back tomorrow or the next day at the latest."

Lord Stanton did, in fact, arrive in town the following day and the day after made a morning call on the Sherwoods. Elizabeth had purposely kept to her room, hoping that he would call, and when she heard that he was sitting with her mother and Charlotte, she hurried down to speak with the butler.

"Williams, when Lord Stanton has finished visiting with my mother, would you show him to the book-room before he leaves the house?" The butler frowned at the impropriety of her request, but she was prepared for him. "I must have a few minutes to speak privately with his lordship, Williams. You know that I have been permitted to do so in the past." As he still seemed unconvinced, she used her final weapon. "Williams, his lordship has rejoined the army and leaves in a week for Belgium. I must speak with him, and you must help me!''

Williams finally relented. What harm could a few minutes do? His lordship was a fine gentleman, and a good friend to the captain. Certainly he could be trusted to hold the line with Miss Elizabeth.

Viscount Stanton was disappointed when he didn't find Elizabeth with her mother in the salon, but he said nothing beyond politely inquiring after her. He and Sir Hugh had called together, and as they were leaving, Williams handed Sir Hugh his hat and gloves but did not offer Lord Stanton his.

"Miss Elizabeth desires a few words with you, my lord, and asked if you would step to his lordship's book-room.''

Stanton raised an eyebrow at this information and turned to Sir Hugh. "I'll meet you later at White's.''

Sir Hugh nodded and left the house, and Stanton went with Williams to the book-room where he found Elizabeth alone and clearly agitated. He crossed the room to her and took both hands she held out to him, although he noticed she was unwilling to meet his eyes. "I was hoping to see you today, Miss Elizabeth, although I had not expected a private interview.''

"Your cousin said that you are leaving in a week, and I wanted to see you again, just in case—''

"In case I didn't come back? Haven't you heard of the Ferris family luck, Miss Elizabeth? You should believe in it more than most, for you have been part of it.'' He continued to hold her hands, and she continued to stare down at them until finally he said gently, "Frightened for me again, Elizabeth?''

Her eyes flew to his face then, and she brought her hands up against his chest in a protective, possessive gesture. "Yes, my lord, frightened. Frightened for all of you.''

And then, without knowing how it happened, she was in his arms, and he was kissing her, with all the insane

231

abandon he had sworn he would never permit himself. During the past two months he had managed to convince himself that he had very nearly gotten her out of his system. And then one look, one touch, was enough to destroy everything. He had no strength, no will of his own, when she was with him. What was it about this girl that made him feel as if all the light went out of the day if she wasn't there? Her mouth was soft and sweet, more passionate than he thought possible in one so young and inexperienced, and he knew that if the world would end that instant, he would have no thought for it, so long as he held this tender girl in his arms.

"Marry me, Elizabeth," he said suddenly, and the words came as a shock to his own ears. "Marry me now, before I leave!"

"Marry you! But you don't wish to be married!"

"Can't I change my mind?"

"Of course you can change your mind. But why? Why now?"

"Because I want you, Elizabeth," he said simply. "Be my wife. I'll settle a handsome fortune on you, then if I don't come back when all this is over, Henry will have the title, but you will be a very wealthy woman."

She laid her fingers over his lips. "Do not say such things, my lord. I would not marry for wealth and position."

"Then marry me because you want me as much as I want you." His arms encircled her possessively, and he drew her body tightly against his own. "And don't say it isn't so, for I would not believe you."

Elizabeth's heart was racing, and her body tingled from the close contact with him, but she forced herself to think clearly—speak sanely. "I cannot deny that I am attracted to you, my lord, but passion is an untrustworthy emotion, I think."

"Ah, yes! Elizabeth—the incurable romantic!" he answered scornfully. "You would hear words of love, then, from the man you would wed?"

"I think I would not marry without love, my lord," she said quietly. If he loves me, I have given him the perfect opportunity to say so, she thought, and then felt crushing disappointment at his next words, which seemed to come to her ears measured and tense.

"I have my answer, then," he said, as he released her and turned away, "for you will hear no words of love from me."

His words hurt her almost beyond bearing, but she would not allow him to have the last word, and she forced herself to answer him distinctly. "I think you will come to thank me for refusing your offer, my lord, when you take time to consider that you may have tired of me before the week was out, and then found yourself with an unwanted bride on your hands. Good day, my lord . . . and may God protect you." She left the room on the words, and a few moments later as she walked along the corridor upstairs, she heard the street door close behind him.

He had said he wanted her. He had offered marriage. Fool! Why couldn't she be content with that? Clearly she wanted all or nothing. Well then, she told herself, you will have nothing, because you are not willing to settle for what he has to offer.

If Elizabeth had entertained the slightest doubt about her exact feelings for Lord Stanton, his kiss had dispelled it. She had previously known security and contentment in his arms, but with his kiss came an unmistakable sense of belonging. The touch of his lips, the wondrous sensations, the new excitement, these were things too complex for her to attempt to define. But the belonging—that was easy for her—for Elizabeth had always known instinctively what was right for her, and with this man, in his arms, was her place in this world, of that she was absolutely certain. And if he would not take her to him, then she would be cast adrift.

The thought filled her with a pervading sadness, but beneath her despair hope glimmered, for Elizabeth was a fighter, in the best tradition of her military family. It would never occur to her to give up the battle so long as there was a single spark of hope. For if he admitted to wanting her, wasn't that a step on the way to loving her? And if he came to love her, then perhaps he could be brought to change his opinions about love in marriage. She would pray that it would be so, for she could see no solution otherwise.

Her rejection by Lord Stanton weighed heavily on Elizabeth's spirits, but she was not the only woman wearing a long face in that spring of 1815. Daily, husbands, sweethearts, sons, and brothers were leaving London, leaving England, to join Wellington's army in Belgium. Elizabeth did not see Lord Stanton again before he sailed, for she had taken care to avoid any function where she thought there would be the slightest chance of meeting him, and he did not call again.

The Duke of Wellington arrived in Brussels on the fifth of April, and everyone breathed easier knowing that he was with the army at last. By the end of April, the British cavalry was landing at Ostend in great numbers, and Jonathan, convinced there would be a major battle in the near future, decided to send Harriet home. He arranged for her passage to Harwich, and wrote asking Richard to meet her there and convey her to London, where she would take up residence with her in-laws.

Harriet arrived in mid-May, and although pleased to see her family again, was clearly regretful at having to separate from her husband. There were hundreds of British in Brussels, she said, and a social season much like any she had known in London. "I didn't want to leave. Very few English have. Most of them feel quite secure since the Duke arrived. But Jonathan insisted that he couldn't rest easy or keep his mind on his work while he knew I was without family in an unfortified city."

"And he was quite right, my dear," Lady Sherwood said. "The hardest part for women is the waiting, but there is little else we can do. And you have not only yourself to consider now, but the child as well."

Richard stayed overnight in London and left for Surrey at first light. He had been gone a week, for Harriet's packet had been delayed in sailing, and he had been detained four days awaiting it. He arrived at Sherwood Manor before noon and found his wife alone in the parlor. She turned quickly as he greeted her, and ran into his arms. "Oh, Richard, I have missed you dreadfully. Our first separation!"

He raised her face with his hand to kiss her tenderly. She saw that his eyes were serious, and when he spoke, his tone was grave. "I fear it will not be our last separation, my love."

She didn't pretend to misunderstand him, and indeed would not have been surprised to have had a note from him, telling her that he was taking the first available ship for Belgium. "You have decided to go, then?"

"Yes. I must. Harwich was a madhouse, and I can only assume the other ports are as bad. Father told me the quartermaster-general still needs experienced men on his staff. I will try for an appointment there."

"When will you leave?"

"In the morning."

Sarah and Richard spent the remainder of the day together. They ate dinner informally at six o'clock, inviting Jimmy to join them. He was clearly concerned when Richard announced his plans to rejoin the army, but he only said, "You will be careful, sir?"

Richard promised that he would be, and after spending the early part of the evening with them, Jimmy said his farewells, promising in a very grown-up way to look after his mother during the captain's absence. Soon after Jimmy retired, Richard took his wife's arm and escorted her upstairs. He had brought the brandy decanter from the library, and he nodded at it significantly, "Come to my room when you are ready for bed, and we will drink to a speedy end to Napoleon Bonaparte."

Henchly had finished packing earlier in the evening, and Richard's room was neat and undisturbed. He was soon ready for bed and dismissed his valet. "I will ring for you early, Henchly, for I wish to be in London before noon."

"Very good, sir. All of our things have been carried down to the hall. It remains only to load them into the chaise in the morning."

"Thank you, Henchly. Good night."

When Sarah came to join him, Richard poured their brandy, and for some time they sat silently near the fire, both occupied with their own thoughts until finally Sarah said, "What are you thinking?"

"I am thinking how much I love you, and how lucky I am." He turned to look at her and surprised a frown on her brow. "I didn't mean for that to make you scowl, my love. What, may I ask, are you thinking?"

"I have been thinking much the same thing, only I regret that I have not been a better wife."

"What foolishness! No man could have a more wonderful or loving wife than I! Believe me, I am perfectly content."

"I know you have never complained," she said, "and I know you never will. But it is not unreasonable for a man to expect his wife to *be* his wife in every way."

"Sarah," he said, possessing himself of her hands and holding them together between his. "We have had this discussion before. You cannot allow feelings of guilt to influence you in this matter. The physical relationship . . . the *best* physical relationship in marriage must grow from

236

mutual love, and mutual need. I will not have you forcing yourself out of some misplaced feeling of duty or guilt.''

"But, Richard, all these times we've been close, and when we're together at night, surely you must wish for more. Don't you find it difficult?''

"Yes,'' he admitted. "I do wish for more. And, *yes*, sometimes it is very difficult, but not nearly as hard as the months I slept alone thinking I had no chance with you. Compared with those dreary days, these weeks since our marriage have been heaven on earth for me. *Please*, for my sake, stop teasing yourself. We are just beginning our life together. We can take all the time we need to adjust to one another. We need not worry if things aren't perfect after less than two months of marriage.''

"But we may not have the rest of our lives, Richard; perhaps we will have . . . no more than tonight.''

"Sarah—''

"No, please,'' she interrupted him. "I have spoken with your mother about this. She told me what it was like for her all those years with your father at sea. She said she knew that each time she said good-bye to him, she might never see him again. Then, when you joined the army and the war in Portugal, she said it was the same feeling again, only the pain held a different place in her heart. Now she has her husband safely home, and it is Jonathan she prays for, and soon now, you again. I have known all these weeks that you felt you should go, and I have stopped myself a dozen times from begging you to stay because I was selfish enough to want to keep you safe. Well, I have come to terms with that, and I realize that you must do what is right for you, and I will not try to influence you otherwise.''

She stopped speaking to regain some control over her voice, and Richard gently brushed a tear from her cheek. "I had decided,'' she continued, "that when the time came for you to leave, I would use your mother as my model, for she is so self-possessed, so brave, and so remarkably strong. It was only today that I realized your mother has something I don't have. She knows everything about your father there is to know. She has given all of herself to him, and has accepted, as her right, all he has to offer. In the early years, she would have had only her memories had she lost him then, but as time passed she had you and Jon, and the girls, *his* children. Please God, we shall have all the years ahead you speak of, but if it is not to be so, then I would not have you leave me now without knowing all I can of you, for I do not think I could bear a life without you, never having known what it was like to be loved, truly and completely loved, by you. Do you understand what I'm trying to say?''

He did not answer her but sat for a long time, staring at her in silence. Finally he stood and held out his hand for hers. She laid her own in it, and he led her to the bed and blew out the candles on the table there. Then, as so often in the past, he helped her out of her dressing gown, and this time her nightgown as well. When he had removed his own things, he joined her in the bed. The first touch of their bodies was electrifying. Sarah came eagerly into his embrace and found herself being kissed with a strange intensity. The room, the world, the past, the future—everything began to fade as she yielded to the passion of his mouth on hers, and soon there was no place in her thoughts for anything but Richard's lips, Richard's hands—and Richard's body.

Sarah awoke before the dawn, aware of a warm glow of contentment. As she moved and came fully awake, she felt her husband's body beside her, and her memory of the previous night flooded back, rich with the joy of their love-making. Never had she imagined that such a feeling of completeness existed in the world. She knew now what the Church meant when it spoke of the oneness of marriage. Richard stirred in his sleep, and she rolled against him, unable to resist touching him, allowing her fingertips to slip over the smooth, hard muscles of his chest, stretching to kiss his neck, and then his lips. Then, suddenly, Richard was awake, kissing her, caressing her, wanting her all over again, setting her body on fire with his touch, and fanning her desire with his own.

Finally, reluctantly, as the sun crept ever higher in the sky, they forced themselves to separate. They shared an intimate breakfast. The chaise was brought round, and while several servants saw the baggage bestowed, Richard drew Sarah into the parlor and pulled her possessively into his arms.

"I don't have any words for last night," he said.

She shook her head. "We don't need any. It was perfect for both of us. That's all we need to know."

He kissed her then, and when he straightened again, he said, "Sarah, I shall do my best to come back to you, but if—"

She quickly raised her fingers to stay the words. "Don't say it."

He gently took her hand away and held it tightly in his. "I listened to you last night, and now I want you to hear me out, for there is something I must say, something I have thought about a great deal since I decided I must go with the army. If I don't come back, I want you to swear to me that you will always remember what we had."

"Oh, dearest Richard," she exclaimed, "I could never forget!"

"No. That's not what I mean. I want to know that you will not stop living if you lose me." He saw a tear overflow and reached for a handkerchief and gave it to her. "This is not a time for tears, Sarah. I fought you for months because you insisted upon seeing all men as you had seen your first husband. You must learn to judge each man for himself, and himself alone. Don't let your memories of me keep you from giving yourself again someday. I am not, after all, the only man who could love you, or even the

239

only man you could ever love." He could see that she was about to protest, but he lifted a finger to silence her. "I have every intention of coming home to you, but if the fates should decree otherwise, then you must swear to me that you will place a limit on your grief, and that you will form new relationships, with good judgment and without fear. Swear it to me, Sarah."

"I swear."

"Good. Now give me your prettiest smile, and a kiss passionate enough to last me the whole campaign."

22

Richard rejoined the army in London, and in a very short space of time was under orders. He arrived in Brussels in the closing days of May and was successful in receiving an appointment on the quartermaster-general's staff. He was kept busy, but found time to spend with both Jonathan and Lord Stanton, both of whom were billeted near Brussels. Richard and Jonathan both wrote to their wives, but their letters conveyed little real intelligence. Brussels continued its social whirl, with balls and parties nearly every night. The Allied armies continued to reorganize, and the tension seemed to mount each day in anticipation of the battle that was to come.

Neither Charlotte nor Elizabeth was enjoying the Season, even though they were both much sought after by any number of men, both eligible and ineligible. Elizabeth had not wanted to come to town initially because she had dreaded meeting Lord Stanton, and now that he was gone, she found little in the Season's amusements to interest her. Charlotte had come to town with the liveliest expectation that Lizzie's prophecy would come true and Charles Warmington would speak to Lord Sherwood at the earliest opportunity. But Charles had not spoken, and since it was now early June and they expected to remove to the country in a few days, she had come to the conclusion that Lizzie was mistaken, and that she herself had misinterpreted Charles's attentions. She had done everything she knew, short of speaking to him directly, to encourage him, but she had not succeeded in bringing him to the point.

"Well, Lizzie," she said one evening as they sat together before retiring, "it seems that we were both mistaken in Charles, for we are to leave at the end of the week and he has said nothing."

"You don't think that perhaps he has spoken to Papa and been rejected?" Elizabeth asked. "He is a younger son, after all, and if Papa thought it an unequal match. . . ."

Clearly this thought had not occurred to Charlotte, and she grasped at it now. "Do you truly think it may be so? I hadn't thought that Papa would interfere, but if he has, then it would explain a great deal. I shall speak with Papa about it immediately, Lizzie. He is still in the book-room, is he not?" She rose as she spoke and abruptly left the room, neither awaiting nor seeming to expect an answer.

Lord Sherwood glanced up as his eldest daughter entered the room, and smiled when she asked if she was disturbing him. "Not at all, child. Did you wish to speak with me?"

"Yes, Papa. I was wondering if Charles Warmington had spoken to you . . . about me?"

"Were you expecting him to, my dear?"

"Well, yes. I thought he might speak . . . rather, I had hoped he might. Lizzie thought that perhaps you would not grant Mr. Warmington permission to address me. Is that so, Papa?"

"No, Charlotte. I have not denied Mr. Warmington, for he has not been to see me. But you must know, Charlotte, that just because a man shows a liking for a woman, it doesn't necessarily follow that he is considering marriage with her."

"I know, Papa, but I have felt that there was more than

mere liking between us. If he comes to you, then, you will not reject him for his lack of fortune?''

"I cannot deny that I would like to see a brilliant match for you, Charlotte,'' her father replied, "but I will always be disposed to look kindly upon any man of your choosing.''

Charlotte smiled and stood on tiptoe to kiss her father's cheek. "Thank you, Papa, but it does not now seem as if Mr. Warmington will speak, for we are to leave town soon and then will not see him for some months, I think.''

She spoke sadly, and Lord Sherwood was sorry to think that she had formed an attachment for a man who did not return her regard. It was puzzling, for he thought himself that Warmington showed a partiality for Charlotte, and he had been immeasurably relieved when Richard had assured him that Warmington was not the spy they sought. If Charlotte had come to him sooner in this matter, he could have discussed it with Richard, for Warmington was a close friend, and perhaps Richard was privy to some information that might be helpful. However, Charlotte had not come, and for the time being Richard was out of reach, and no doubt had more weighty problems to deal with than Charlotte's romantic hopes. Time enough to think of Charlotte's future after they had dealt with the threat of Bonaparte.

At the end of the first week in June, the Sherwood ladies removed to the country, leaving Lord Sherwood behind in London. Both Harriet and Elizabeth were depressed by the constant talk of impending war, and Lady Sherwood felt they could all benefit by leaving the gossip and rumors of town behind. She was also concerned that Sarah had been so long alone, for Richard had been gone nearly three weeks.

During the third week in June, news began to trickle into London of the French advance across the frontier and a major encounter with the Prussians at Ligny and the Dutch-Belgians at Quatre-Bras on the sixteenth of June. Some

243

hours later, Lord Sherwood received the information that the 1st Guards had been engaged late in the day at Quatre-Bras. He considered sending off a quick note with this news but then decided against it. There was no reason to alarm them at home until he had more information. But when, some days later, he did have confirmed information, he found it was something he could not bring himself to write, and so instead he sent a message to Charles Warmington, asking him to call.

"You have some news, my lord?"

"I have news, Mr. Warmington, that must be conveyed immediately to Surrey, and since I cannot myself leave London, I was hoping you would act as my deputy." Lord Sherwood's voice was unsteady as he continued. "It is not such news as I would wish to write. The Guards were engaged on the sixteenth, and Jonathan is included on this casualty list." He handed a paper to Charles as he spoke, but Charles took it without looking at it as his lordship continued. "It will not be an easy errand, Mr. Warmington, but you are a friend of the family. My wife . . . the girls . . . Harriet. . . . I would rather not send a stranger." He paused briefly and then added, "There is no news of Richard or your cousin Stanton. As I understand it, no cavalry was engaged at Quatre-Bras, and although we held the ground, our losses were heavy. The Prussians were soundly beaten at Ligny and have fallen back before Bonaparte.

Charles tried to express his regret to Lord Sherwood, but his words of sympathy sounded empty even to his own ears. Sensing that his lordship would rather be alone, Charles promised to leave for Surrey immediately and quietly left the room. He went home to change into riding clothes, ordered his horse brought round, and within half an hour was on his way. When he arrived at Sherwood Manor in the late afternoon, he found that Charlotte and Sarah had driven to the village and that Harriet was resting.

Lady Sherwood and Elizabeth were therefore alone in the parlor when he was shown in.

Both ladies rose instantly to their feet as Charles was announced, and Lady Sherwood stepped forward, but his name as she spoke it was more question than greeting. "Mr. Warmington?"

"How do you do, ma'am. I have come with a message from Lord Sherwood."

His countenance and his tone could leave her in little doubt of the nature of his news, but she asked automatically, "You are bearing ill tidings, I think, sir?"

"Yes, ma'am. . . . The worst," he said quietly.

"Richard?"

He stepped forward to take her hands in his own. "No, ma'am—Jonathan."

She nodded mutely and allowed him to lead her to a sofa. She sat down slowly, closing her eyes and folding her hands in her lap.

Charles transferred his gaze to Elizabeth and found her staring at him in stunned silence. Then after several minutes had passed she went to her mother and laid a hand on her shoulder. "Mama, we must tell Harriet."

Lady Sherwood roused herself from her abstraction and raised her eyes to Charles. "You will stay to dinner, of course, Mr. Warmington, and if you need not return to London immediately, then you must stay the night as well." She pulled the bell-rope as she spoke, and when the butler appeared at the door, she said, "Jepson will show you upstairs, Mr. Warmington. I am sure you would like to freshen up after your long ride."

They all left the room together, and as they ascended the stairs, Elizabeth turned to Charles and asked quietly, "My father has had no word of Richard or your cousin?"

"No, none."

Elizabeth nodded, and when they parted at the top of the stairway, Charles gazed after the women as they moved away down the hall, marveling at the courage they displayed in the face of such a devastating loss. He couldn't know that they were each trying to be strong for the other, but at Harriet's door, Elizabeth's courage failed, and she grasped her mother's arm painfully. "Mama," she said, her eyes filling with tears, "I don't think I can face Harriet. How can you be so calm?"

"We must be brave, Elizabeth. We have no other choice. We all knew we could expect this kind of news, and we must accept it."

"Why must we accept it?" Elizabeth cried. "It's not fair! Jonathan was barely twenty-three, with his whole life before him, his child soon to be born! And it's only the first battle, Mama! Are we to accept it if Richard is next, and then Lord Stanton?"

Lady Sherwood took her daughter by the shoulders and shook her. "Elizabeth, calm yourself! Jonathan is dead. Nothing we can say or do will change that. He was fighting to protect his family and his country, and he knew the risks inherent in the profession as well as any man. War is the greatest evil on earth, and it leaves no one untouched. I carried your brother within me, and I brought him into this world, and no one could love him more than I, but he served his country proudly, and it is with pride that we will remember him, for that is what he would have wished." She paused for a few moments and then continued gently, "I will speak to Harriet alone. Why don't you go outside. Perhaps take a walk in the garden. Do not deny your tears, Lizzie, for we are not forbidden to mourn, but do not allow yourself to become bitter, for such an emotion is unworthy of you." She kissed her daughter gently on the cheek and then turned to enter Harriet's room as Elizabeth hurried down the hall and then down some service stairs and out a side door into the garden.

Harriet did not take the news well, and Lady Sherwood sent a message that they would not be down to dinner.

Sarah, Charlotte, Elizabeth, and Charles sat down to one of the cook's best efforts, but it was a desultory meal. None of them had any appetite, nor could they think of anything to say, but since they were all equally disinclined for conversation, no one seemed to mind the silence.

They adjourned to the parlor together, Charles declining any offer of port. Sarah asked Charles to tell them what he knew of the action on the sixteenth, and though he knew little more than what Lord Sherwood had told him, he shared this information with them. Elizabeth interjected an occasional question, but Charlotte sat listening in stony silence, until suddenly she leaped to her feet and ran from the room. Sarah rose to follow her but Charles stayed her.

"Please, Mrs. Sherwood, let me go."

Charles didn't see Charlotte on the stairs, but he heard a door close down the hall and realized she must have gone to the library. He followed her there and entered quietly, closing the door behind him. As she turned to face him, he saw she held a slender volume in her hand that she had apparently just taken from the shelf.

"Jon gave me this book of poetry on my last birthday," she said. "There were only thirteen months between us, you know, and as children we were loyal comrades. I can remember when we were very young—we got into terrible scrapes and nearly drove our nurse to distraction. I can't believe that he's gone."

Charles crossed the room to stand before her. "Why did you run from the room just now?"

"I couldn't bear to listen anymore. I was looking at Sarah, thinking how horrible it must be for her with Richard over there, and as worried as I am for him, I suddenly realized how lucky I am that you hadn't gone, and I felt guilty. . . ." She stopped speaking abruptly as she realized what she had said, and she looked up to see an arrested expression on his face.

He brought up one finger to wipe a single tear from her

cheek and then cradled her chin in his hand, gazing intently and steadily into her eyes. And then, very slowly, he bent his head and gently touched her lips with his own. Charlotte's response was instantaneous, and as she raised her arms about his neck, he took her waist and drew her to him. For some moments they remained so, caught up in the waves of emotion pouring over them, and then suddenly Charles put her from him, and she stared in surprise to see him shaking his head vehemently.

"No, Charlotte, this will never do. I'm sorry. I didn't mean to. . . . I must go. It is highly improper for us to be here alone. Will you come back to the parlor?"

She gazed at him in some confusion but only said, "No, thank you. I would rather stay here."

"Very well, then," he replied stiffly. "I shall bid you good night." He turned and was gone on the words, and when Charlotte finally quit the library, she did not return to the others, but instead went upstairs to the privacy of her own room.

Charles left Sherwood Manor the following morning, promising to return should he have any further news. But it was Lord Sherwood himself who arrived two days later with the news of Napoleon's complete defeat by the Allied Forces just south of the village of Waterloo on the eighteenth of June. The British and Prussian armies had not been able to join forces, he said, and the British and some Allied troops had fought valiantly all day to hold the position until the Prussians could come up in support. The battle had raged for more than eight hours, but by nightfall the French Army was in full retreat. The Allied Forces had been victorious, but the price had been dear, the losses on both sides staggering. He had no information on the casualties of that battle and was sure it would be several days at least before they had any reliable word. He returned to London the following morning, and several days later the casualty lists began to come in. There was no mention of either Lord Stanton or Captain Sherwood.

The interminable days of waiting continued, and then finally news arrived in an unexpected way. One evening, just at dusk, a chaise turned in at the gates of Sherwood Manor, and a few moments later the women were drawn into the hall by the sounds of an arrival. Sarah was shocked to see her husband being more or less carried into the house supported between Charles Warmington and Henchly. His left leg was swathed in bandages above the knee, and he appeared unable to rest any weight upon it. His face was pale, but he smiled at Sarah's worried frown as he bent his head to kiss her briefly.

Charles hastened to reassure her. "He looks much worse than he is, Mrs. Sherwood. The jolting of the coach these last few miles was too much for him, I'm afraid. I tried to convince him to stay in London for a few days, but you know what he is. Said he would come home to you straightaway and wouldn't listen to any sage advice."

"Yes, Mr. Warmington, I know what he is. To travel at all in such a state is unthinkable." She tried to keep her voice lightly critical, hoping that her tone would in some part hide the overwhelming relief she felt in knowing that Richard was alive.

"He will be better here at home than elsewhere, ma'am," Henchly added. "The number of wounded in Brussels is appalling, and there is no way to care for them all properly. Those wounded who felt they could travel were encouraged to do so."

Richard insisted that he could hop up the stairs, but there was a general outcry and Charles refused to be bullied. With the help of two footmen, they lifted the captain bodily and carried him up to his bedchamber. Once there, he desired to be placed upon a couch and insisted that if he should be given a glass of brandy, he would do nicely.

With his arms finally freed, Richard took his wife into

249

them and kissed her properly, heedless of all eyes upon them. Then he accepted in turn the embraces of his mother, his sisters, and his sister-in-law. As Harriet bent to kiss his cheek, he took her hand. "Sit a moment, Harriet. I have a message for you from Jon." Silence fell in the room as Harriet sat facing him, and for a moment it seemed to the two of them that they were alone. "I saw Jon the day before Quatre-Bras. He was in high spirits—excited that we were to see some action, but he did get serious for a few moments and he said, 'If I don't make it through this, tell Harriet that I love her. And tell her to name our *son* after me.' "

Harriet smiled crookedly through her tears and said, "I will, Richard. I will."

A short time later, Lady Sherwood took Harriet away, and Charlotte, made decidedly uneasy by Mr. Warmington's presence in the room, went with them. Elizabeth, no longer able to control her anxiety, blurted out, "Do you know anything of Lord Stanton, Richard? We have heard nothing."

"I'm afraid I know very little, Lizzie, for I left Brussels early on the morning of the nineteenth. Julian was attached to General Grant's brigade. When the Prussians fell back from Ligny on Havre, we were forced to fall back to Waterloo to maintain communications. All the cavalry was kept to guard the retreat, and the 7th Hussars were heavily engaged at Genappe on the seventeenth. I know he came through that, for someone told me they saw him the next morning, but I have heard nothing since. We took a tremendous beating on the eighteenth, and our losses were heavy. By the time the Prussians were able to join us, many of our units were fighting as a last line of defense, with no reserves whatsoever. But they stood their ground to the last, against some of the heaviest artillery fire I have ever seen, and massive attacks of both cavalry and infantry. When the French mounted their final general advance sometime after seven, the Prussians had arrived in some force on our left, and we were able to turn the French from the field. Their army was fairly routed, and the Prussians took up the pursuit as they retreated. Most of our fellows dropped right where they were for the night, too exhausted to take a step in any direction.

"I arrived in Brussels during the night and was sent out with some of the first wounded that were able to travel. The town was already overflowing with wounded from Quatre-Bras. I can't imagine how they are dealing with the masses of wounded from Waterloo."

Richard noticed that Elizabeth had become alarmingly pale, so he hastened to add, "If Julian hasn't been on the casualty lists so far, Lizzie, that's a good sign, for bad news travels fastest."

Henchly had been hurrying about the room preparing the captain's bed, and at this lull in the conversation he made so bold as to say that he thought the captain would be better between sheets. Sarah agreed, so Charles bore Elizabeth off, promising to stay long enough in the morning to take his leave of them.

"Why don't you leave me to Henchly, Sarah," Richard said. "He can scrape some of this dirt from me and get me into bed."

"I would much rather stay and help."

"And I would much rather you stayed, my love, but I think it would shock Henchly profoundly if you did." He smiled as he spoke, and she relented and went away.

When she returned some time later, she found him washed and shaved, in a clean nightshirt, and snugly tucked up in bed. "Are you hungry?"

"Yes, and I have already sent Henchly to fetch me something from the kitchen."

Sarah sat gently on the edge of the bed and laid her hand on the coverlet over his leg. "What is the nature of your wound, and how did you come by it?"

"It was a musket ball, lodged deeply in the thigh. It bled freely at first, but I managed to tie a cloth above it and that helped some. I did well enough until my horse was hit. I don't remember much, but he must have come down on the same leg, for it's badly bruised, and I remember someone saying that I had to be pulled from under him. By the time I regained consciousness, I had been carried to Waterloo, and the ball had been dug out and the leg dressed. I was lying under the prettiest elm you can imagine. I don't remember ever finding a tree so attractive, but after six hours on the battlefield, the relative quiet behind the lines seemed like heaven.

"Henchly helped me to sit up against the tree, and we stayed there until after dark. There were quite a few wounded waiting to be conveyed to Brussels, and we managed to keep informed of how the battle was progressing by shouting to an occasional officer or troop that passed by, or from information from the wounded who were continuously streaming back from the front. By the early hours of the morning we had received positive confirmation in Brussels that the French were in full retreat and in such disarray that the Duke thought it unlikely that they would be able to make another stand before the Allies hounded them into Paris.

"Lizzie looks terrible. Is it Jon?" he asked.

"Partly Jon, and partly her concern for you and for Lord Stanton. She is in love with him, Richard."

"Oh, no," he said on a sigh. "I have been afraid of that, but I kept hoping that it would not be so."

"I think it is the waiting that is hardest. At least if she knew one way or the other, she could begin to deal with it."

"It is amazing to me that anyone could come unscathed through that battle. Never have I seen such violent conflict or such staggering losses. It was a sight I shall not soon forget. And then Jon. . . ." A shadow crossed his face, and he reached out a hand to his wife. "Come here, Sarah."

She leaned closer, and he pulled her against his side. As she laid her head on his chest, he slowly lowered his chin into her hair, closing his eyes and allowing his body to relax. He savored the warmth and softness of her body in his arms and the familiar and comforting scent of her hair, and they sat so, in companionable silence, until Henchly arrived with the captain's dinner.

The following morning Charles entered Richard's room in the company of the village doctor. The doctor examined Richard's leg and said that he saw nothing amiss and was convinced it would heal splendidly if the captain kept all weight off it for a full two weeks at least. He was amazed at the extent of the bruising and remarked that the captain was fortunate that his horse had not broken the leg when he fell on it.

The doctor was soon gone, and Charles reached out to take Richard's hand. "Well, I'm off, then. I'll stop at Mount Street to tell Lord Sherwood that I saw you home in one piece."

"Thank you, Charles, for all your help. And please, tell my father also to let us know immediately if he has any news of Julian. We are all concerned for him."

It was another three days before they had any word of Stanton, and then the news didn't come from Lord Sherwood, but from Charles, who had met in London a wounded Hussar from the 7th who had seen Julian on the nineteenth of June.

. . . He said that aside from a few flesh wounds and a rather nasty saber cut on his right forearm, Julian was well on the morning of the nineteenth. He had come in to have the cut stitched but insisted upon returning to the brigade and moving on with them to Paris. I don't think we need concern ourselves for him. Please convey my compliments to your family. I will write again if I receive further news.

Yours, etc.,

Charles

Richard read this aloud to Sarah, and when he finished, she reached to take it from him. "May I take this to Lizzie?"

"Yes, please do. I think she went riding with Jimmy this morning."

By the time Sarah made her way to the stables, Elizabeth and Jimmy were returning from their ride. Dismounting, Elizabeth turned to see Sarah hurrying toward her with a letter in her hand, and she turned suddenly pale.

"It's good news, Lizzie," Sarah called to her. "Lord Stanton is well, and still with the army, following Napoleon back into France."

Elizabeth, who had wept unreservedly for Jonathan on the day they learned of his death, had not allowed herself to give in to such weakness since, but after the intervening days of anxiety and the sleepless nights, she could not deny her overwhelming relief, and she threw herself into Sarah's arms, weeping like a child. Sarah cradled her in her arms until the sobbing subsided, and then as Elizabeth raised her head, Sarah brushed a few loose strands of hair from her face. Elizabeth was dabbing her eyes with a large man's handkerchief.

"Where did you get that?" Sarah asked.

"It's Lord Stanton's," Elizabeth explained. "He lent it to me a long time ago, and I never returned it. I keep it with me most of the time. I know it's foolish, but I like having it."

"No, Lizzie, it's not foolish, but I think you have kept these feelings to yourself long enough. When you see Lord Stanton again, you should tell him how you feel. If he

knew you loved him, it might change things between you."
Elizabeth shook her head, but Sarah said quickly, "Don't
say no. You can never be sure of anything where love is
concerned. Look at your brother and myself. Richard didn't
allow his pride to stand in the way of telling me he loved
me, and it's a good thing he didn't, for otherwise we would
never have found the happiness we now share. If you tell
him how you feel and he still rejects you, you can feel no
worse than you do now, don't you see? You are the one
who is always saying that honesty is important above all
things. Well then, practice what you preach! Tell him the
truth, and see what he will do with it."

23

Bonaparte's brief reign had come to an abrupt end. He was banished to the bleak island of St. Helena, and Louis XVIII was once again placed upon the French throne by the Congress of Vienna. During the summer, great numbers of men were demobilized, and Charles wrote to Richard that Julian had come home at last, tanned and healthy, and in excellent spirits.

Lord Sherwood finally came to the country for a well-deserved rest, but he was less than pleased with the conditions he found at Sherwood Manor. Richard was up and about the affairs of the estate, and it was plain to see there was nothing amiss with his marriage, but Charlotte and Elizabeth were both looking poorly, and he could not help exclaiming to his wife when they were alone.

"The girls are looking burnt to the socket. What ails them?"

"I have tried speaking with Elizabeth," his wife said, "but she will not confide in me, and Richard says that I should not press her. Charlotte admitted that she has formed a *tendre* for Charles Warmington. She said she had spoken to you."

"Yes, she did. She seemed surprised that the young man had not approached me, for she felt he returned her regard. I had decided to speak with Richard, and I will do so immediately. He is in a better position than most to know where Mr. Warmington stands in the matter."

Lord Sherwood spoke to Richard at length that very evening, and although he did not share the substance of their conversation with his wife, he told her that Richard felt the situation between Mr. Warmington and Charlotte did not look promising.

But two days later, all thought of Charles Warmington was put out of their heads by the precipitate arrival of Sir High Broughton just as the family was gathering in the drawing room before dinner. He was shown in immediately, greeted everyone politely, but seemed disappointed as his eyes swept the room. "Julian is not here, then?"

"No," Richard replied, puzzled. "Did you expect him to be?"

"I suppose not really, although I had hoped he might stop here. I shall push on to Stanton Castle immediately and hope to find him there. We have had the most unsettling news in London this morning. It seems that Henry Ferris is a spy for the French—has been for years." Sir Hugh was speaking to Richard and could not fail to see the look that passed between Richard and his father at his words. Sir Hugh turned to Lord Sherwood and asked brusquely, "Did you know, my lord?"

"No, Sir Hugh," his lordship replied. "Richard and I knew that there was a traitor among our acquaintance, but we didn't know who, until now. The night of our ball in Mount Street some delicate papers were tampered with in my book-room, and on the night that Lord Stanton and Elizabeth were shot, we made an attempt to capture the man, but he overpowered the footman who had been set to watch for him. Most recently, he broke into the house in London and ransacked the entire room."

"I can't believe it," Richard said in a dazed voice. "Not Henry. We fought together. He put me on his own horse when I was wounded in Portugal. It's just not possible."

"I would have been the first to agree with you," Sir Hugh said, "but I am afraid it is true, nevertheless. They discovered some papers in Paris that showed Henry's activities without question. Right up until Waterloo, he was sending the French whatever information he could about our troop strength and movements. When they faced him with it yesterday at the Foreign Office, he made no attempt to deny anything but astonished everyone by leveling the nearest minister and casting himself through a second-story window. Before anyone could respond, he had disappeared into the side streets, and nothing has been seen or heard of him since. The story was all over town this morning, and I was with Julian when we first heard it. He would not believe the rumors but went immediately to the Foreign Office and demanded to be told the facts as they knew them. When they were finished, he never said a word but only walked out to the coach. When I tried to follow him, he said that he wished to be alone and that he must go home to Giles.

"That was the last time I saw him. I spent the better part of the day trying to run him down in London. All I know is that he did go home, but Giles had already heard the rumors and left the house. Whether Julian ever found him I don't know. His servants were being awfully close, even with me, but I could see for myself that Julian's curricle and team were gone, so I concluded that he had left town, but I can't imagine where he has gone."

"I doubt that he has gone to Stanton Castle, Hugh," Richard said, "and I see little reason for you to seek him there. You know Julian. If he wants to be alone, you can be sure he will go nowhere he would expect to be found. Stay to dinner, stay the night, and go back to London in the morning. When he has come to terms with this, he will go back there, I have no doubt of that."

"I'm sure you must be right," Sir Hugh answered. "The thing is that I never should have let him out of my sight. I have racked my brain trying to think where he may have gone, but I can come up with nothing. I can't rid myself of the idea that he has gone after Henry, and I shudder to think what may happen if he catches up with him.''

Giles Ferris heard the rumors about his brother Henry almost simultaneously with Stanton. Unlike Stanton, he had no thought of having the allegations confirmed. By the time Stanton had parted from Sir Hugh and arrived home, he found that Giles had ordered the post chaise and left the house nearly an hour earlier. Stanton instantly ordered his curricle and team. He did not doubt for an instant where Giles had gone, for he had had the same thought himself. The only safe place for Henry was France, the quickest way to get there—across the Channel.

What Stanton and Giles knew, and no one else, was that Stanton owned a piece of property on a stretch of lonely coastline in Kent. It was no more than a modest manor house on the edge of the marsh, presently let to a tenant. Julian and Henry had spent several summers there as boys, and once, when Giles was seventeen, Julian had taken him there and shown him where he and Henry had played at being pirates and smugglers. It sickened him now to think that Henry had probably found the place convenient for meeting his confederates from across the Channel.

Stanton changed teams often and made good time into Kent. He abandoned his carriage at Tenterden and hired a horse for the last twelve miles of his journey. He had no intention of stopping at the manor house and gave it a wide berth. It was growing dark as he directed his horse out of a stretch of timber and onto the broad expanse of the marsh. He followed a narrow sheep track that wound erratically over the ground. In all these years, he thought, the path had not changed. It had neither widened nor narrowed and seemed not to have moved an inch from its original meandering trail.

It had by this time grown quite dark, and sensing that he was close to the shepherd's cot he sought, Stanton dismounted and tied his horse a little way off the path to a thorn bush. It wasn't a very substantial tethering place, but the animal was tired, and the viscount judged that he would not attempt to break free. He had walked only a few paces when he heard a sound to his right, and, peering through the twilight, saw a horse tethered nearby—probably Giles's, or perhaps Henry's. A few more minutes brought him to the tiny hut. Although it had been carefully shuttered inland, there were several cracks with light showing toward the southeast. Stanton approached soundlessly and made his way round to peer through one of the chinks in the wall. His brothers were both inside, apparently alone. He heard Giles's voice raised in righteous wrath.

"None of what you are saying makes any sense to me. You can't feed me any rubbish about loyalty to the Empire! Julian was engaged at Waterloo, wounded there! He could just as easily have been killed, and you would have been instrumental in your own brother's death! My God, Henry, so many of our friends died there! Your friends!"

"I have no friends in this country." Henry's voice was passionate; he spoke with finality. Giles took a menacing step forward, and Stanton saw for the first time that Henry held a pistol, leveled almost nonchalantly at his young brother.

Hoping his arrival wouldn't startle Henry into unwary action, Stanton called out, "Henry, it's Julian. I'm coming in." He lifted the latch as he spoke and bent his head to enter the dimly lit interior. Obviously viewing Stanton as a more tangible threat than a mere schoolboy, Henry pivoted, aiming his weapon at his eldest brother.

"I thought this place forgotten," he snapped. "I did not expect to have my entire family descend upon me!"

"I shouldn't think that anyone beyond we three knows of its existence," Stanton replied. "But I must ask you either to use that pistol, Henry, or put it down. You are wondering if I am myself armed, and the answer is yes. But there is no provocation that could induce me to fire upon my own brother, so you may rest assured that I will not make the attempt.''

Seconds passed, and then slowly, Henry lowered his pistol and laid it on the table before him. He watched his own motions carefully, staring at the piece as he put it down, and then suddenly looking up to meet the viscount's eyes defiantly. ''Well, I am waiting to hear your tirade of disgust and incredulity, Stanton. I have already endured one from this whelp. I am sure you will be more eloquent than he.''

''I have not come for that, Henry. You know what you have done, and I know full well that your activities were not accidentally entered into or taken lightly. I am sure that you are fully committed to your cause, in every way that a man can be.''

Giles started to speak, but an uplifted hand from Stanton silenced him immediately, as he continued.

''I know how much you hated my father, and I also know how deeply you loved Mother. To a large degree, we share those feelings. I disliked Father intensely and decided early on that he was a perfect model of the man I would never wish to be. As for Mother, I loved her, yes, but not with the dedication you felt. It was not an unbreakable tie for me. I want you to know that I understand your position; we are, after all, half French. You had a choice to make, and you made it. But even though I understand your sympathies, Henry, I cannot forgive your activities on these shores. You have forsworn an oath of allegiance to the king. You are a traitor to this country and to your family here, and I will not protect your life at the risk of my own or Giles's. I plan to call on the district magistrate at dawn, with the intelligence that I own property here, property with which you are familiar, and which you could

261

be using as a place of concealment. If you have friends over the water, I hope that they plan to collect you tonight, for after tomorrow morning I have only one brother.''

He turned to look at Giles as he spoke these last words and could see that the boy was trying hard to control his emotions, but his eyes were glistening, and one tear had already coursed a track down his cheek unheeded.

"But . . . we are brothers," Giles stammered, "and we love one another. Does that not count for anything?" He was vainly seeking answers—solutions that would fall short of tearing them apart forever. The cold reality was that after tonight they would never see Henry again, and he did not want to face it. He looked from Henry to Julian, but he could not speak.

"Love between brothers counts for a great deal, Giles," Stanton said, "but there comes a time in each man's life when he must follow the dictates of his conscience, and sometimes in order to do that, he must sever old bonds. Henry has severed his bonds with us, and if the truth be told, he did so many years ago."

They stood for a few moments in tense silence, and finally the viscount spoke again. "Is that your horse a little way down the path, Giles?" His brother nodded mutely, and Stanton continued. "Go to him, and wait for me there. I will be along shortly." Giles stood his ground anxiously until Stanton took his shoulder and turned him toward the door. "Go now, Giles. We will be fine, and I will come soon, I promise."

As Giles left and Stanton turned back, Henry came from behind the table and took a step forward, leaving less than two feet between them. "Julian . . . if you could think of the good times, when we were young, and we didn't have much except each other . . ."

"I won't forget them, Henry. Our father did us a great disservice when he brought our mother to England. He cast the dice for us even then." He held out his hand as he

262

spoke and was not surprised to see it shaking. Henry took it in his own, but as if by mutual consent they felt it not to be enough, they embraced each other suddenly, and then, just as suddenly, stood apart. "Good-bye, Henry. If you see Mother, give her my love, and tell her that she need lack for nothing so long as I live." For the first time in his life, Stanton experienced the sensation of hot tears rising to his eyes, and he turned away quickly, passed through the door, and found himself struggling for breath in the cool night air.

He soon came up with Giles, and they walked together to where Stanton's horse waited. As he mounted, Giles finally found his voice. "Julian . . . I feel . . . I can't describe it."

"Sick—and empty," Stanton supplied. "But there is no help for it, Giles. We must learn to live with it, and hope that in time it will fade."

"Do you truly intend to lay information in the morning?"

"Yes. I won't say that I suspect Henry of being here, but only that I own property in the area. You needn't worry for Henry. There are at least a hundred places where he can hide until they come for him, and he knows them all. We haunted this marsh for three long summers. We left no stone unturned." He stopped speaking suddenly, and Giles knew he was remembering those carefree summers, and he, too, relapsed into silence. They rode on side by side without speaking for many miles.

After several weeks passed with nothing being heard of Henry Ferris, most people assumed that somehow he had escaped to France. If he was willing to change his name and settle quietly in some remote village, it was unlikely that anything would be heard of him again.

Lord Sherwood returned from a short visit to London with the information that both the Prince Regent and the

Duke of Wellington had personally communicated with Lord Stanton regarding his brother's activities. "They both felt that he should hear from them directly, so he would understand that there was never any question of his loyalty. The Prince said something to the effect that the Ferrises had been loyal subjects of the Crown for over two-hundred years, and there was no reason to doubt them now simply because there had been one rotten apple in the barrel."

"I think it showed great sensitivity for His Royal Highness to speak to Lord Stanton," Lady Sherwood said. "It must be reassuring for him to know that his allegiance is not in question."

"Yes," added Elizabeth, "but I'm not sure that I understand. Was Henry Ferris an agent for the French, or a traitor to Britain?"

"He was a British subject, Lizzie," Richard answered, "and as such owed his allegiance to the king. But there is little doubt now that his sympathies have always been with the French, and therefore to some degree you are right—he was a French agent, and no doubt highly valued by them."

"Still, it must have been a great shock for Lord Stanton to discover that his brother was a French sympathizer," Charlotte added, "for I think that he and Henry were fond of each other."

"Yes," Richard agreed, "they were very close."

The following evening, after dinner, while Harriet and Charlotte went for a walk in the garden, Elizabeth found an opportunity to bring up the subject of Charlotte's floundering affair with Charles Warmington. "Papa, is there nothing we can do to encourage Mr. Warmington to ask for Charlotte? She is so miserable."

"She is looking poorly," Lord Sherwood agreed, "but there is nothing we can do, Lizzie."

"But couldn't you talk to him, Papa? Explain that the

money isn't important when weighed against Charlotte's happiness?''

Lord Sherwood looked across at Richard. "I have talked to him, Lizzie," Richard said. "I got nowhere. He is determined that Charlotte can do better for herself. He will not make an offer."

"Did you tell him that Charlotte loves him?"

"No. I didn't think I had the right, since I was speaking without Charlotte's knowledge. But I think he knows how she feels."

"Is he really so poor, Richard?"

"No, actually. His house in Kent is very well—much like the one we grew up in. And with Charlotte's fortune, I am sure they would be very comfortable there. But we can't force him to offer for her, Lizzie."

"He can't really love her," Elizabeth said with conviction, "or he would not allow such foolish scruples to stand in his way. If there was just some way we could get around this stubbornness of his," she mused, more to herself than to her family. "Perhaps we could devise a way to have him compromise Charlotte. Then he would be forced to offer for her."

"Really, Elizabeth!" her mother objected. "I must beg you not to voice such improper thoughts. Whatever will you say next?"

Elizabeth was silenced, but Richard was much struck by her casually uttered words and he met his father's eyes speculatively. Shortly thereafter, Lord Sherwood and his son went off together to the library, and his lordship left a message with the footman in the hall that he wished Miss Charlotte to join them as soon as she returned.

When Charlotte came into the house nearly an hour later, she was directed to the library, where she found her father alone.

"You wished to see me, Papa?"

"Yes, Charlotte. Do you remember, some weeks ago, speaking to me about Mr. Warmington?"

"Yes, Papa."

"You said you thought that Mr. Warmington might speak to me concerning you. Why did you think that, child?"

"I thought he might be interested in asking for my hand, Papa."

"But why?"

"I suppose because we enjoyed each other's company. He seemed to seek me out, and I thought, as did Lizzie, that he showed a decided partiality for me. I suppose also that I hoped he cared for me."

"Because you care for him?"

"Yes, Papa."

"So it was all conjecture on your part? Did he never say or do anything to make you certain that he cared?"

"Why are you asking me this, Papa?"

"I am merely trying to obtain a clear view of the situation, Charlotte. *Did* he say or do anything?"

Charlotte did not answer immediately but instead stared down at her hands, and Lord Sherwood felt a faint glimmer of hope as he asked again, "Well, Charlotte?"

"At the time I spoke to you, Papa, no, he had done nothing. But since that time, something has happened that made me more certain that he cares."

"And what was that?"

"When you sent him down with the news of Jonathan . . . I was upset . . . and I blurted out how I felt about him . . . and he kissed me." She raised her eyes to her father's, and he saw that they were full of tears. "For a moment I thought he would admit that he cared for me, but he didn't. He just said that it was wrong, and apologized, and left. I was confused, Papa, and I didn't know what to think. All I know is that I love him."

"Where did all this take place, Charlotte?"

"Here. In the library. I had come to find the book that Jon had given me for my birthday, and Charles followed me."

Lord Sherwood rose from his desk and walked over to embrace his daughter. "Take heart, Charlotte. I intend to see Mr. Warmington and have a talk with him. If there is anything that can be done to advance your cause with him, you may believe that I shall do it. But you must promise to stop moping. No young lady ever won a man's heart with a worried frown and with dark circles under her eyes. Have some faith in your father, who loves you more than anything, and who will do all in his power to see you happy."

Charlotte soon left him, and Lord Sherwood returned to his desk, very pleased with himself. Lizzie's remark, Richard's suggestion, and his inquisition had yielded the weapons he needed to proceed. He sat for some moments in contemplation, and then, choosing a quill, pulled a piece of writing paper forward and began a letter to the Honorable Charles Warmington.

Lord Sherwood received an immediate answer to his letter. Mr. Warmington replied that he would be happy to visit Sherwood Manor and hoped that Thursday next would be a convenient day for his arrival. Charles arrived late in the afternoon and was not surprised to find himself the only house guest.

After dinner that evening, the ladies retired to the parlor, and as a footman set the port upon the table, Richard rose and excused himself, and Charles had the distinct feeling that he was about to discover Lord Sherwood's purpose in summoning him into Surrey.

"You will have port, I believe, Mr. Warmington?" his lordship was saying.

"Yes, thank you, sir," Charles answered automatically, and then noticed that Lord Sherwood signaled for the footman to leave the decanter, and motioned him from the room.

"You will no doubt have guessed that I have something of import to discuss with you, Mr. Warmington?" his lordship asked.

"Yes, my lord."

"It concerns Charlotte."

Charles had also suspected this, but he said nothing and waited for Lord Sherwood to continue.

"Charlotte confided something to me several days ago that has caused me considerable disquiet, but I have determined to make no judgment in the matter until you have had ample opportunity to defend your position."

A frown creased Charles's brow, but he continued to regard Lord Sherwood steadily as the older man continued.

"Charlotte has told me that during your visit here in late June, you shared a conversation with her in the library."

"Yes, sir. I did. She was grief-stricken over Jonathan, as we all were. It was not a pleasant evening for us."

"Charlotte has admitted to me, Mr. Warmington, that you and she were quite alone in the library, and that you did more than talk." He paused meaningfully and waited for Charles to respond.

"What exactly are you saying, Lord Sherwood?"

"I am saying, sir, that I asked you to come to my home because I thought you a man to be trusted. My wife, daughters, and daughter-in-law were all residing here without the protection of any male relative. I had expected that you would deliver my message in good faith. I did not expect that you would take advantage of the situation to make advances to Charlotte."

Lord Sherwood watched as Charles's jaw hardened into a firm line, and he answered stiffly, "Is that what Charlotte said? That I made advances?"

"She said, Mr. Warmington, that you kissed her, and I

hope you do not expect me to doubt her word, for Charlotte would not lie to me."

"No, sir, I would not expect you to doubt her. I did kiss her. I don't deny it."

"Then, may I ask you, sir, what you meant by it, and what your intentions are toward my daughter?"

"I meant nothing by it, my lord, and I have no intentions toward your daughter. I apologized to Charlotte, and I will apologize to you if necessary."

Lord Sherwood rose suddenly from the table with all the appearance of a man overcome by righteous indignation. "You force your attentions upon a young, unmarried girl in her own home, when you know she has no protection by; you take advantage of her grief, and then have the audacity to sit there and tell me that it meant nothing and that your intentions are dishonorable! You are insulting, sir!"

Charles rose to his feet as Lord Sherwood finished speaking and spoke in a steady, carefully controlled voice. "I do not mean to be insulting, my lord, but I do not know what you would have me say."

"I would like to hear the truth from you, young man. Why did you feel yourself constrained to kiss my daughter?"

"I kissed her because I find her very desirable."

"And . . . ?"

"And because I am in love with her."

"May I ask if Charlotte returned your embrace, Mr. Warmington?"

"Yes, sir, she did."

"In my day, young man, when a gentleman loved and desired a young, unattached woman and went so far as to kiss her and receive her kiss in return, there was one more requirement that went along with the desire and the kissing."

"An offer of marriage," Charles said flatly.

"Yes, sir. An offer of marriage!"

"And you are demanding one from me?"

"I expect one from you, Mr. Warmington, if you consider yourself a gentleman!"

There was a pause before Charles spoke again. "Charlotte would be throwing herself away on me, my lord."

"The day the daughter of a simple sea captain throws herself away on the son of an earl is the day hell will freeze over, my boy. You and Charlotte have both admitted that you love each other, and you have taken the first step toward a physical commitment. There is no honorable way to turn back now. . . . I am waiting."

The two men stood staring at each other across the width of the dining room table, and finally Charles spoke. "I would like your permission, Lord Sherwood, to pay my addresses to Charlotte."

"You have my permission, Mr. Warmington, and you may do so without delay." As he spoke, he moved to the door of the parlor and, throwing it open, strode in. Charlotte was sitting with Harriet near the empty fireplace, and he spoke to her directly. "Charlotte, will you step back into the dining room for a few moments? Mr. Warmington would like to speak with you."

All five women stared at his lordship in silence, and Charlotte rose mechanically and walked past her father into the dining room. He pulled the doors to behind him, leaving her alone with Charles. She stopped just inside the doors, and Charles stood beside the table, fifteen feet away.

"Charlotte," he began, "your father has given his permission . . ." And then when he saw the joy in her eyes, he could only say "I love you." He was walking toward her then, and she met him more than halfway as he folded her in a hug that took her breath away and left her in no doubt whatsoever of his intentions.

24

Two days later, the engagement of Miss Charlotte Sherwood and the Honorable Charles Warmington appeared in the columns of the *Post,* and two days after that, Lord Sherwood and Captain Sherwood were still chuckling over the way they had used Charles's overly fine sense of the proprieties to turn his own hand.

Charles realized, of course, that he had been manipulated, but having once admitted his love for Charlotte, he could not wish any of it undone, and he confessed ruefully to Richard that he should have given in to his friend's initial arguments. "I should have known that if the entire Sherwood clan united against me, I would have no chance. You are a ruthless, disreputable lot, and it is clear to me now that you will go to any length to win."

Lord Sherwood agreed to a wedding date in late December, allowing for six months strict mourning for Jonathan, and insisting that the ceremony be private and simple. Charles spent much of the remainder of August in Surrey, but early September found Lord and Lady Sherwood, Charles and Charlotte back in London with plans to remain. Lady Sherwood, of course, would come down for Harriet's lying-in. Elizabeth vaguely planned to spend some part of the Little Season in London, but for the present she chose to remain in Surrey and work around Harriet's schedule, whatever that might turn out to be.

One sunny afternoon, just four days after she had seen her parents and sister off to town, Elizabeth was alone in the hall, arranging some late-summer flowers that she had gathered, when a knock sounded on the door behind her and she turned to see Viscount Stanton admitted to the house. There was a shattering crash, and she stared down in amazement at her feet. Her flowers were scattered in every direction, the lovely blue-glass vase broken into several dozen pieces. She looked up again as she exclaimed, "My Lord Stanton! This is a surprise. We did not expect you."

"Apparently not," he said, smiling. "I am sorry if I startled you. I hope it wasn't a valuable piece?"

She gazed at him uncomprehendingly for a moment and then recalled the broken vase. "No . . . no, not at all. How foolish of me." She stooped immediately to collect the flowers, and then unthinkingly swept her hand over the marble floor, gathering the broken slivers of glass.

Stanton bent quickly, grasping her wrist in concern. "No, ma'am, you must not. You will surely cut yourself. Leave it for the servants."

She stared for a moment at his hand on her wrist, and then, looking up into his eyes, suddenly realized she was acting a complete fool. It had been such a shock to see him standing there. It was nearly five months since she had last seen him—the longest five months of her life.

She rose unsteadily and, recalling her manners, invited him into the parlor. "Richard and Sarah are visiting with the tenants at Ellis End, and Harriet is resting, so I fear I am the only one to entertain you. Will you have some wine?"

A footman responded to her pull on the bell. He was sent for refreshments and soon returned. While he was in the room, serving the viscount, Elizabeth's mind was racing. The last time she and Lord Stanton had been together he had proposed to her, and in the months since then she had passed through a wide array of emotions: her realization that she would never be complete without him; her terrible concern when he and her brothers had gone with the army; the shattering news of Jonathan's death, followed by days and nights of tortured waiting for some word of Richard and Stanton, praying constantly for their safety, fearing them dead; Richard's safe return home, and news that the viscount was alive; and finally, the discovery of Henry Ferris's treason. She knew it must have been devastating for Stanton, and she wondered how he was coping with it. She wanted to say something now, but no words would come, and as the footman left the room, she heard herself ask, "What brings you to Sherwood Manor, my lord?"

"You . . . and Richard, and Jonathan's wife. I wanted to tell you all how sorry I am about Jonathan. I wanted to come sooner . . . but I couldn't. I called on your parents yesterday and found Charles there. I have rarely seen two people happier than he and your sister seem to be. I am pleased that things worked out the way they did, for Charles is the perfect man for Charlotte, and he will make her happy, as she deserves to be."

"And she will make him happy as well, my lord."

"Yes. I am sure she will. How is Jonathan's wife handling his loss?"

"As well as can be expected. None of us will ever stop missing him, but we are learning to accept that he is gone. He was buried on the battlefield, you know, as were thousands of others, but Papa has put up a memorial stone, and we pretend that he is here with us. Harriet has been very brave, and in about two weeks her baby is due. I think it will be a great comfort for her to have Jon's child."

At that moment Richard and Sarah returned home, and the tête-à-tête between Elizabeth and Lord Stanton came to an end as greetings were exchanged. The viscount took Sarah's hand briefly in his and then grasped Richard's warmly.

"Charles said you had a nasty leg wound, but I see no evidence of it now."

"No, none at all," Richard responded. "Not even a limp. It healed beautifully. How did you come? In your curricle? Will you stay?"

"Yes. I drove myself. And, yes, if you will have me, I would like to stay, overnight at least. I was hoping to have your permission to ride with Elizabeth this afternoon, and I was also hoping that you could lend me a horse."

Elizabeth looked startled at the suggestion, and Richard gazed at her inquiringly. "Well, Lizzie?"

"Yes . . . of course, my lord. . . . I should be happy to ride with you if you wish it."

"Then have John saddle Sultry for Lord Stanton, Lizzie, for I shan't need her today."

Elizabeth nodded to her brother and turned to the viscount. "I will go and change and shall be down directly." She left on the words and hurried to her room to don her riding habit. She wasn't sure she was doing the wise thing, but the opportunity to be alone with him was too tempting to be denied.

Elizabeth had told no one about the offer of marriage she received shortly before Stanton left for Belgium. She had very few secrets from either Sarah or Richard, but that offer was one of them. Lord Stanton desired her physically and had admitted as much. He had made his proposal based upon that desire. It had been painful for her to receive such an offer from a man she loved with her whole heart, and that pain was too intimate, too humiliating, to share with anyone.

When Elizabeth returned to the parlor and Lord Stanton rose to join her, she caught Sarah's eye across the room and suddenly remembered Sarah's words on the day they had learned that Stanton was safe. "When you see Lord Stanton again, you should tell him how you feel." Elizabeth wasn't sure that Sarah was right—wasn't sure she could make such an admission even if she wished to.

"Which way will you ride?" Richard asked.

"Over the Downs, I think," Stanton answered. "I am in a solitary mood."

Elizabeth turned to him in surprise. "Are you sure, then, that you want company, sir?"

"Yes, indeed," he promptly replied. "For either I shall include you in my mood or you shall shake me from it. In either case, I desire your company." He turned to Richard. "You won't worry if we are gone for some time?"

"No. I won't worry."

As Elizabeth and Stanton left the house and walked across to the stables, Richard moved to the window and watched them go. "He will refuse to take a groom along, and he will keep her out for hours," he said thoughtfully to his wife. "He's troubled. Anyone can see that."

"Troubled over what?"

"Over his feelings for Lizzie."

"Romantic feelings? Do you think he has any?" Sarah asked.

"I think he is attracted to her, yes."

"You have never said so before. What makes you think it?"

"You never knew this, Sarah, but on the night Julian rescued Lizzie from Granbrooke, he challenged Granbrooke to a duel. I had every intention of taking the same step myself, despite the promise I had made to Lizzie on the night of the ball. The man had gone too far—something had to be done about him. I was surprised by Julian's challenge, because it was not his place to defend my sister's honor, and I have never known him to provoke a fight. In fact, I have heard him speak out strongly against dueling. But I accepted his explanation that the provocation had been great, and I also believed that he was acting in my interest, thinking that the blow I received would make me a poor candidate for such a deadly sport. I accompanied Julian and Hugh to the dueling ground on the appointed morning, but Granbrooke never appeared. Julian was furious, angrier than I have ever seen him, and his unusual behavior made me begin to question his involvement with Lizzie. His anger seemed disproportionate for a breach of honor, cowardly though it was. I had the impression that he was looking forward to shooting Granbrooke, and that his anger stemmed from the lost opportunity. My suspicions were strengthened shortly after Lizzie and Julian were shot.''

''Why then?''

''Lizzie's maid told me that Julian came to Lizzie's room in the middle of the night and stayed at the bedside for more than two hours watching her sleep.''

''Perhaps it was a vigil,'' Sarah suggested. ''She was very ill, and she had saved his life.''

''It could have been that, of course, but I don't believe so, for she had already passed the crisis and was resting peacefully when he made his visit. He stayed with her for two hours at a time when he was still very ill himself and in considerable pain. Something drew him there at that time of night, and I don't think it was anxiety or even gratitude. I think it was something closer to curiosity. He was asking himself, as he had asked me earlier, why she had done it. Perhaps by being there, close to her, he thought he would find the answer.

''There was one more incident,'' he continued. ''When we were in Leicestershire, the relationship between those two seemed strained to me. There was one day when Lizzie had walked to the village, alone, and when it started to snow and she hadn't returned, Julian went to fetch her. They arrived home safely, but I could tell instantly that something had taken place between them, for you know how attuned I am to Lizzie. I don't think they had argued or even disagreed, but the air seemed charged between them. That day I began to suspect that Lizzie cared for him. He left suddenly soon after that, on the slimmest pretext. My conviction grew steadily from that day—a conviction that there was strong attraction, on both sides.''

"Why has he come today? Do you think he intends to make an offer?''

"I can't say. I know he has little use for marriage. I was astonished when he offered for Charlotte—it seemed out of character somehow. He seems to lack the confidence of a man ready to make a declaration. My guess is that he wishes to spend time with her to more carefully weigh his feelings and perhaps try to discover hers.''

"I advised her to tell him of her love,'' Sarah said.

"Really?'' he asked in surprise.

"I cannot see who is served by her keeping it to herself,'' Sarah answered defensively.

"Such a confession by her could destroy their friendship if he doesn't return her love.''

"As it destroyed ours? You faced a situation similar to Elizabeth's, yet you did not withhold your feelings from me.''

"No. I admitted my love for you, and I destroyed our friendship in the same moment. There were many times when I regretted my impulsiveness, Sarah, and wished to have my friend back again. I gambled on a chance to win all—and when I lost, I was left with nothing—no lover, no friend, and very little hope.''

"But, don't you see, Richard, Lizzie is just like you. She doesn't want Lord Stanton as her friend, she wants more, as you did. And, for my part, I hope she goes after it, and I wish her luck. Lord Stanton will be giving your father ample ammunition to force a declaration from him,'' Sarah suggested. "Riding unchaperoned for hours over deserted commons is a great deal more compromising than a brief kiss in the library.''

Richard turned to his wife and took her into his arms, smiling down at her. ''The tactics that my father employed on Charles would never serve with Julian. He is not the man to allow himself to be tricked, coerced, or threatened into any action. If ever he offers for Lizzie, it will be of his own volition, his own choice, freely made.''

The horses were soon saddled, and Stanton himself put Elizabeth up. He moved to Sultry's side, and as he gathered the reins and prepared to mount, the mare turned her head round and gently nudged him. He smiled at her and reached to stroke her muzzle. ''What's this? Disapproval?''

''Curiosity, I should think,'' Elizabeth said. ''No one ever rides her but Richard. I am sure she is wondering who you are.'' Elizabeth was surprised when Stanton told the groom they would not need him, but she said nothing, and they rode off in silence, neither of them speaking until the road had diminished to a cart track and the horses had begun to pick their way up the steep ridge of the Downs.

It was a cool, sunny day, with only a light breeze, a beautiful day for riding. They rode side by side, their legs occasionally touching, and finally the silence became too much for Elizabeth, and she spoke suddenly. ''My lord, there is something I wish to say to you, but I cannot think how to begin.''

''Something concerning Henry?''

''Yes,'' she said gratefully, for now that he had spoken his brother's name, it seemed somehow easier to continue. ''I was concerned—we all were—when Sir Hugh told us about your brother. We were so shocked; Richard was incredulous; and we realized how hard it must have been for you. I wish you had come to us then. Perhaps we might have helped.''

He smiled at her tenderly. ''Perhaps so, but I think it was

278

best that Giles and I dealt with it ourselves. Strangely enough, I didn't have that much difficulty accepting Henry's French ties. What I found so hard to overcome was my own blindness and insensitivity where he was concerned. Here was a man, my own brother, who I thought I knew better than any other person on this earth, and I found that I didn't know him well enough to understand those things that were most important in his life. When we were young, we were very close. My father was a wastrel. He made my mother's life miserable, and the less we saw of him, the happier we were. Giles was much younger, but Henry and I were inseparable as boys—and even as young men. We knew each other so well that I sometimes felt we were thinking with the same mind. But now as I look back, I can see that things changed for us when my father died and my mother returned to France. We grew apart, even though I told myself that we were as close as ever. We had become men, and we each chose the life that was right for us. Henry chose the side of our mother's blood. We have both lost brothers, Elizabeth. I wish that I could have lost mine honorably, as you did."

"But surely you must know that no one attaches any blame to you for Henry's activities," Elizabeth said. "Papa told us that both the Prince Regent and the Duke spoke to you personally. Surely that reassured you!"

"Believe me, Elizabeth, having them speak so only made matters worse."

"But why? If they said that your loyalty was not in question—"

"Elizabeth, you don't understand! I let Henry get away! When everyone was looking for him, I guessed where he had gone, as did Giles. We found him, and I let him go. I didn't help him, but I didn't hinder his leaving the country."

"And you think that was wrong?"

"Wrong? It was treasonous!"

"But what could you have done instead? Shoot him?"

"Yes! That is exactly what the Prince or Wellington would have expected me to do!"

"But, Julian," she said, forgetting in her anxiety to use his title, and addressing him as she had thought of him all these months. "We are speaking of your *brother*! Certainly when such horrible decisions must be made, love must be the first rule to govern us."

"As it was when you purposely intercepted a bullet meant for me?"

"Yes," she answered without hesitation. "As it was then."

He pulled Sultry to a standstill, and she did the same as he continued, "Had you no thought for your own safety?"

"No. I thought only of protecting you and didn't count the cost to myself."

"There is a name for that kind of selfless giving, Elizabeth."

"Yes," she agreed. "Sarah says I must have loved you even then, although I didn't realize it at the time." She kicked her horse into a walk again, unable to bear his steady regard.

"Oh, Elizabeth," he said, and the words were almost a groan. "Everything is so simple for you. You can say you love or hate a person, as easily as you discuss the weather. Everything for you is either right or wrong, black or white. To me the world seems always gray, and telling someone I love them is harder for me than leading a cavalry charge against impossible odds."

"You loved your brother a great deal, didn't you?" she asked simply.

"Yes. I love both my brothers, although I daresay I have never said as much to either of them. And now, for Henry at least, it's too late."

"No. It's not too late. Surely he knows why you let him go. Only love between brothers could have seen you through the difficult moment that must have been."

280

"Giles said, 'We are brothers, and we love one another. Does that not count for anything?' And I thought to myself, It should. It should count for everything."

They rode on for several minutes in silence, and finally Stanton continued, his voice low and unsteady. "Elizabeth, the last time we met, the day I asked you to marry me, I know it must have hurt you to think I didn't care for you, and although it can't change anything between us, I think that the truth can't be any more painful than the lies. I love you, Elizabeth, and I have for a very long time." He turned to look at her, but she seemed unwilling to return his regard and kept her eyes firmly fixed on the meandering path ahead as he continued. "I suspected your feelings for me after the shooting incident." A sad smile crossed his face. "I wasn't sure until today. I have tried to keep my feelings in check because I have nothing to offer that you could ever be content with. I tried to explain to you once before how different we are. That hasn't changed. We want different things from life. I cannot make the kind of commitment you want, because I know that in the end I would fail you and make you unhappy."

"I cannot believe that you really love me," Elizabeth said quietly in a dazed voice. "I have prayed that it would happen, but I never believed it would."

"Oh, you can believe it!" he said. He pulled both horses up suddenly, reaching to take her chin in his hand and forcing her to look at him. "I love you madly, passionately. . . . I lie in bed at night and torture myself wondering what it would be like to hold you . . . touch you. I would like nothing better than to keep you to myself and protect you from the world. But it would never work, Elizabeth! I know you so well! You would always stand by me. Constancy is part of your nature. But it is not part of mine, and wishing will not make it so. If I could be sure that I would always feel the same . . . but I cannot be sure . . . and I will not risk hurting you."

281

"But you are hurting me now!"

"Yes. I know, and I'm sorry. But you are young, and if you stay free of me, in time you will forget."

"I don't want to forget!" Elizabeth returned passionately. "You ask for too much, my lord. None of us is ever guaranteed happiness. Think of Jonathan and Harriet! But certainly we will never be happy if we never *try*!" You may not win every battle, but you cannot make me believe that you ever led your men expecting to lose. You make plans to win—and sometimes you do!"

"Yes. And sometimes you lose," he replied dampingly. "And always the cost is dear."

"I would rather have whatever time you are willing to give me," she insisted, "than none at all. If it is marriage you fear so much, then take me as your mistress. Then, when you tire of me, as you seem so certain you will, there need be no bonds to tie us."

"This is no time for jest, Elizabeth."

"I am not jesting. I care not for my reputation. I don't think it likely that I will ever love any man but you, so why shouldn't I be with you while you want me. Then I will be able to say that at least once in my life I knew what it was to be loved.

"I will pretend you didn't say that, Elizabeth," he said wrathfully, "because I am convinced that you are too innocent to fully realize what you say. I wish never to hear you repeat such a sentiment again. You will never be my mistress, nor any man's. Do you understand?"

Elizabeth had expected him to be flattered by her offer, not angered, and she looked away in confusion, only nodding her head in answer to his question. Several minutes passed before she spoke again. "I think I understand the difference between the kinds of love we feel. My love for you seeks to remove the obstacles and find solutions. Your love for me views every stone in the path as a boulder, and you fear real problems and imagined ones as well. You

282

lack faith in us," she said sadly, "and faith, like love, cannot be taught. It is something that must be experienced, and shared."

He gazed at her wonderingly. "How can you see so much so clearly at your age?"

"I have always understood love," she said. "I cannot remember a time in my life when I didn't feel completely loved and secure."

"I envy you that."

"You may say you envy me, but you don't want the same thing for yourself," she pointed out. "Otherwise you would not hesitate to take the love I am offering you—which is all, and everything, I have to give."

They rode on in silence for some time, each of them realizing that the conversation had come to its inevitable conclusion. There was no more to say. There was no solution, no future. Finally Elizabeth spoke again. "Would you tell me about your life when you were young, and about your relationship with Henry during those years?"

"Yes, if you like. And later, you can tell me what it was like to grow up in a seaport, and what mischief you got into as a child."

She turned her head to smile at him and said saucily, "I was a perfect child."

He returned her smile. "Now, why do I doubt that?"

Lord Stanton and Elizabeth rode for more than four hours, and to Sarah, they seemed to return in much the same manner as they had departed—amiable but strained. It was impossible to tell what had passed between them but easy enough to see that they had not made any commitment to each other. If Elizabeth had found the courage to tell him she loved him, it clearly hadn't changed the gentleman's opinion about marriage, for there was no joy between these two, only resignation.

Dinner was a fairly pleasant meal, if one didn't take into account the fact that Lord Stanton ate little, and Elizabeth ate nothing at all. Exercise generally improved her appetite, but apparently it had not been so today, for she simply pushed the food about on her plate, refusing to be tempted by any of it.

The post that day yielded a letter from Charlotte, and as Richard was best at deciphering her scrawl, he had agreed to read it after dinner. Taking the letter from a table in the parlor, he crossed to a chair near the fire and sat with his back to the blaze, allowing the light to fall over Charlotte's scribbled news. Elizabeth sank to the carpet near his knees, the soft folds of her pale blue muslin spreading about her on the floor. Charlotte's letters were always amusing, and Elizabeth looked up expectantly as Richard broke the seal and spread out the pages. Sarah knew that the Sherwood children had always gathered so about their mother's chair whenever there had been a letter from their father. Elizabeth's pose was perhaps too informal for company, but she was consistently uninhibited in the viscount's presence, treating him more like a member of the family than a guest.

Elizabeth presented a charming picture, Sarah thought, with the firelight shining softly upon her uplifted face. Sarah turned her gaze to Lord Stanton and saw that his eyes, too, were fixed on Elizabeth, but the look she saw on his face both startled and shocked her. Surely she saw great pain and longing in his eyes? He is as much in love with Lizzie as she is with him! she thought. Then, why are they both so blue-deviled? And what is keeping them apart?

The remainder of the evening passed uneventfully, and after the tea tray had been removed, Sarah and Elizabeth rose to retire, Harriet having been encouraged to go much earlier. The viscount took Sarah's outstretched hand. "I will say good-bye now, Mrs. Sherwood, for I plan to leave very early in the morning. I must thank you for your hospitality toward an unannounced and uninvited guest."

"Nonsense, my lord. You know you are always welcome

here. We are pleased to have our good friends call to see us."

Stanton turned to Elizabeth and took her cold hand in his warm one. "Will we have the pleasure of seeing you in town for any part of the Season, Miss Elizabeth?"

"I think not, my lord. I am determined to stay to help Harriet with the baby, and I find that London has little appeal for me. I much prefer the country."

Elizabeth was aware of her heart pounding painfully in her chest, but still the viscount held her hand as he spoke again. "Thank you for riding with me today. I enjoyed it a great deal." When she didn't answer, he said, "Good-bye, Elizabeth."

"Good-bye, my lord." His fingers tightened on her hand, and as she looked up to meet his eyes, he bent, and to her surprise, kissed her lightly on the cheek. It was a brotherly kind of caress, but it was so unexpected that it brought sudden tears to her eyes, and taking her hand from his, she turned and fled the room. Hurrying across the hall, she was already started up the stairs before Sarah could catch up with her.

"Lizzie, please wait." Elizabeth turned in obedience to the pressure of Sarah's hand on her arm, and Sarah was shocked to see tears pouring down the girl's face. "Lizzie, please, tell me what has happened."

"I can't, Sarah." Elizabeth sobbed. "Not now." She turned on the words and fled up the stairway, while Sarah stared helplessly after her.

The following morning, Viscount Stanton left for London. For several days, Sarah could not bring herself to press Elizabeth for an explanation of the ride she and his lordship had taken, but slowly, as the September days passed, Elizabeth began to confide in her, and little by little, Sarah came into possession of the facts. It was a weighty problem, for, like Elizabeth, she could see no clear way to overcome Lord Stanton's resolution.

25

On the twenty-second of September, Harriet Sherwood was delivered of a strong, seven-pound son. Her labor, although difficult, had been blessedly short, and both she and her son were prospering. Elizabeth and Sarah delighted in the new baby as much as did Harriet, and Richard made his wife blush one evening at dinner by saying that if she had such a liking for babies, he must see about giving her one of her own as soon as possible. In addition to her husband and herself, both Elizabeth and Lady Sherwood were present at the table, and Sarah was moved to expostulate, "My goodness, Richard, have you no delicacy?"

"What? Have I embarrassed you? But I assure you, my love, that Mama knows where babies come from, and so does Lizzie—I believe. *Do* you know where babies come from, Lizzie?"

"Yes, certainly I do, dear brother," Elizabeth answered promptly. "And I have not the slightest objection to another niece or nephew. I think it would be splendid!"

Sarah's eyes met Lady Sherwood's resignedly, but her ladyship only said, "It is as I have always said, Sarah. There is no way I will ever be able to moderate Elizabeth's behavior so long as her brother encourages her thus. But so it has always been," she said in mock dismay. "No one pays the least heed to me. They will all go their own way." She rose from the table as she spoke, and Elizabeth immediately leaped to her feet.

"I am off to the nursery to help with Jonathan Edward," she said. "I will join you at tea-time."

"Tea-time! Honestly, Lizzie," her mother objected, "the child is only three days old. He sleeps most of the time!"

"I know. But I like to watch him sleep. And I promised to read to Harriet. We are in the middle of a romantic novel. The villain is about to get his just deserts." She left the room on the words, and Sarah turned to her mother-in-law.

"She seems somewhat improved these last several days," Sarah said, "but her mood underneath remains the the same. Richard and I have discussed it, and if you have no objection, I would like to accompany you to town at the end of the week. I have taken a leaf from your book, ma'am. I think it is time one of us approached Lord Stanton, and I think it should be me. Matters can become no worse, and perhaps I will be able to help, because I think that better than anyone else, I can understand his pain."

On the last day of September, Lady Sherwood and Mrs. Sherwood arrived in London. Sarah immediately had a message carried to Lord Stanton's house in Park Lane, informing his lordship that she would appreciate the opportunity to speak with him at his earliest convenience. She went on to say that she would be at home that evening, and the following morning as well, should he find an opportunity to call.

This communication from Mrs. Sherwood was conveyed to the viscount while he was dressing for dinner, and it puzzled him. He hadn't known that she was in town and thought it strange that she should write to him requesting an interview. When he had finished dressing, he sent a footman round to Sir Hugh Broughton's rooms in Ryder Street, begging to be excused from his engagement for the evening, and then set off to pay a call on Mrs. Sherwood in Mount Street.

Lord Stanton was shown into the salon, where Lord and Lady Sherwood greeted him warmly. He then took Sarah's outstretched hand. "You wished to see me, ma'am?"

"Yes, my lord. I would like to thank you for calling so promptly."

"I believe my daughter-in-law wishes to speak with you privately, Stanton," Lord Sherwood said easily. "So, if you will excuse us, my wife and I will leave you."

Lady Sherwood rose as he spoke, and they quit the room together. As the door closed behind them, Sarah said, "I am sure you must be wondering why I have asked you here, my lord. Please, won't you sit here by the fire? Will you have some brandy? Richard and I always enjoy it at this time of night."

"Yes. Thank you," he said, reaching automatically to take the glass she offered him. "Richard did not come up to town with you, Mrs. Sherwood?"

"No, my lord. He did not come, and I have not come to stay. I came only to see you, and I may leave again as early as tomorrow. . . . Lord Stanton, there is something I wish to tell you, and although it may seem strange to you at first, I beg that you will bear with me, for in the end it will all become clear to you, I believe."

He regarded her with polite interest as she continued. "Unlike you, my lord, I was not born to wealth and position. My parents were simple country gentry, my father the son of a village rector. I was an only child, and from the moment my parents decided that I would be handsome, they thought of little else besides selling me for a title. When I was barely seventeen, they discovered Sir Winston's son, my first husband, James. It was not the peerage my parents sought, but when Sir Winston died, I would be a lady at least, and they decided to settle for that. I was not consulted in the matter of my marriage. My husband, like my father was . . . a worthless man, and Sir Winston is little better. I had no use for men, any men, until I met Richard Sherwood.

"From the very beginning I found myself drawn to him, for I saw something in him, and later, in his family, that I did not know existed. When I was with him, or with them, I felt as if I were standing outside a window in the cold, looking in on them, seeing their warmth, and their love, and feeling as if they were part of another world—a world in which I would never belong. I wanted desperately to pass through that window, and yet, I was afraid that, once inside, I would discover that it had all been a mirage, and I would find the same desolation and humiliation that I had known in my childhood and my marriage.

"Nevertheless, I was drawn against my will to Richard, each day needing him more, each day missing him more, each day wondering just a little more if perhaps life had something to offer that I had missed. And then, when my wanting him became a pain equal to the pain of my memories, I said I would marry him. I was terrified of giving myself to him. I felt as if I were standing on the edge of a deep pool, unable to swim, knowing that if I jumped in, I would surely drown. And yet, there was Richard, asking me to jump, telling me to trust him to keep me safe. And finally, I did decide to trust him, and I found the courage to go to him. Partly, I suppose, it was because of my son, Jimmy, who loved this man with such intensity, and who encouraged, nay, begged me, to allow myself to love him, too. And partly it was my need, which had become an ache nearly impossible to bear. But most of all it was my response to Richard's need, which he had never hidden from me. I found it impossible to live with the pain my rejection was causing him.

"But now I come to the end of my story, my lord. I

jumped into that pond, and the feeling was exactly as I had imagined. The water was cold and terrifying, and it closed over my head. But when I rose to the surface, I discovered I could swim! I needed help. I needed guidance and teaching—but I *could* swim. I saw the love in that family, and I took a chance that Richard would be able to show me the way to find it, and he has. I'm not saying that it will always be perfect. I know there will be troubles, but I'm not afraid to face them, because my love has kindled a strength in me that I never knew I possessed.

"The last time we were together, I saw the way you looked at Elizabeth. I saw the combination of pain and longing in your eyes and recognized it. I can't be certain how you feel about Elizabeth, but I think you love her a great deal. She has told me that she is in love with you, and that she has told you so—so there can be no misunderstanding on that score. I think perhaps you are afraid of your love, afraid that the feelings you have, the images you behold, will vanish if you reach out to take them. I, too, felt that way. The very day of my wedding I felt as if I was moving in a dream; that the fates were playing a cruel trick on me; that Richard was no different from any other man; that my love had made me blind; that I was seeing an illusion, an image of what I wanted my lover to be. Imagine my shock on my wedding night, when my husband came to me the same tender and gentle man I had married—not changed beyond recognition into the embodiment of my fears. My commitment had not endangered me, it had set me free."

Sarah paused, but Stanton did not speak. He was staring now into the fire. Finally she continued. "I think that we are not offered love so often in our lives, my lord, that we can allow ourself the privilege of snapping our fingers at it. Elizabeth is young, but she knows her heart, and she has given it to you." He looked up at her then, but she continued without pause. "Hers is not a volatile nature, and her feelings will not easily be swayed. If you continue to reject her, she will continue to suffer. For now, she is devoting all her energies to Harriet and the new baby, and Harriet needs her support, so she feels somewhat fulfilled. But the days will come when Harriet needs her less and less. Jonathan's loss in time will fade, for Harriet has no hope and knows that he will never come back to her. The pain will lessen, the sorrow become easier to bear. Lizzie will not be so fortunate. For her, the hope, and therefore the pain, will live on, and she will never give up hope, my lord, so long as you are free.

"I truly think that in the end you must go to her. I think that, like me, you will find yourself drawn against your will. But I also think that because you are much stronger than I, you will fight your inclinations longer than I did, and you will both suffer unnecessarily as a result. Does this make sense to you, my lord? You say nothing, yet I feel I have come close to the truth."

"I feel as if you have crawled into my head, Mrs. Sherwood. It is a queer feeling, I can tell you. You have correctly interpreted the look you saw, and you see my fears far clearer than I see them myself. Elizabeth said that a complete love requires faith, and you are telling me that a proper commitment requires courage. But I do not think I possess your courage, ma'am."

"I did not find the courage within myself, Lord Stanton. I found it in Richard—and you must seek it in Elizabeth."

Sarah returned to Surrey the following day but had nothing concrete to report to her husband. Lord Stanton had listened politely to all she had said but had given her no indication that he would change his mind about involving himself in Elizabeth's life. "I think perhaps he will reconsider his decision," she said, "but I cannot be sure. I don't think there is anything more we can do except give him time to come to terms with his fear and hope that in the end he will decide that he needs Lizzie enough to come to her.''

But as the autumn days of October passed, and then the weeks, any hope that Sarah had held of having altered the viscount's resolve faded. Elizabeth did not mope about the house. She had too much pride to wear her heart upon her sleeve, and her youth and natural liveliness helped her to deal with her rejection. But beneath the surface, all could see the change in her. The perennial optimism that had been her trademark was often absent. She took long walks and rides alone, refusing to take a groom with her and sometimes worrying her family by not returning for hours. When Richard remonstrated with her, he did not meet with the spirited argument of the old days but with a meek apology and a promise to be more considerate in future. She objected vehemently to any suggestion that she go up to town for part of the Season, and she was adamant in refusing any and all invitations to various house parties.

The month of October was drawing to a close, Charlotte and Charles's wedding was now less than seven weeks away, and one afternoon while Richard sat in the study, going over some accounts, he looked up as the door opened and the butler announced, ''Lord Stanton, Captain Sherwood.''

Richard rose and moved forward to greet his guest. ''Julian! What brings you to us this time? Or can I guess?''

''I have come to see Elizabeth, but I wish to speak with you first. You know, of course, that your wife came to see me nearly a month ago in town.'' Richard nodded, and Stanton continued. ''Do you share her hope, Richard, that Elizabeth and I should marry?''

''Yes, Julian, I do.''

''Not so very long ago you made it quite plain that you did not desire me as a brother-in-law.''

"At that time, we were discussing your position as husband to Charlotte. Elizabeth is not Charlotte."

Stanton smiled ruefully. "No. Elizabeth is not Charlotte. Then you would not object to my asking for Elizabeth?"

"You don't need my permission, Julian."

"No. I know I don't. But I know that Elizabeth is your favorite, and it is important for me to know that you approve."

"I approve wholeheartedly, my friend," Richard assured him. "I have known for months that Lizzie's happiness lies only with you."

"Where is she?"

"She and the baby's nurse usually take him for an outing at this time of day. You will probably find them in the gardens behind the house."

One of the footmen showed the viscount the direction Elizabeth and Nurse had taken, and he was not long in finding them. As he came round the end of a tall hedge, he saw them seated on a rustic stone bench, the baby on Elizabeth's lap.

Both women glanced up as they noticed someone approaching, and Elizabeth's heart thumped uncomfortably when she recognized who it was. She rose to her feet as Stanton came closer, still holding the child in her arms. He stopped about ten feet away, and they stood staring at each other, neither of them willing to speak.

Finally Nurse broke the silence. "Shall I take the babe back to the house for you, Miss Elizabeth? He will be hungry soon, I think."

Elizabeth dragged her eyes away from the viscount and forced herself to attend to Nurse. "Yes, of course you may have him." She handed the child to the older woman as she spoke, tucking the shawl closely around his tiny face as he settled into Nurse's arms. Nurse walked quietly away, and Elizabeth turned back to Stanton.

Slowly he covered the space between them, and she held out her hand instinctively. It was her right hand, ungloved, and as he took it in his, her diamond ring caught the afternoon sun and brought a rush of memory. It seemed years ago that he had taken it from her injured hand the night Granbrooke abducted her from Vauxhall. And then he had returned it the night she saved his life. He continued to regard the ring steadily until Elizabeth startled him by saying, "I have not taken it off, not since the night you put it there."

His hand tightened painfully on hers, and he drew her roughly into his arms, bringing his lips down on hers in a kiss that was hot and hungry and demanding. And then, suddenly, he released her mouth and crushed her against him in an urgent embrace. His breath was quick and rasping, and she could feel his body tremble against hers. His fingers were gripping her so tightly that she knew she would be bruised by them, but she didn't care, and she clung to him, allowing the wonderful intimacy of the closeness of their bodies to wash over her. For so many months she had felt desolate and alone. She had yearned to have him hold her, dreamed of having him want her, and now, in his arms, she knew she had come home.

Long minutes passed as he held her close. Slowly his breathing evened, and finally he loosed his hold and put her a little from him. She looked up to meet his eyes shyly. "You have not come into the country for solitude this time, I think, my lord."

"Certainly not! I have come for companionship. Will you give it to me?"

"Gladly."

He took her face in his hands and allowed himself the pleasure of running his fingertips over the softness of cheek and chin. Then, very slowly, he bent his head and kissed her again. The kiss was as different from the last as midnight was from noon. It was infinitely soft and sensual—a brush, a touch, a whisper—a lingering, languishing caress, a kiss so intimate that Elizabeth was breathless and blushing when he finally held her away. He drew her to the stone bench and down onto it beside him, holding her hands firmly in his.

"I once made you an offer of marriage, Elizabeth, and I couched it in such terms as to make it totally unacceptable to you. I intend today to make you another, and I hope to do better this time. First I will tell you that I love you—more than I thought it possible to love any person or anything in this life. I told you once before that I wanted you, and that also is true, even more so now than it was then. But there are several other things that I want as well."

"What is it that you want, my lord?"

"I want you to be the first thing I see each day when I open my eyes, and the last thing I see each night before I close them. I want you to teach me the secret of making love grow each day. I want you to prove to me that I am the kind of man that can love one woman truly and honestly all his life, and I want you to give me a reason to prove it to myself as well. And most of all . . . I would like to see you hold a child of mine in your arms."

"I want all those things, too," she whispered, her eyes suddenly filling with tears.

"Elizabeth, will you be my wife?"

"Yes."

"When?"

"Whenever you like."

"As soon as possible?"

"Yes. As soon as possible."

He took her once again in his arms and held her close, and for the second time in his life felt the threat of tears. But this time, he made no attempt to stop them, for he no longer feared them. All the faith, all the love, all the cour-

295

age that he needed in his life was in his arms at that moment—all that he would ever need to make himself complete.

More romance from Regency and...

RACHELLE EDWARDS